PRAISE FOR ANTHONY CARTWRIGHT

How I Killed Margaret Thatcher

'A bittersweet elegy to Britain's battered working classes ... mournful, moving' *Metro*

'A suprisingly complex nuanced narrative' *Financial Times*

'An impressive novel redolent of a more tender David Peace' *The List*

'Brilliant ... an angry, unforgiving novel' *Independent*

Heartland

'This is what fiction should be and what readers want it to be: passionately engaged. The ambition and achievement shine forth from every sentence' David Peace

'A writer with a wonderful ear for dialect and an unblinking sense of Britain as it is today. Anthony Cartwright's patient, attentive storytelling shines a glowing light on areas of our common experience that the English novel usually consigns to darkness' Jonathan Coe

'Impressive ... a parable for tensions and anxieties of multicultural Britain five years after the bright New Labour dawn' D. J. Taylor

'This impressive novel succeeds in giving voice to a part of the country that is more frequently spoken about than listened to' *Guardian*

'This brilliantly realised novel expertly interweaves the stories of friends on either side of a stricken community's social and religious divide' *Esquire*

'Movingly traverses the territory of the human heart' *Independent on Sunday*

The Afterglow

'Anthony Cartwright's first novel depicts modern life in the Black Country and shines brightly for British regional fiction' Zadie Smith

'A painfully honest and accomplished first novel' Philip Callow

'Anthony Cartwright's characters are wholly believable; he has an instinctive talent for using description to create subtle shades of mood' Carol Birch

'With great tenderness, Cartwright reveals the tentative dreams and aspirations for a better life that underlie the seeming heartlessness of his quiet heroes' *Independent*

'Combining sharp social observation and compassion with the compelling narrative focus of Jon McGregor's *If Nobody Speaks of Remarkable Things*, this is a most impressive debut' *Guardian*

IRON
TOWNS
ANTHONY
CARTWRIGHT

First published in Great Britain in 2016 by Serpent's Tail,
an imprint of Profile Books Ltd
3 Holford Yard
Bevin Way
London
WC1X 9HD
www.serpentstail.com

1 3 5 7 9 10 8 6 4 2

Designed and typeset by Crow Books
Printed by Clays, Bungay, Suffolk

The moral right of the author has been asserted

The characters and events in this book are fictitious. Any similarity to real
persons, dead or alive, is coincidental and not intended by the author.

A CIP record for this book can
be obtained from the British Library

ISBN 978 1 78125 538 4
eISBN 978 1 78283 201 0

We come through our black labyrinths, massed shadows. The fires are all out now. We are the smoke that patterns the brick. We are the iron roar that you thought you'd silenced. We sing to twisted metal and down long, flooded tunnels, across empty water and fields of rubble. We sing of better days.

'Dee Dee, that you?'

She knows who it is before he speaks, with what she takes to be the line's prison hiss, in the energy of a phone ringing when it shouldn't have. All these years spent willing it not to ring.

'You know it is,' she says, and walks down the hall, through the empty bar, chandeliers catch the morning light through a half-closed curtain, out into the yard. Red sky at morning over dead cranes at the Lascar docks.

'I wanna see her, Dee Dee.'

'Where are you?'

'I wanna see my baby.'

'You can't.'

'I wanna see my girl.'

'There are people here who'll kill you. You know that, don't you? Understand that?'

She thinks of her uncles, the way they used to sit around a table in the back room. She'd watch them through the blue smoke, the half-open door. There has always been a look that comes when people find out who she is, the people she is from. Their power has long gone. There is no one to kill him. He knows that full well, wherever he has been. And she has no intention of conjuring up a vanished world now. Back at school there'd been kids who'd said she was a witch. There have been plenty of times since she has wished it true.

'I'm gonna see her.'

'Where are you, Goldie?'

'I stayed away, Dee Dee. I kept away.'

'You stay away then, you hear, you keep it that way.'

It is hard to breathe. She thinks of the rattle the asthma pump makes as you shake it, the fizz of life as your lungs open. The pump is in the bathroom cabinet, feels a long way off.

'I'm already here,' he says, and she steps forward with a jolt into the rosy brightness of the yard. The smell of bleach rises from the concrete, a sense of things wiped clean. She looks at the jagged glass stuck in concrete atop the wall, half expects to see him come over it, his face, spiteful and handsome, across nearly twenty years, counting.

'You try anything, I'll kill you myself, I swear to god.'

Then comes the old manic glee in his voice.

'I'm already here Dee Dee, I never went nowhere. And I'm coming now, you mind that, darling, eh.'

Upstairs, the bureau is open in the spare room, dark wood against the yellow wallpaper. A square of sunlight comes through the net curtain and onto the wall. The furniture in here is all her nana's relics. Alina works at the bureau sometimes, sitting in the high-backed chair, face illuminated by her electric pad's screen, some art thing she's carried on with even though she's finished at college now. Dee Dee wants to ask her about it, holds back.

There is a photograph on the desk's green inlaid leather. There are photos stuffed in all the drawers, snapshots from when Dee

Dee was a kid, a posed portrait of her great-grandad wearing a turban and salwar kameez, with a waxed moustache, in sepia, is propped against the wall. She has intended to get a new frame for years. Alina told her that they made the colour by grinding little sea creatures into a paste.

She pauses for a moment. A passing lorry rattles the window-frame, she sees the roof of the 29 bus slide by, and is startled to see herself twenty years ago in the picture on the desk, though she has never made any effort to hide these photos. She sits with her arm in Sonia's. Their hair touches as they lean into each other. They wear identical outsized T-shirts, Dee Dee's yellow, Sonia's blue, which fall off their shoulders. The boys are standing, moving. Mark Fala and Goldie lean in the same direction, each with a foot raised as if to run or dance. They grin, the edges of their bodies blur with movement, a little out of focus, as if they are not fully there. Liam is caught in the act of rising, unfolding his long arms and legs, his skin unmarked. He looks at Dee Dee.

She looks away. The flyover in the distance creates a bar across the window, a horizon. In the mornings there is the dark shadow of the hills beyond. The afternoon sun dissolves them. She looks back.

They are on the roof at the flats, you can see the Lascar cranes in the background. The Falas' flat was in Stevedore House. She could lean out of the window now and probably make out this same block, this roof. *Is*, not *was*. They used to sunbathe up on the roof; it would be a good day for it today. She hasn't been down there for years, a distance of a mile, no more.

There was always the five of them back then. Who took

the picture? A shadow cuts across the frame. It is Mark's mum. Within a few months of taking this she will be dead. Within a few years, Sonia too. Goldie is looking somewhere off the roof. She is struck by how he and Liam look so similar in this picture, like her and Sonia. Her hand shakes. She wants to push Goldie, to send him running over that low wall and down to the ground below. Everything would be different. Everything is different now. His cracked voice across the years has changed the light in this room. If she had pushed him Sonia would be here. Alina would not be. Dee Dee considers this. This is why she does not look at old photographs, tries not to answer the phone. Everything would be different.

The Anvil Yards football ground. Irontown Football Club. An empty dressing room at the middle of summer. Out of season and out of luck. The sun shines through a narrow open window, onto the wooden benches, the bare treatment table, the tiled floor. The room smells of fresh paint and disinfectant, but linger, and underneath that is the smell of ancient liniment and sweat and thick winter mud that has soaked into the wood through the years.

The thin window shows an oblong of pitch. Gulls peck at the centre circle. They think it is a beach, perhaps, miles inland. They are the descendants of the birds who would follow the boats up the estuary and river and canal to the Ironport. Now they live on the council tip out towards Burnt Village, under the motorway. They hang in the dust that rises from the middle of the pitch. The club has opened the iron gates at the Greenfield End and run a car boot sale every Sunday since May. The sun has baked the mud.

The handle of the dressing-room door turns and turns again. From behind it there is a bang, a grunt, a sigh.

'Ted, Ted,' calls a voice. 'He's only painted this door shut.'

'What?'

'The door's slammed shut and the paint's dried. I told him to wedge it open. It won't budge.'

'Give it some iron.'

'I have. It's tight shut.'

The door handle rattles again.

'Jesus. The lads'll be here in a minute. The gaffer's here already. I've seen his car in the car park. He's got to meet them Portuguese. They've got that kid with them, the triallist, he looks about ten years old, I swear to god. They'll have him for bloody breakfast. I've got to get this kit laid out. We can't look any more of a shambles than we already am.'

'Liam's here somewhere. He's signing shirts in the Players' Lounge. Liam'll save us.'

In the empty room the men's voices fade as they move away down the tunnel. There is the occasional rattle of a seat in the grandstand above. Footsteps sound along the walkways. There are the ghost sounds of thousands of feet in the aisles, the ghost cries of great crowds, echoes of old songs, the clang of metal, the roar of a furnace, rattle of a tram, a siren across the docks.

Silence.

A clock ticks and then more voices come, clear now from behind the door.

'I'll have to force it.'

'Do what you've got to do, mate.'

There is a thud and the wood around the door handle splinters. The door is locked. The bolt twists and shreds the wood and the door bursts open into the room. Liam Corwen stands there in the light, rubs his shoulder, blinks.

Two men, half his size almost, crouch and haul the kit baskets into the room across the splinters.

'I thought you said it was stuck? You just needed the key.'

'Ah, well.'

'Don't worry about it, Liam. Thanks our kid.'

'Thanks Liam. You've saved us.'

He shrugs.

'You playing today, Liam?'

The big man shrugs again.

'Up to the gaffer. He says I need to rest, my age. I tell him I ain't got much time left, Ted. He might as well play me.'

'Good lad, Liam, good lad. Enjoy yourself if yer get on.'

Liam Corwen's is a face from a cigarette card, though they have not made them for forty years. They had something similar in boxes of teabags for a while when Liam was a kid, went the same way as the Austin Allegro and Saturday teatime wrestling.

In the dressing-room quiet Liam flicks back and forth from the magazine's cover, *Human Animal: People, Culture, Places, Trends*, to the pictures of him inside. He sits under his number 5 shirt on its peg, captain's armband slung on the hook. He doubts that he's starting, but sitting here, in his usual spot, will put him in Ally's eyeline and that might remind him to get him on at some point. It is possibly a good game to miss, all triallists and kids against a team of part-timers.

In image and biography, he is the acme of the modern footballer, Liam reads. *Body art, brushes with the law, two ex-wives, his first, Dee Dee Ahmed, former rebel in girl band Aurora and backing singer for nineties bands such as Massive Attack and Ocean Colour Scene, the other a Scandinavian underwear model. A career that failed to live up to its early promise (he holds the record for the shortest ever international career: less than a minute as an England substitute when he was eighteen). Now he's playing out his last days at Irontown, after returning from the obscurity of FC Kallevelo, of the Finnish Veikkausliiga. His hometown club, for whom he has made more appearances than anyone in their proud but luckless history, and for whom he has the extraordinary record of converting thirty-nine successive penalties across nearly twenty years, has fallen on the hardest of times.*

Look closer at those tattoos, though, and a different picture begins to emerge. Not the gothic script or Native American warriors of his contemporaries, but an entire history of football inked on his impressive frame. Great figures from the sport's golden age, such as Alfredo Di Stéfano and Eusébio, sit alongside more personal choices, from a chipped penalty that made Czechoslovakia European Champions in the seventies, to now obscure greats from before the First World War.

Why do it?

I'm a football man. I wanted to show myself as that, to celebrate it. It's been my life.

The photos make him look good, he gives them that. The

words don't matter. No mention of Tony, though. Tony has done every one of the tattoos except the one of Jari Litmanen. He got that done in Finland. Tony added the other Ajax players later. Edgar Davids autographed it after he'd played against him last season. Tony went over the signature that same night to make it part of the piece.

The piece. The work. That's what it's become.

'It's a piece of work, that,' is all his dad had said when he'd gone swimming with him at the Heathside Lido when Greta and Jari were here in the summer.

He wonders for a moment what Greta would make of being described as a Scandinavian underwear model. She'd probably just shrug. I did model underwear once, she might say. He doesn't know. She might have. She is hard to read. She is not his ex-wife. They are still married. He doesn't want to think about this right now. Dee Dee never sung for those bands either. Finland isn't even in Scandinavia. They never get it right.

As for brushes with the law, one driving ban and a caution for indecent exposure after pissing in a plant pot at the Hightown casino the night they won the old Division Three – a hundred points, a hundred goals – does not make him Ronnie Kray. It does not even make him the Ahmeds or Goldie Stone. And how has that memory drifted into his thoughts? He spends a lot of time not thinking about things. He stuffs the magazine under the bench out of sight. All reading material is banned from the dressing room.

. . .

The air parts for him as he runs, this kid. Defenders chase him like hounds after a stag in a medieval tapestry. Di Stéfano is just about old enough to be his dad, feels like it right now. It is two years since Hampden Park, might as well be twenty. Another European Cup Final, another northern night, Amsterdam, and the sky a darkening blue beyond the floodlights. The ball skims the turf, see the soles of Eusébio's boots as he hurdles into a follow-through. The ball flies inside the post. The crowd call his name. On the touchline a thin Dutch ballboy tries to move just like him.

A look goes between them, Di Stéfano and Eusébio. Some torch passed? Maybe this is the night, Di Stéfano thinks, his legs heavy as he strides back up the pitch, tries not to show it, two nil up, five three down. Maybe he thinks nothing of the sort. Great men, and the not so great, always believe that they have one more act, one more victory in them. But maybe this is the night he becomes an old man. An old man, who for a long while has been the best footballer in the world.

. . .

Joseph Stalin Corwen likes to drive up out of Black Park and above the Far Valley on the back road to get to the ground. He drives past the end of the terrace where his dad still lives, shored up with props against the lee of the hill, the house he grew up in. Joey knows all the lanes that web the hills, learned them twice over, as a boy and then in all his years as a postman. Up ahead are the Cowton high-rises. He knows them too, shudders at the thought of the November wind funnelling down the estate walkways, feels it now in his hip, and smiles at how he manages to conjure ideas of winter from a blue sky. White butterflies pattern the hedgerow.

His old man Eli refuses a lift to the match, refuses to acknowledge football at all until the cricket season is done with, has complained about the overlap for as long as anyone can remember. In some distant past football began the week after the Oval Test Match. Joey saw him this morning, left him sat in a deckchair by his back step, listening to the start of play on the radio and watching his cabbages with a glass of home-brew. Joey feels his dad's presence in the car, there in the passenger seat. Liam's too, as a boy, and more recently. Since Liam's driving ban Joey has ferried him around. He has no idea how he is getting to the game today, has not had any reply to his texts.

'Has he still not been in touch?' Liz asked him. 'Always the same, that boy. I don't know what went wrong.'

He pictures Liam riding there on the bus or the tram, can't quite put it past him, as if some Brylcremed ghost. Half the team used to travel on the 29 bus when Joey first started going to matches, 56-57. That was the year they played the Busby Babes in the cup. Same year they played Bishop Auckland six times with all the replays. It's why they're playing them today, a tradition revived. You can think what you like about Ally Barr, and Joey does not think much these days, but he likes to follow tradition.

Back then they would walk up out of the valley to Wrexham Road after his dad's shift had finished, catch the bus to the castle, then squeeze on the tram, the old tram that clattered through busy streets, through the Lowtown Bull-Ring and Lascar and across the river into the Anvil Yards. The air became heavier, wetter, as you came down the hill, closer to the rivers. The tram windows would steam up. When the works were open the fogs were worse. There'd be half a dozen Saturdays every season when you'd descend into it. He'd watched games when you could only see a third of the pitch, Stanley Matthews come slicing out of the gloom like Excalibur from the lake. There are moments now when Joey thinks they have all outlived themselves, him and his dad. Liam too, truth be told, still playing at almost forty, kids old enough to be his sons alongside him, skipping by him.

. . .

There is no Iron Town.

They are plural – Anvil Yards, Iron Towns – but the years have reduced them.

Back in the seventies the authorities made them singular, an act of rationalisation, enclosure.

You used to see the letter s graffitied on signs along bleak slip roads on the way out of Cardiff and Birmingham and Liverpool. Older people would scrawl addresses in bold: Anvil Yards, Iron Towns, and that used to make Joey Corwen smile on his post round. You don't see it so often these days. The Anvil Yards are close to empty. Joey is retired. The anger has died off, turned inward, assumed a hundred thousand different forms. Take the shiny new tram that goes nowhere in particular, from the Spider

House to the Heath, and see the messages on the bridges and the crumbling Victorian brick.

Lascar Intifada, Ddraig Pengwern, Kowton Bullet Krew.

The people of the towns tell themselves they have greater concerns than an abandoned letter s.

There is Hightown, with its cliff and ruined castle keep that looks west for insurgents who never come. There is Lowtown and its Spider House and markets. Oxton and Cowton, with their Rangers and Celtic supporters' clubs, high-rises of third generation Glaswegian families who once thought they were moving south for a better go of things, the Sheep Folds beyond them where the roads run out. There is Salop, and Calon, with their avenues of sycamores and 1930s villas. And pit villages all along the Far Valley and Welsh Ridge. There are no pits. The villages are emptying out. The Iron Towns are shrinking. Lascar and the Ironport have their vacant docks and rusting cranes, Chaintown has its dark terraces that have dodged the wrecking ball. There's the Pengwern estate, a lost pebble-dashed valley edged by canals and scrap. Then there's the Heath, remnants of wildness and witches and common land, and the long roads of Heathside on its fringes, with its golf club, and Tory councillors, and dreams of a different England.

And there along the valley bottom, between the two rivers, is the Anvil Yards, a maze of ancient works and roofless brick factory buildings. The blocks of the old Greenfield Ironworks stand at its heart like some secret kaaba. Names from the glory days of a revolution appear on road signs and raised in metal. Newcomen and Stephenson and Darby and Boulton and Watt. And there at its edge, hard against the bank of the River Chain, is the football ground, built to look like one of the factories, still going, creaking into life for another season, one more year. There is talk of tearing it down, that the club will fold soon, the same talk there has been during all its years in the wilderness, much of the last hundred years. But it's there for one more season. And even now, people come through the spaces between the empty factories, just not so many of them any more. They shuffle up the remaining terrace and sit on clacking seats in the stand, huddled, laughing and grumbling against whatever might come next.

. . .

'Are you Dee Dee Ahmed, pet?'

She drops the tray of freshly washed glasses at her feet. They clatter across the lino behind the bar and by some miracle don't break. Not one. There are half-hearted cheers from the few drinkers in the lounge.

'Sorry my love, I'm sorry. I never meant to startle yer.'

The man leans against the bar and talks in a soft north-east accent. Dee Dee looks at him, realises he is not some ghost come to haunt her, but just a man standing at a bar early Saturday afternoon having a pint before the football.

'Yes. Yes I am,' she says, wipes her hands on her apron, bends at her knees to crouch and put the spilled glasses onto a shelf.

'Someone told me you ran this place.'

She nods. Sun comes through the pub's high windows.

'I saw you sing,' the man says, 'a few times I think. I was a roadie for a bit. Charcoal, The Carnations. Newcastle bands, you know?'

Dee Dee nods again, not quite sure where this is going, folds her arms. He does not look like a friend of Goldie's, not at all, in his Hendrix T-shirt, tugging at his earring.

'I don't sing any more.'

'Well, life moves on, I suppose. King Tut's, I saw you. Then that Primal Scream gig in Newcastle. I don't have much to do with it either now. Not at all?'

'In the shower, maybe.'

He looks down at his pint and smiles. She thinks he might even be blushing above the start of a beard.

'Well you had a lovely voice, Dee Dee, pet. I'm sure you still do. That's all I wanted to say.'

He sees his drink off and looks at her and smiles. Warm, she thinks, kind.

She mumbles thanks.

'You take care of yourself.'

'I'll try,' she says, 'I'll try.'

He's already gone. There's a group of them down from County Durham for the afternoon from what she can tell. The man's companions get up from their table by the door. An old bloke in a flat cap, maybe his dad, and a young lad in a blue-quartered football shirt, his son, she reckons, a couple of other men, short sleeves and tattoos, different ages. It's a long way to come on a summer's afternoon, for a pint in the Salamander and a game of football at the Anvil Yards. It happens all year, though, from places like Rochdale and Hartlepool and Mansfield.

Names from the football coupon. At least they can enjoy the sunshine today.

She keeps her arms folded across her chest. Running a pub is no way to hide yourself.

· · ·

The club was founded by bearded Victorian men, Methodists, cricketers after some winter training. They stare out of old photographs like Marx and Nietschze. The only Anglican of the group, the fifth James Greenfield, heir to the Greenfield Ironworks, was an old Etonian. That's why the club's shirts are Eton Blue. Ted hangs them on the dressing-room hooks. Eton Blue is pale green against wood panelling.

The gas lamp under which Iron Towns Football Club was formed in November 1874 had been preserved until the late sixties, when the square on which it stood was demolished to build the flyover. Mount Zion, the chapel, was taken down brick by numbered brick and reassembled a few miles down the road at the Heritage Museum. There is talk of doing similar to the closed East Stand and its iron railings, a joke that they might have to do the same to Liam Corwen.

· · ·

Where the lane meets Wrexham Road Joey hears drumming come like squalls of rain across the fields. At the junction he winds down the window. He sees a police girl, a wisp of blonde hair astray across her cheek. She walks in the middle of the road, her right arm up to slow the traffic. In front of her Joey sees a broad back and a bowler hat. The Orangemen, of course. He's forgotten all about them. It's still marching season. They linger on past all thoughts of the Boyne and into early August here. Everything goes on too long, Joey thinks.

He recognises the bulk of the man who limps out in front, sees him in profile as he turns his head. Pink veins mark his face, comb lines run through his steel coloured hair. His white shirt collar has rubbed a red line on his neck. Joey gets a strange sense of looking at himself. Not that this kind of thing is his cup of tea.

The sash my father wore, they sing, tuneless and lost in the wind.

It's Billy Kerr, he knows him from years back. Billy's dad had been a miner, worked the same shift as Joey's at Black Park. The sun shines on Billy's Brassoed ceremonial chain. He walks like he's got corns. Half a dozen others straggle along with him. An old boy limps with the flag held out in front. A handful of kids march along the verge. They wear berets. There's a boy on a drum, a boy on a flute. A handful of scattered spectators stand on the corner by the shops. A woman comes out of the butchers' with a bag of square sausage, puts her arm out for the bus, oblivious.

'To see my British brethren all of honour and of fame.'

Joey looks at these men, red blotches the shapes of empire on their faces.

The road dips away here and the Iron Towns spread out beneath them. The castle stands bone white against its hill and the ground falls away again beyond it to a patchwork of dark buildings and the green bowl of the hills. There is a glimmer of the rivers and the canal and docks at the Ironport. Joey tries to pick out the floodlight pylons at the ground. From here it all looks the same as it ever did. No smoke, no fire, of course, but the shape of it is the same, more or less. He can see all the way to the Goat Wood, past the training ground, at the far end of the Heath, where when he was a kid they said witches met in the clearings, where the people killed a German parachutist during the war, stuffed his body in an old mine shaft and never told anyone about it. His ghost joined all the others. There is no noise from the valley like there once was, carried up the rivers on the wind, just the notes of a flute and rattle of a drum drifting off into English summer air.

'If the call should come we'll follow the drum, and cross that river once more.'

He has no doubt they would, despite their ragged look. Under the castle, there in the wall that marks the boundary with Lowtown, is the Crusader stone. It's where they met to leave to go to Worcester and follow the Lionheart on his holy war. Joey likes his history. The stone itself is much older, left by Druids on their exodus west, patterned with lichen and faint Ogham lettering. They say Manawydan forged shields on it. This had been one of the cities of the legions, its name lost in time. The Pals Brigades would touch the stone for luck before they left for the First World War. They would have looked just as ragged, men and boys full of a strange anger, dreaming of Jersualem and Mons, followed by patient crows.

A few cars line up behind his. A horn sounds. The police girl follows the heavy union flag into the turning for the shops and the Cowton Orange Lodge, which sits flat-roofed on a car park of sparkling broken glass. She waves everyone down the hill. There is nothing more to see.

. . .

The city and the country Eusébio was born in are no longer there. Or rather, their names have changed, as has so much else with time and war. They are different places. It used to say *This is Portugal* high up on the dock buildings, and in the look in people's eyes, for better or much, much worse. It wasn't, of course, wrong continent, wrong hemisphere, except in some ways it was. Such is empire.

That night in Amsterdam, the shooting at home is soon to start, has already begun in Angola, where his dad was born. His brother is ready to lift his gun. Eusébio has left the hammering sun and the glitter of the bay of Lourenço Marques. *This is Portugal* he would see as he ran with his feet barely touching the ground.

And Barracas, Buenos Aires, too is changed utterly, transfigured by rust and the years of the generals. Di Stéfano remembers being taken to see the old iron bridge pulled down. The men spoke in hushed Italian dialects. His dad was from the island of Capri, his mother was German, Irish. Europe was finished for them. He is Argentinian, becomes Colombian, becomes Spanish. Barracas is a place of shadows now, empty factories and stock yards. Trains clatter through, don't stop.

But these are men of movement, do not look back, keep the world spinning with their footsteps.

. . .

Paul, her bar manager, puts his head round the corner of the lounge.

'You've got a visitor at the off sales, Dee Dee.'

'What?'

'Don't worry. Just your usual Saturday dinner gentleman caller.'

She doesn't know why she's kept the hatch open. She tells herself it was what her nana would've liked, but times change. Dee Dee used to sit on a stool in the space between the bar and the lounge on long ago Sundays and watch her nana serve at the hatch which opens onto Meeting House Lane. At 3 o'clock they'd lock the doors and she'd always do a song or two in the empty lounge bar under the chandeliers before they went upstairs for dinner.

Mark Fala stands at the counter. He's spread a pile of change across it. No more than a pound, she can see, runs her hand over it. There are a couple of washers, an old Italian coin. Lira doesn't even exist any more. She can't tell if he's serious, pulls a bottle of sherry from the shelf and some cans of cider from the chiller nevertheless. She takes down forty Superkings too, her own, not even the pub's, although it's the same thing she supposes. She bought them at the new Ukrainian shop.

'All right, Mark,' she says.

'Thanks Dee Dee. I appreciate it.'

'You take care of yourself,' she says, looks at the shadow under his eye, can't decide if it's a bruise or not.

He doesn't move straight away, sways a little, as he arranges his bottle and cans into his plastic bag. He stuffs the cigarettes deep into his overcoat pocket. He used to go weeks without speaking at all. He has always shown up here though, always early in the afternoon on matchdays. She wonders if he used to walk down here with his dad when he'd been a kid, something pulls him back, not just a few handouts. There are plenty of people who'll give him them.

'You got anything for me dog, Dee Dee?'

'Your dog? I didn't know you had a dog, Mark.'

He shrugs.

'Sometimes.'

She reaches to the back shelf, pulls a couple of bags of scratchings off the thin cardboard display.

'Thanks, Dee Dee,' he says, 'thanks. I'll see you soon.' And he turns and limps away. She'll get him some shoes, she thinks, but doesn't know if he'd accept them. He doesn't have to dress like he does. He's not down and out. She knows he still lives in the flats, although they're slated to come down when they begin the work. When he turns the corner at the sagging wall his shadow angles across the road and a smaller, lower shadow follows.

She has kept the hatch open for Mark Fala, of course. That's how things work. People do things for him. She stands and catches the sunlight on her face, mouths a song to herself, slow and quiet, hears the bell ringing for service in the lounge.

. . .

There is no match traffic. There isn't when the season is in full swing, so certainly not today. Clouds move up the River Anvil, high and slow over the cars and floodlights and cranes. An ice cream van has pulled into the kerb by the car park entrance. Joey considers buying one. A lone figure stands nearby with a pile of new copies of the fanzine. New season special! The fanzine is called *46 seconds*. It angers Joey every time he sees one. His boy played for England and all people do is take the piss. They say he never touched the ball, even, but he did, he won a header, a flick-on. People never get anything right.

He puts his hand up to acknowledge the seller, a young, balding man, prematurely aged, wears a hearing aid, and whose name Joey can never remember, with the new away shirt spread across his belly. This shirt's official colour is chocolate, another legacy of the Greenfield family. James Greenfield played cricket, briefly, for Surrey, and the shirt is the colour of their county cap. Like dog shit on a lawn, Ally Barrr once said when the team had been given a hiding somewhere, Plymouth or Yeovil was it? Some team in green. Everyone says they hate these brown shirts, but they are the only thing at the club that turns a profit. They get orders from Salt Lake City and Mannheim and Daegu, men young and old buying a piece of football folklore.

Joey turns in through the club gates. In front of the offices, a couple of Mercedes shine in the sun and Ally's BMW, a new car for the new season courtesy of Lionel Ahmed, who had probably intended it for Liam. The Mercedes must belong to the Portuguese, already here. Joey decides against pulling into the space marked *Club Captain/LC*, drives instead across the tarmac to the unpaved ground under the fence by the canal. He sits in the meshed shadow for a while, thinks about moving the car to the shade. It looks cool under the solid end wall of the old Watkins Cylinder Works. Ivy has grown and spilled down a length of the wall. Elder branches arc over the towpath. Everything is still. From the tunnel of branches comes a man, limping, limping and swaggering in equal parts. He wears a long overcoat in spite of the weather and a football boot on his left foot, an unlaced brogue on his right, a carrier bag of drink swings from his wrist. The shoes account in part for the limp. His face stays in shadow but Joey knows full well who it is.

Mark Fala's walk has retained some of the old character it used to bring to a football pitch, although he's not stepped on one for nearly twenty years. Wasps swim out above the water, zigzag against the pattern of the brick, as if they move for him. Joey would not bet against it. That boy. Mark drops his head and disappears from sight under the bridge. Joey sits for a while.

A fox walks along the towpath in the same direction as Mark, nose up, a patch of grey-orange fur missing from its flank and its ribs sticking through, but shiny eyed and alert. Following him, Joey thinks, not just chance, trotting along there with his nose up, on to a scent. Joey tries not to believe in bad luck. They say there's a curse on the ground. He missed that fucking penalty on purpose, for one thing, is what Joey thinks. The fox goes on its way into the gloom under the bridge. More thoughts of carrion.

· · ·

They are not Portuguese. None of them are, even the young lad himself, Luis, who is from Cape Verde.

'This is Liam Corwen, club captain,' Ally says. Liam shakes hands with the two men who have stepped from the Mercedes. He sees himself and Ally reflected in their sunglasses. Another man sits in shadow in the rear of one of the cars, does not move. Liam turns to the young kid who stands next to them in his green tracksuit. His hand feels like a little boy's. Liam thinks of Jari, thinks of his hand in his.

'Liam, these are Luis's representatives.'

'I'm sure they are, gaffer.'

Ally gives him a look, but what to say?

Ally worked at Sporting Lisbon, coached there under Malcolm Allison, so this Portuguese bit at least sounds true. The rest is a mystery. One thing Liam is certain of is that only he and this slight boy he now leads down the corridor's torn lino to the dressing room are not set to make something from this little pantomime. Steve Stringer's absence only adds to Liam's suspicion. The club secretary holds the place together, haunts it in his baggy, grey suits, invisible most of the time, filling out forms and talking on the phone in his office, which sits gloriously out of time, with stencilled lettering on frosted glass, inside the West Stand. The directors meet every now and again for some sausage rolls and a chat about the season. The club is owned by the last of the Greenfield family – Dorothea Greenfield-Carter – who lives out her old age in the Madeira sun. The last of the line, she refuses to invest, or sell, or do anything at all with her absolute control of the club.

Liam knows the look that comes from behind the glasses. Older men watch much younger ones and calculate what they might make from them. Reflected glory, reflected youth, cold, hard cash. Not that Luis's representatives, as Ally calls them – Ally is good with the jargon – are that old. Liam is maybe even giving them a few years, smooth skinned men in expensive suits, the world shining in their glasses. They are of indeterminate ethnicity, a phrase Liam read in the paper, but then aren't we all, he thought at the time. And the boy looks about fourteen. What must he make of this, on his route from Cape Verde to Lisbon to who knows where via the Anvil Yards? Liam ushers him towards a corner of the dressing room.

'You know Eusébio?'

'Eusébio?' The kid has no idea what he is talking about.

Liam untucks his shirt and lifts it to show two men inked onto his right flank. Eusébio and Di Stéfano look at each other at a moment of passing, the 1962 European Cup Final, Benfica 5 Real Madrid 3. Eusébio has just scored.

'Eusébio,' Luis grins, says the name again but it sounds different this time.

'He played here, you know. Trained here. Three times. For the Rest of the World, for Portugal in the World Cup, and with Benfica, before the cup final against United. Played here.'

'Here?'

Luis looks around at the dressing room, widens his eyes. He is quick, Liam senses. He bets he can run like water.

'Right here, yeah. You think I'm pulling yer leg.'

Liam smiles and so does the boy. The Eusébio stuff is all true. In the sixties the club was in the second division but the Greenfield family still had some say at the Football Association, told everyone that the Iron Towns were an easy drive to Wembley.

Liam points again at the picture.

'Real Madrid,' Luis says.

'Yeah, Di Stéfano.'

'And this one?'

The boy points to a dark-eyed figure, a glitter to his eyes and a toothpick clamped in the corner of his mouth, his gaze equal parts magic and menace.

'Billy Meredith.'

'And this one?'

The dark-eyed man looks at a pale-faced boy in an old-fashioned England shirt, his face open and innocent.

'Steve Bloomer.'

For a while he and Tony had concentrated on pairs, on great players as they passed each other on the way up, on the way down. There's one of Van Basten coming on as sub for Ajax, Cruyff coming off, holding his hand out to shake.

'I don't know this ones.'

'Old players.'

'You have Ronaldo?'

'The old one, the Brazilian one. I'm not allowed players who are still playing.'

It is true, but Liam sets the rules himself. He feels good saying it, though, like this was some bigger thing than himself.

Liam unbuttons his shirt, takes it off, stretches his arms out to the sides and turns to show Luis the image of Ronaldo between his shoulder blades, arms outstretched too, as Christ the

Redeemer above Rio. They copied it from a tyre advert but put him in his Barcelona shirt.

'I like Ronaldo. This one. But Cristiano is better.'

'You play like him?'

The boy laughs. 'More like Messi, maybe.' He grins.

Liam likes this lad. God knows what he is doing here.

. . .

The film is from a January morning. Alina has recorded so much now that she is months behind with what she watches. This one is possible, though. Although possible for what she is not sure, some exhibition that exists only in her head. When there was no cloud those winter mornings were good, better than the summer glare, something to do with the angle at which the sun comes over the hill at Burnt Village. To think she didn't know the sun rose at different places, from different angles, until she'd started this work. Hardly work, really. She didn't know what to call it, thinks instead of a word to describe the light and is left scratching her head. Sunrises, sunsets were not thought of as appropriate subject matter at art school, but still. The sunrise is not really the subject. We are flying through space on a giant rock.

There is a thin line of blue above the far hills. Yellow streetlights pattern the foreground, then there is the dark mass of the docks and the Anvil Yards. Venus shines bright above a black hill. The blue line broadens, lightens slowly. A red sun comes up into the blue band. Plane contrails form between what clouds there are. On the far hillside Burnt Village looks just that as the sun appears to swallow it. The outline of charred houses is silhouetted against the sun. Light and shade ripple across the valley, then the light evens, as the sun, golden now, rises behind clouds.

It's fine. It's OK. The light is good. The way it comes green down the hillsides might make you think of a time there were no towns here at all. But it's not what she wants.

Then she has a thought, simply plays it backwards. The sun sinks back towards the middle of England. The light fades, slowly, slowly, then fast. The hills burn again, then that last band of blue takes ages to disappear. But time has reversed, run back on itself. And it is so very simple. She wonders now if this is too simple, too easy, no soundtrack, no other explanation, nothing. But that is exactly what she wants: time running backwards, time lapsing, folding in on itself.

. . .

'Blisters, fucking blisters, but.'

The dressing room is hot and silent.

'Blisters. Unbelievable. Professional footballers who cannot think to look after their feet.'

They sit and stare at the tiles. Julius Williams has a wet towel over his head. Steam rises from it. Kyran Blackstock, one of the kids who has come up from the youth team, grins and tries to catch someone's eye to highlight this phenomenon. Liam gives him a look and he puts his head down, eyes to the floor. Kyran won't last five minutes, Liam thinks.

They are not all professionals. Ally's wrong on that

score. They're still playing triallists, got a couple of lads over from Ireland, an attempt to get a few more warm bodies in before the season starts.

They are two nothing down to a team of part-timers. The pitch is a moonscape. Ally needs something on which to focus his anger. Liam watches him. The man is chewing, red faced, as if sick of the world and the injustice of it all, but Liam can tell he is trying to work himself into this anger, moving his false teeth up and down his gums. He's had enough. This, with everything else, does not bode well for the season ahead. It's as if Ally knows what he should do, knows how he should be feeling, knows the rage these players expect and deserve, as he looks from face to face, but the anger isn't there. He's finished, Liam thinks suddenly to himself. Ally breathes hard, looks at the wall, pulls at his shirt collar. He's in his third spell as Irontown manager, is sixty-six now. One more season, he told himself, back in May, kidded himself if he could get a decent couple of players in they might be good for the play-offs, delusional. Finish with one last promotion. One last bit of pride. He is a man who believes he was destined for bigger things than this. He played on the fringe of the Lisbon Lions team, the Quality Street Gang after that, grew up in Finnieston, like Danny McGrain who always got picked before him, chased the ball on the cinders under the crane as a kid, a Protestant boy who played proudly at Celtic, like McGrain and Dalglish, like Jock Stein himself. He has half a team complaining about their feet.

'Fucking blisters.'

This is how Liam comes to get on that afternoon, not that things improve much. They let in another goal ten minutes from the end after a scramble in the six yard box following a corner. Liam loses his man, their big striker, and he hopes Ally does not see it in the dust storm.

The kid barely gets a kick. Liam has almost forgotten about him in the humiliation, the day's touch of glamour, this boy on his way into or out of Sporting Lisbon, as if, and somehow playing here en route. Then in the last minute Liam thumps a clearance from twenty yards inside his own half, more out of frustration than with any intent, and he is there, Luis, and sways into the ball, takes it on his right thigh, dead, swivels and flicks it with his left foot past the moving defender, takes a step, hits it on the volley, all in one movement, with his laces. The ball fizzes and dips twenty-five yards, as if it's a different object from the one that has bobbled around for the previous ninety minutes, clips the outside of the post with a satisfying ping and rebounds back to the edge of the box off the advertising boards with a deep thud before their keeper has even moved.

It was Cruyff who claimed he used to sometimes try to hit the post on purpose. Cruyff is the pale Dutch ballboy. He tries to move like Eusébio, like Di Stéfano.

Half the crowd have already gone. From the ones who remain, many weren't looking. There is a jolt from a few, and a handful of oohs and applause drifts across the pitch. Some of the young lads behind the goal begin to sing *Sign him up*. These are the boys who sometimes come to matches wearing a fez, a homage to an old newspaper headline 'Ally Barr bars baa baas', a reference to the time Ally tried to get the livestock market to close on Wednesday match days. That was in the days when Ally thought he could do anything, took the club from the bottom of the third division to that missed penalty kick in the play-off final away from the Premier League. He could do little wrong then. The market has gone for good now anyway. The boys laugh as they sing, because they know that there are bigger forces at work. This kid, listed as 'A.N. Other' on the programme, in a nice Edwardian touch, is not destined for the Anvil Yards.

Liam glances up at the grandstand. Spits out some of the dust. They don't know what they're looking at, most of them, the punters, he is convinced. If they see anything as good as that for the rest of the season they'll be lucky. The ref blows for full-time before they take the goal kick.

. . .

Di Stéfano traps the ball as it falls from the keeper's kick, rolls his studs over it (over *her*, he writes in a book years later called, *Thanks, Old Girl*). He turns to his right, with his back to goal he is moving left, but he keeps turning, almost a complete circle, away from the Eintracht player, and now takes a couple of paces. Strange how his legs seem longer when he has the ball. He feints, sways as if to strike it wide for Canário, but stops, almost entirely still for a moment. His opponent runs from him and he moves forward now, builds momentum, pushes it to Vidal, gets it back, has to check his run, but from his heels springs forward, slides it towards Puskás with the outside of his boot, looks to sprint for the return, but as Puskás opens himself the defender has nicked it away. The defenders are not often so lucky.

It is like this all night, *la furia*, changes of pace, of direction, unrelenting. Like this, he moves through people's dreams. When he gets the ball the blood quickens in the eighth of a million people inside the stadium. They have laid down their iron on the banks of the Clyde to come to see him in the European Cup Final, to see the great Real Madrid make it five in a row. He walks, he sprints, he stands still. Hampden is his time, his space, to do with as he wishes.

. . .

Liam sits on the bed in the room. He has lived at the hotel for three weeks now, since pre-season training began, since Greta and Jari went back, got a deal from the manager, Amir, an old school mate. He thinks he might never leave.

He stands for some time at the window, stretching his calf muscles, looks out across the Anvil Yards. A crow flies from the floodlight gantry to the East Stand roof. The gulls wheel over empty dock water.

In a few minutes he'll turn on the laptop. The bedside clock blinks and tells him it is still too early. She said seven o'clock, nine in Finland. Long blocks of shadow fill the view. He imagines the white Northern light filling rooms; the light across the lake fills the house, Greta and Jari move through the rooms. She is combing his hair while he stands in his pyjamas. Liam's body aches. She lets Jari stay up when they're at the lake house. He can feel the grooves of the pine jetty under his feet. He has a blister on his right heel. He can hear the sound of the water lap-

31

ping against the wood. You can't open the windows here in the hotel. He wants some air, wants to hear the sound of the gulls, the sound of traffic, of cars going somewhere else; the sound of water on a thin beach and the silence of great forests beyond. He cannot see a single human movement across the whole of the Anvil Yards, Saturday teatime, no one there. He looks at the ruin of the old Assembly Rooms, where his own parents met the year of the World Cup, talked about Eusébio. They used to hold under-age club nights there before the dancefloor fell into a hole. He remembers queueing up to get in on a summer night, Dee Dee and Sonia in the line in front of him, and Sonia turning round and looking at him over her bare shoulder.

'What a fucking mess,' he says, and his words colour the glass.

A dirty St George's flag that hangs from the corner of an old warehouse moves in a sudden breeze, pigeons rise and veer together across the old docks wall and away towards the Greenfield Ironworks. His face has caught the sun, his nose and cheeks have reddened. He enjoys the small burn of it. That pitch, a corner of which he can see here over the river and through the gates at the Greenfield End, is a desert. He pictures Laurel and Hardy in the Foreign Legion, going in circles. A helicopter comes down the line of the hills and river, angles in at the corner of the window, moves away to turn and head back up the valley towards Cowton or Oxton. He tries to make his mind as empty as the pitch, the dock, the long stretches of wasteland that radiate out from the old ironworks.

There is Greta on the screen. He can tell she's made an effort, has done her hair, some make-up. That's good, he thinks.

Something has happened to the sound, so he watches them moving in the patterns of the water reflected from the lake. Jari refuses to stay in front of the camera, Greta reaches for him, her arms bare. Liam sobs, lets it out now, leans away so he is out of the picture. One time last year he started, couldn't stop.

'Daddy sad,' Jari said.

'Never do that again, never,' Greta hissed down the phone a few days after that. It was when things had been bad, worse than now.

'Daddy,' Jari says. The boy's face, his hair. He holds a blue plastic robot. It's the one he chose on one of the last days of their visit when Liam's mum and dad had driven them out to the ToysRus by the motorway.

The small amount of English that Jari had learned is fading. Greta says she uses it with him but Liam doesn't believe her. He never learned Finnish. Greta speaks Finnish, Swedish, German, Russian. There'd been no need for him to learn, he picked up the odd phrase, he was always the Englishman, the big man, always set apart, in the corner of the dressing room, in the centre of the pitch. It had suited him, he thought. Now he looked at his son babbling away into the camera. They would not speak the same language.

'*Kaunis poika*,' he says, beautiful boy. He knows a few words, should get those tapes out again, god knows he's got enough time on his hands. They say it's one of the hardest languages to learn. Jari is a beautiful boy.

Then he is gone, there's just that flickering light from the lake and Greta, distracted, a quick goodbye, neutral. Just stay, he wants to say, leave the camera on, go about your business, I'll just sit and watch from here. They arrange to speak during the week.

He looks at the blue plastic bag on the table he'd meant to put in the bedside fridge. The cans of beer inside sweat, there are a couple of bottles of Lucozade and a packet of jaffa cakes next to the bag. He'll run the beers off on the Heath tomorrow, dress the blister, take it easy and stretch himself out for Monday's training. Archie Hill's got him on a special programme. The aches are starting. He can feel his heel, his hip, his back, all start to go. He'll watch the rest of the cricket highlights, read his book, about Real Madrid in the fifties. He can read about Di Stéfano, Puskás, Gento. He can do that. He can phone his dad to talk about the match if he wants to. He wonders about that boy, Luis. Ally's car is still in the car park. The Mercedes have gone. He stands at the window and watches the blue evening fade.

· · ·

INTERVIEWER: But you are hopeful, Ally, for the
    season to come?
ALLY BARR: It's August. Listen son, in August there's
    always hope.
INTERVIEWER: Even in Irontown?
ALLY BARR: Even in the Iron Towns.
LIAM CORWEN (aside): Wait until September.
(Laughter)

· · ·

A dead pigeon hangs in the mesh suspended from the giant concrete awning. The Lowtown bus station is choked with fumes and lit by yellow strip-lights, even though the sun shines brightly on the building's open side. Goldie waits for his bag, muses on the pigeon. He wants to feel something, something to make it all seem real. Twenty years can be a lifetime, as well he knows. Though the twenty years in his head seem longer than the ones that have passed here. Prison time lasts longer in some ways, in other ways does not pass at all. It wasn't like he'd been in prison all that time anyway, less than half if you added it all up. He had made a life in Birmingham with Nadine, and look what that had come to now, same as everything else. The pastel coloured murals, the daytime twilight, the food stalls, are all the same as the last time he came here. He remembers now, waiting for Sonia and Dee Dee to come back on the London bus from an audition, a Friday night not long after he first got a car. Excited, all of them. Liam and Mark were with him, must have been June, outside the football season, otherwise Liam would've been tucked up behind the net curtains in his nice Black Park bedroom. It might well be that he has come back to slit Liam Corwen's throat.

On Fridays a big van used to pull up on the waste ground outside, where the football coaches parked, and set off racing pigeons. They would rise with their wings sounding like applause. He'd had a row once, stupid, in the workshops at Winson Green about whether pigeons and doves are the same bird, different colours. *This is what it sounds like* . . . There was a Prince tape he wore out playing in the car and on the roof at Mark's flats. It was the one that was playing when they crashed. Pigeons can fly, he

35

thinks, and wonders why these ones choose to stay here, pecking at scraps of burger and dying in the rafters.

'This yours, chief?' A Brummie accent, the driver wants to get a move on, has to go back the other way in twenty minutes or so.

'Thanks, mate.' Goldie hauls the kit-bag onto his shoulder, an army surplus, he bought it at a kiosk in the Rag Market. He thought it might make him look like a soldier back on leave. It just makes him look like who he is, what he is. He can see his reflection in the glass barrier. When he looks away he sees the departure board. Buses to Manchester, London, Holyhead/ Dublin. He has been to none of these places. He could head to the ticket counter, go for whichever bus comes first. He can do what he likes. He feels the same weightlessness he had that morning, walking down through Digbeth, leaving the city that had been his home in one way or another for much of the past twenty years, his adult life. He can go wherever he wants. But he knows what he's doing. He asked for a ticket to Lowtown.

'Return, love?'

'I ain't coming back.'

But coming back is exactly what he is doing. The bus only took an hour and a half, came the long way too. He is deflated by the paltriness of the distance, the way time collapses. In his head it is like the crossing of a great continent. There was traffic on the Hagley Road.

He wants this to feel like an occasion. He puts his hand to his jacket pocket. There's a roll of notes, a couple of half-smoked spliffs and a little tub of diazepam. One of Nadine's brothers must have borrowed the coat. Goldie hasn't smoked for years.

He doesn't need any more paranoia. He thinks they might come after him. He can sell the tablets. The place won't have changed that much.

There used to be a bar just here, been done out as a café now, you can see in through the windows and out to the market on the other side. There are plastic tables with umbrellas out on the concrete. The windows were blacked out in those days. The Eight Ball, it was called. Sometimes Stan Ahmed himself would sit there at the bar, his thick arms resting on it. A few times Goldie was told to call in there, get his instructions, explain himself. More usually it was at the bookies at the corner of the docks road in Lascar. Goldie tried to read the signs, what a meeting here or there might signify. He could never tell whether he was being spoken to because he had done something well or not, if he was on his way up or down.

He feels something now. He looks in through the window at the young girl serving, scans the faces at the tables quickly. Maybe that old man there, maybe, with his blue eyes staring out of the window towards the markets, is that a flicker of recognition? It jolts him. He knows that Stan Ahmed has long gone, to his villa first, and then a private hospital somewhere near Marbella. Stan's brothers too, sold up, moved out, or ruined, inside, or dead, a little bit of all these things in the aftermath of a fallen empire. Lionel's still around, he knows that. He is exposed here, looking at his own shadow. The old man stares through the window, takes a sip of tea, his eyes pass over Goldie, look through him. Something like disappointment makes him sag a little. He wants to hide, wants to be seen.

He wanders through the light and shade of the market edges. This is dangerous now, the Lowtown Bull Ring. Things don't change that much here. Maybe twenty years is not so long. The woman there at the fruit stand with the perm, didn't he used to collect money from her on a Friday?

'Tell him, he'll have the rest next week, chick.'

'He won't be happy, darling, I can tell yer that for nothing.'

And there at the taxi rank, where the drivers lean against their cabs and flick through the papers, stroke their phones, wasn't he one of Lionel Ahmed's little crew? The man turns his thick neck out of the sun, puts his hand on the car top, see: only three fingers. People said that Lionel had cut his mate's fingers off over a girl they both liked, but that was crap, a length of steel cable had torn it off at the Ironport. It's him. Goldie cannot remember the bloke's name, ducks his head, weaves between the shoppers. It all hits him now. He keeps his head down. Every glance now, he's like a kid in a story lost in a wood, faces in the branches stare out at him. And he feels the darkness creeping in at the edges of his vision as sweat runs into his eyes. There, and there, and there, and that girl in her summer dress just there, Sonia's face looks back at him. Sonia's face back then, still twenty years old and full of life. He edges past the man with henna in his beard, selling batteries from a pink plastic bucket, meets the fence, walks along it, away from the market, expects to hear his name called, expects footsteps behind him, feels the weight of the bag on his shoulders, although god knows what is in it for it to weigh like this, everything he owns, and the money from behind the panel at the back of the airing cupboard, and his knives. He worked in the kitchens at the hospital when he first came out on licence, was lucky to get a place doing anything, taught him how to use a knife. They will come after him. He walks with the market behind him now, lines of buses between him and the bus station. This road runs down into the Anvil Yards. And here, there's a gap in the fence, signs warning of dogs and security, but he'll take his chances. He slips through the gap, sun bounces off the bus windows, and he glances back at not a soul around, goes down a set of crumbling blue brick steps where nettles and dock leaves grow, and into the shadows again.

. . .

There are rooms in this house that no one has stepped inside for years. No one has ever been in that extension, she's sure of it, since the builders finished years ago. By the time that was done Dee Dee and Liam were already coming apart. Dee Dee chose the child over him and that was the end of that.

This is a family home. Liz looks out of the leaded window at the turn in the stairs, looks out at the green hills turning blue in the distance, the roses in the garden below. That lawn is dying. This house is more than most people dream of, she thinks, the kind of house people might climb the hill to get a glimpse of, drive past on summer evenings, on Sunday afternoons, and say one day, if all our ships come in, we'll live somewhere like this. Liam bought it from a consultant at the Bethel, Mr Jenkins, same one who'd operated on Joey's mum that first time, small world they said. Small world for sure, it was Mr Jenkins's replacement,

Mr Ali, who spoke to Liz in that hot, side-room off the ward and discussed procedures and ways forward and strategies to contain and then eradicate her cancer. You knew it was bad if they ushered you into those little rooms. They never used to use the word itself. Your nan is very ill they said to Liam and the girls when it was Joey's mum's turn; Molly is very ill they would tell people, and people would nod and understand.

Liam and Dee Dee were twenty-one, same age as when she and Joey got married, except they'd moved into his mum and dad's back bedroom, waited on the council list. She remembers having no idea how Liam could afford it, but he'd played for England, Dee Dee had been on *Top of the Pops*. It was the very start of those years when the banks lent money hand over fist. They had the money. They had everything.

This was the kind of house where children ran back and forth across the lawn, laughing and playing, protected from the Iron Towns by the high walls around the garden and the money in the lanes that led down to the stables and the tennis and golf clubs at the edge of the Heath. She has told him she'll just come once a week from now on. She gets tired now much more quickly than before, maybe her strength will build, but more because there is nothing to clean.

This was the kind of house that should be full of voices on a Sunday night, brothers and sisters and uncles and aunties and cousins and grandparents, laughter rising out of open windows and across the hills like those fire lanterns that have become popular now. She half expects one to drift down the valley from a birthday party on one of these lawns one Saturday and burn down the Anvil Yards. If only, she thinks, if only. She has spent her life getting away from the place and still only made it halfway up the hill.

Liam barely speaks to his sisters. Their girls have a cousin who they don't know, an uncle who takes no interest in any of them. He is not a good son, has not been a good husband.

The house could not have been colder when she was here with the boy. Little Jari, her grandson, her own flesh and blood, half a world away even when he was here in the summer. She kept speaking to him in their language, explaining what his nan and grandad had said to him. Finland. You may as well say Timbuktu. She knows Liam asked her to stay here with him. You think she'd be happy to move from the cold, the dark. He has mislaid two wives and a son now with this carelessness, that's what she thinks, but by the time she's finished the banister rails, she's back to lamenting how those girls were not good enough for him. It was they who refused him, her once beautiful blue-eyed boy.

. . .

She sings at funerals. That's what she could have told the man at the bar. A few through the years now, that's for sure. Her nana's, of course, a couple of her uncles'. Dee Dee imagines when Stan dies they'll fly the body back, can't arrest a dead man. She sang at Sonia's, at the wake, though, that she and Liam organised. The service had been plain, barely any ceremony, police stood discreet at the back of the chapel of rest. Sonia's parents had not wanted any of them there at all.

Liam drove back across the Heath after the service, pulled into a clearing off a back lane. She wore black tights too hot for a summer's day, torn them off herself, climbed in the back, only a few hundred yards from where the car had gone in the river, not even much of a river there. They tore at each other. She dug her nails into his arse, bit his neck. They froze at the noise of a tractor going past, animals in their burrow.

'Don't worry, it's nothing, just fuck me Liam,' she said. For years afterwards she felt ashamed of that half an hour or whatever it was, no longer than that, for sure, under the trees, the day of her best friend's funeral, the car roof sticky with sap. It made more sense as the years went by. She thought of it now in moments of quiet, one of the true things of her life.

Dee Dee loves that line from Dylan Thomas, *After the first death there is no other*. Not as a negation of what comes after, more that whatever comes afterwards simply amplifies the past. She tries not to think of Sonia at all, then looks at Alina, her daughter, *her* daughter already past the age at which she died.

Were they older then, somehow? Dee Dee was more certain of herself that's for sure, certain of the world, already married a year, of course. I'll take care of her, she said. It was years of hating him for not going along with it before she realised she had never even asked him.

She sings at funerals, likes Dylan Thomas, doubts every single thing she has ever known. She could've told him that, the handsome stranger at the bar.

'Are you Dee Dee Ahmed, pet?'

'I don't know, love. I honestly could not tell you.'

. . .

Mark Chapman: Of all tonight's ties, none are more
loaded with history than the one at the Anvil
Yards, Irontown against Wolverhampton Wanderers.
Redolent of another age. Pat Murphy is there for
us.

Pat Murphy: Yes Mark, it's thirty years or more
since a rather uncharitable former manager of
both of these clubs said that if the Wolves were
sleeping giants then Irontown were a comatose
pygmy. He had just been sacked, mind you, by the
once all-powerful Greenfield family, very much
absentee landlords these days. Dorothea Greenfield-
Carter, last of the dynasty, lives out her days
in Madeiran exile and refuses to sell or invest.
Nothing soporific about tonight, though, as you
can probably hear. The Anvil Yards is full. Its
capacity is just over ten thousand these days,
with the closure of the East Stand and other
health and safety issues. Gone are the days of
fifty thousand plus and the old 'iron roar'. The
crowd is boosted by a large contingent from the
nearby Black Country, hopeful of a new dawn under
Kenny Jackett. There used to be a big rivalry
between these two, of course, but they haven't
played each other regularly since they slid down
the leagues together in the dark days of the
1980s. One last thing, for those of you of a
certain age, Liam Corwen, he of England infamy and

43

```
Irontown legend, forty next year, is on the bench
tonight and is currently laying out cones for
the warm-up, a rondel, Barcelona-style, in front
of the away fans. The PA system is playing 'My
Sweetest One', sung by his ex-wife's girl band.
Perhaps he's wearing earplugs!
```
Mark Chapman: Thanks, Pat. Updates from the Anvil

Yards and elsewhere throughout the evening . . .

. . .

This is more like it. His dad has even lifted his summer ban for the night. The Wolves at home in the League Cup under the lights.

One of the last great crowds here had been when they had the League Cup run in the early eighties. They'd played Liverpool in the semi-final, there'd been traffic all up to Hightown before the first leg, young lads scaling the walls at the Greenfield End. He remembered the way the ground used to look for those night matches, the glow of the floodlights, and the bigger glow of the Anvil Yards beyond, lighting the clouds that came up the river. The sound, the roar. And the lighting of the whole sky. If you came along the Monmouth or Wrexham Roads back in those days, from way out, looking over the hills, it was like you were approaching the crack of doom itself, matchday or not. The red valley they used to call it then. But then that couldn't be right. By the time of that Liverpool game the works were already closing. They had a red flag that filled the away end, sang *Dalglish* all night until they started on *You'll Never Walk Alone*. It was Rush, though, who'd scored twice. Liverpool had won three, four, was it? Won the second leg six-nothing. They were sat in line with Rush's second goal, he'd fouled big Archie Hill, clipped his heels as the ball was played and then left him for dead. Joey remembered Liam alongside him, eight, nine years old, screaming at the linesman to stick his flag up.

. . .

'We are English, Welsh, Black Irish,' Mark Fala's dad would say to him, tugging at his dark curly hair, 'pirates from the Spanish Main, gypsies at home in any hedgerow,' tell him stories of where their name came from. The stories would always start and end in the same way. A young man would leave his valley for the last time, sometimes with his brothers, sometimes alone, to the sound of wolves howling across the mountain snows or the sun coming patterned through the cork trees. His route, and all the generations that followed him, eventually brought him here on the road between the Ironport and the Anvil Yards, to the sound of iron being struck.

It would depend on how much his dad had drunk, how long and complex the way became, but there was always the flight from the mountains, from wolves and bandits and hunger and vicious landowners. And there was always a first glimpse of the sea.

Sometimes it was a fishing village set among the green cliffs, sometimes the harbour of a great city. One version had the young man arriving in Lisbon as the Armada massed, and signing up for a place on one of the impossible floating castles, bigger than the village the lad had left, that sat out in the estuary. Another longer, even taller tale had the man and his brothers join other ships and cross the Atlantic to the slave markets and jungles and great cities of gold. The man returns with jewels and chocolate and a tame crocodile but somehow loses all this and can't find his way home and is blown by a storm into the rainy north. There is always a storm and a shipwreck. In the Armada story, defeat and bad weather has the ships floundering off the Irish coast and just as the hull splinters on some rocks the man leaps and swims ashore, led by mermaids whose names are Estrildis and Habren, through the waves to a deserted beach, where he lies on the edge of the water half dead but still somehow escapes the soldiers who wait to kill him.

There is always Ireland in the story, in some guise or other. The man is his sons and grandsons and great-grandsons and so on. He is hundreds of years old. He moves inland through the mist and silent fields and peat bogs. He is chased like a fox by the English, goes out of his mind with hunger when the famine comes.

He sets sail again, to New York, to Australia, to the Liverpool docks or Lancashire mills or Midland factories.

'We are English, Welsh, Black Irish,' his dad would say to him, take a sip of his mild ale. He smelled of chemical soap from the works, and he'd look up out of the valley where he'd always lived to the limestone hills and appear every inch a man of the Iron Towns. A man made of coal and iron and wiry muscle.

The man in the story was a miner, a tinker, a docker, a puddler, a horse trader at the Stowe fair. Somehow the road would

wind nearer and nearer, merge somehow with the real, like figures stepping out of a comic book. Mark's great-granny lived
at Merthyr Tydfil. They would go and see her at Easter and he
would pull at his elasticated tie and look at cousins whose names
he could never remember.

And there they'd be, beside the River Chain, the man would
become his own dad, off to work at the Samson Foundry every
morning at six, a small black shape against a raging fire, that was
how Mark would see him on the few times he'd been down to
the work gates, kicking his tennis ball against the kerbs on the
way.

When he almost signed for Torino, the club had that money
to spend after selling Lentini, the whole thing was cursed, they
were going to take Liam with him, and he guessed Dee Dee
might have come too, the lawyer in the beautiful suit, his fat head
leaning forward behind his glasses across the contract like the
emperor of the toads spoke to him.

'Fala, a good name. Venetian, I think.'

Mark shrugged. 'I'm not sure, I don't think so.'

'Spain? America? Ireland?' His mum laughed whenever he
asked her. 'Your dad's never been further than the donkey rides
at Weston and you can only see the sea there when the tide's in.'

.　.　.

We came when you enclosed our meadows and drowned our
valleys. We came out from our little forges in the sun-dappled
woods. We came from fields of dead potatoes and soldiers, from

Clydeside tenements with the promise of work, we came no distance at all, our ways of life swallowed, harried off our land by your gamekeepers and lackeys. We are English, Welsh, Black Irish, Scottish. We were none of these things once upon a time, and we shall not be them again. We take many forms. Some of us once watched from ditches by the river, or from the higher peaks, waited for Roman soldiers to pick us off one by one. We are patient as the stones.

. . .

The players are born within the sound of hammers. Whether a great boom across rivers and docks or the tap, tap, tap from backyard workshops, the sounds of metal and stone are always close by. The rattle of the railway and tram, the tapping of the nailyard, chainyard, pottery, the blasting of stone from quarries, the hacking of coal from deep underground, the roar of a furnace. They hold in them the energy of fire and dammed rivers. Di Stéfano and Billy Wright look out on their iron bridges, Beckenbauer's dad delivers his post through the snow and ash of ruined Munich while Jack and Bobby Charlton's father lies deep underground scraping coal. There are exceptions, sure. Pelé was born in a city of cows, where lanes filled with sacks of coffee hauled by mules, but he was soon off to the port.

In the end, they all come from iron towns.

. . .

'Liam, Liam, will yer sign this?'

He looks into the enclosure. They've split it between rival fans tonight. There's a Wolves flag hung over the wall, a line of people in wheelchairs behind it. He steps off the pitch and sees the hands holding an England shirt and a pen towards him, watches his step on the narrow gravel track in front of the stand. They are watering the pitch like crazy. It's turned to a kind of grey soup on top and then is still rock hard underneath.

'What they still watering for?' Julius mutters, struggling to trap a ball that skimmed off the surface.

'Suit our slick passing game,' Liam replies.

It's true that Ally does get them to try to play, to pass it out, play through the fullbacks, press. They do not have the players for it. He wants them to go after the ball too far up the pitch for a man nearing forty to leave an acre of space behind him.

Liam is not starting again.

'I've got a game in mind for you, son,' Ally said yesterday as they did a warm-down on the training ground at the Heath, stretching and looking across a yellow field. Liam watched a ball, tiny against the sky, as it climbed and fell, missed the fifth green at the golf club.

That might mean he will start on Saturday in the league game, which is how it should be. Or it might mean that Ally has some vague notion of a fixture in November when he thinks he'll need him. Anyhow, what's certain is he won't start against the Wolves, probably the last chance he'll have to play against them. He tries not to let his face fall, wonders what is coming next. 'When the pitches get heavy, that's when your season starts,' or something like that, he's heard all sorts of crap before. The truth is, he's still the best player at the club, no one will convince him otherwise. He should start alongside Devon at the back every opportunity, every time they're both fit. They should just defend deeper. It's their only hope of staying up this season.

'I've got a game for you,' Ally said, stretched, looked at the man hacking around the rough grass searching for his ball, turned to run back to the changing rooms.

Liam reaches for the pen with one hand, the shirt with the other. The pen is snatched back from his grasp.

'What would I want your autograph for, yer prick?'

The words come hissed and sharp like a slap. Liam looks across the wall to see the face of a younger man leering back at him. There's a chorus of laughter, jeers, from the seats around the man, the boy, who speaks to him. Faces crowd in, he sees knuckles whiten on a fist gripping the handle of a wheelchair. The bloke jerks back in his chair and tugs the shirt which Liam still has hold of. Liam leans across the wall, keeps his grip on it, knows he should let it go. 'Prick,' the bloke says again, his long face twisted in a grimace. The man brays like a donkey. Liam doesn't know if he's laughing or reviving an old taunt. Still he holds the shirt. He feels the mood of the crowd shift. Faces press forward now. Men stand three and four rows back.

'Give him his shirt, mate.'

'Give him his shirt, yer bully. Picking on a kid in a wheelchair, I ask yer.'

This last a woman's voice, high and shrill. Heads turn, there is the clatter of seats flipping up as the people stand now in this corner of the ground. Liam sees an orange-coated steward walk towards him, another move down the steps. He should let go of the shirt. There are other hands gripping it now. The same white knuckles from the wheelchair handle. He feels the shirt begin to tear. The steward is next to him looking into the crowd. Liam leans forward slowly, uncoils his grip and the shirt rests on top of the wall. He holds his palms up to the faces in front of him, smiles. Someone spits past his ear. The steward has his arm round him, pulls him back, just as carefully, as gently, as he let go of the shirt.

'What's going on here, Liam, eh?' the young man says softly, softly, he has a split lip pressed to Liam's ear. Liam thinks he recognises the steward from Billy Ahmed's gym, a good kid, Tyrone he thinks his name is, from the Pengwern. It is unusual to look at a man the same height, bigger under that padded jacket. He can still hear the woman's voice but can't make out what she says. The young man has turned him round. Liam faces the pitch now, starts a sprint to catch up with the others, who have almost reached the tunnel. He glances back once, thinks of Cantona, that moment when he crouched, cocked his ear and went charging into the crowd. Liam is surprised that it doesn't happen more often. His blood is an outgoing tide now and he laughs as he sprints through the floodlit glare. He can hear Dee Dee singing.

. . .

The men in the good suits come, puffing on their cigars. Eusébio is to join Sporting Lisbon. There is an agreement, Sporting

Lourenço Marques is tied by a colonial umbilical cord. That much is clear from the name alone. Di Stéfano will go to Barcelona and play with Kubala. An Argentinian and a Hungarian will shine for Catalan nationalism. The truth is that the players do not much care for flags. The men in good suits come. Samitier smokes his cigar, talks to Di Stéfano, parties, pours another brandy, although it's not clear through the blue smoke whether Samitier really is for Barcelona, or maybe now for Madrid. Nothing is clear at all. Di Stéfano shrugs and looks at the papers. Europe will be an adventure, a grand stage. The shirt he wears won't make that much difference. The game will come to him. He is sure of his footing.

They take Eusébio to a house on the Algarve. He runs to the sound of the sea. He runs the same, whatever the continent, the hemisphere, his feet barely touch the ground. The sea sounds the same. He gets his haircut, talks to Guttmann. The men in good suits come.

Behind them, invisible, the men in uniform.

Eusébio signs for Benfica, Di Stéfano for Real Madrid.

. . .

They are three nothing down inside twenty minutes. Ally tells Liam to lead the subs in a warm-up. The usual spot is in front of the enclosure, right in front of the kid in the wheelchair. He takes them the other way instead, trots towards the Greenfield End.

'Where's our Liam off to?' Eli says. The last communist of the

Far Valley has lifted his football ban for the evening. He sits next to Joey.

'Leading a breakout,' a voice calls from behind them.

'Come back,' pipes up another, 'you can't get out of it that easy!'

There's localised mirth and then a collective groan as the ball goes in the box again and almost falls to a Wolves forward.

Joey feels a tap on his shoulder.

'Why ain't Liam started, Joey, is he fit?'

Joey shrugs.

'Keeping him for Saturday, I expect,' says another voice and saves Joey having to invent an answer.

'I should bloody hope so.'

Joey knows that these voices are kinder towards his boy when he's not in the team, that he becomes several times the player when he is not out there. Plus, their voices soften when Eli is with him. If Liam makes a mistake when Joey is there alone it always seems to him that there will be some sense, in the silence or the comments around him, that he is at least in part to blame. He is responsible for delivering such an abject son to the football club. When Eli is there, it's as if they do not want to hurt him, this old man, the grandad, who is tougher than them all, Joey has no doubt.

Liam continues the run towards the Greenfield End. Noise builds. He raises his arms above his head, signals to no one in particular, into the glare of the lights, for the fans to sing up, to lift them somehow. He is applauded. *Iron Towns, Iron Towns*, they sing. The Greenfield End have never dropped the s. They segue into *One Liam Corwen*, which was not Liam's intention at all, and he knows he'll get a bollocking from Ally later on. If not from Ally then from his dad.

'What is he fucking about for?' Joey asks the concrete and chocolate wrapper and puddle of tea between his feet. He fears his son has always craved the attention. Joey fears that his son enjoys the idea of being a footballer rather than playing football and that has been his downfall. He pushes this thought away. Then takes it up in another form, his old man enjoys the idea of being a human, rather than being human.

They stretch on the far touchline, with the silence of the closed East Stand at their back. Liam feels like he is being watched. Not by the thousands of eyes on the other three sides but from the darkness behind him. Irontown have a rare attack but the ball bobbles through to the keeper. The noise at the Greenfield End keeps going. Archie Hill waves and points at them from Ally's shoulder. He makes a motion of dragging them back around the touchline. From this distance Archie looks like a man gesturing the installation of a noose. Liam glances up into the shadow and starts the half-lap back round the pitch.

. . .

This to win it, the cry of boys on darkening streets and scrubby fields all over, to be champions of Europe.

Panenka takes a run-up of eight, nine strides, as if he might try to blast the ball back to Prague, off the penalty spot, across the brilliant green pitch and over the concrete stands and Belgrade high-rises named for Partisans. He shapes to do so as well. The goalkeeper Maier moves before he makes contact, forward and to his left, sees how Panenka's body remains slightly open. When his foot comes down on the ball Maier is off the ground. And Panenka doesn't strike it, but digs his foot underneath the ball, stops it, so the ball springs up and floats in a gentle arc and everything slows down. The ball hangs a few feet above the turf. Everything stops, except Maier who accelerates, flies almost past his left-hand post, like one part of an experiment in advanced physics. As the ball slows, his momentum increases. Everything else is dead still.

There is all the paraphernalia of mid-seventies European football behind the goal, caught for that moment that the ball hangs in the Belgrade night. There is an orange running track in shadow, the crowd is miles away beyond it. Not that this huge bowl lacks atmosphere. They nickname it the Marakana when Red Star play at home. A line of photographers stands at an angle to the goal, there's a wheelie bin, temporary advertising boards, some in Dutch (the Czechs had shocked Cruyff and his beautiful blue-eyed boys in the semi-final). There they are, time stopped still.

Panenka accelerates now, surges into a follow-through so he almost catches up with the ball. Maier raises his right arm, hits the ground. The ball floats into the middle of the goal. Maier is already standing, he looks back at the ball, shakes his head, and Panenka turns and continues his run with his arms aloft. There he is, still running.

．　．　．

Liam plays in an area ten yards square in front of Devon and this young lad McLaughlin. His job is to protect them, the kid anyway. Devon's got his hands full dealing with the forwards and the crosses coming in and talking the boy through the match. He is not good enough, but neither is this midfield. Liam closes down, harries, runs short bursts, gets goal-side, barely even puts in a challenge, but stems the flow, stops them pouring straight through. There are no thoughts of a comeback. This is damage limitation. They defend off the edge of their own eighteen yard box, give no space behind them. When Liam gets the ball at his feet he kicks for territory like a rugby fullback. The intensity leaks from the game. The clock ticks down. They get through the second-half without humiliation.

'I don't know why he didn't play our Liam from the start, I'm sure I don't.'

'Two games in a week, Dad. It's tough the age he is. Anyway, that kid McLennon, he looked good in the reserves last week.'

'Two bloody games in a week!?' Eli leaves every other comment he could make hanging in the summer evening.

The game is drifting, the atmosphere of earlier has gone with it. People shuffle along the rows to get away. Eli changes tack. Both men have this conversation while keeping their eyes on their son and grandson who shuffles backwards a few yards to watch their right-winger, who steps inside to look for the scraps.

'You went to the reserves last week?'

'Yeah, they're playing home games up at Cowton, trying to save this pitch a bit.'

'You've got a wife to look after at home, you know.'

They stare at the pitch, their heads move in unison as the keeper kicks from his hands. Liam wins the header but it skews off his head and bounces out for a throw. Joey slumps. He feels heavier in his seat than a few minutes ago. A man stands up half-way towards the corner flag and begins an essay in bile aimed at no one and everything and the stewards move towards him.

'Give it a rest,' Joey says in the direction of the shouting man, quiet enough for him not to hear.

.   .   .

Panenka runs across Liam's left shoulder. Liam cannot sleep, lies there on the bed with the curtains open. He sees the floodlights go out with the shadow on the hotel bedroom roof. He thinks of Panenka as he runs up to take the penalty, thinks of Mark Fala, out there, somewhere in the night. He read somewhere that Panenka knew before the match that this is what he'd do if he got the chance, no doubt in his mind.

The room is too dark with the floodlights at the ground switched off and Liam reaches across to turn the bedside light on. A plane blinks against the clouds over the hills. Getting to sleep after a night game has always been a problem, but these days it's nearly impossible. He thinks of Panenka and Maier to ward off thoughts about Greta and Jari. Football will heal him. His body has started to ache. At least that means the adrenaline is fading and he might sleep soon. He should stop thinking. He tells himself that men who head footballs for a living should not think at all.

He turns the TV on again, flicks through the channels with the sound off, another cricket rerun, some tennis. One of the news channels plays a report from Australia. Aboriginal people have been thrown off their land for a giant open-cast mine, the usual story. He knows that he has seen all these pictures before. Drink cans scattered across the red earth, people with angry, bewildered looks on their faces. The young men wear vest tops with the names of Aussie beers scrawled across their chest, T-shirts with pictures of Michael Jackson and Ayrton Senna, and then he sees the faded chocolate football shirt, jolts upright. A long-limbed boy wears it, fifteen years old or so, he reckons, but a head taller than everyone else, the same shape Liam had once been himself. The shirt is long sleeved, and the sleeves only reach halfway down his forearms, but the body looks big on his thin frame. The shirt is dirty, smeared with red dust, the one with the name of the sponsors who went bankrupt, press studs at the collar, and he knows, a fraction before the boy turns in the searing desert light, that he will see in fading print on the back, the number 5 and the name Corwen. The boy's eyes look at him from the screen, staring back over his shoulder, a can of beer in his hand, utterly lost. Liam's heart thumps, scared to be part of the world.

. . .

When he came to the valley James Greenfield knew that this was the place. There's a painting which hangs in the Hightown Town Council chamber, a copy you can buy as a postcard at the Heritage Museum, of this first James Greenfield stood at the head of the valley like Moses. He has walked up out of the Sheep Folds, leans a hand against ancient oak. The scene is deep English pastoral. The brass plaque beneath the painting reads 1722. The rivers meet, cows drink from the banks, sheep drift along the steep hillsides. The glade in which he stands is where now the last of the Cowton estate runs out, where they trampled that boy to death, a shepherd's hut is just visible through the greenery. The shape of the Heath is clear in the distance where the valley opens out and beyond are the blue hills and the sky a lighter blue above that.

He already knew the valley well, of course. His family were farmers, smallholders, he had cousins spread across the Midlands and border country. His dad's family farmed land near Bridgnorth. When the family fame grew, a story attached itself to them that an ancestor of his mother's, a milkmaid, helped King Charles hide as he fled through Worcestershire. This country was no great biblical revelation. And it was not empty, there were mills all along the rivers, farmhouses and hamlets, forges out in the woods. Hightown Castle and the Lowtown markets which clustered below it came with the Normans, fortuitously beyond the crest of a wooded hill in the painting. The castle had been built on an old abandoned fortress; the earl's masons worked standing stones into the castle walls. Offa had contemplated his dyke here. Blue men had once watched columns of centurions appear through the river mist.

He'd been apprenticed to Darby at some point, had followed Chamberlain and Baylies out to the Dolgun furnace at Dolgellau, realised there were hundreds of valleys like the one at Coalbrookdale.

That the future was made of iron he was certain.

Alina gets the 29 to the bus turnaround at Cowton sometimes. There are often plastic flowers tied to the stile, the odd card in the spring, where the fight had spilled into the scrubby field. She can't remember the boy's name now but it had been a big thing at the time, he'd been the same age as her. She can't remember what he'd done or was meant to have done or if anyone was ever caught, which shames her every time she sees the shrine, and thinks to herself she'll have found out for next time, but still never does. She does not think they left flowers and teddy bears for her mum. She used to want to, pestered her mum, her mum now, would not let it drop one year. Was it the year that Diana died or was she still too young to understand then? To take her down to the roadside and lay some flowers. Dee Dee said no, wouldn't relent. Her mum had a plaque at the crem and a rose bush. They could go there instead. It was not what people did back then, the laying of roadside memorials, another of the many ways the actual fact of her death fell away into the past.

She walks the paths up where the fields start, looks for the place where the view becomes Greenfield's. It isn't there, of course. Or if it is, it is so changed you may as well say it was there in the next field, or under that line of trees up on the ridge, or exactly where the last kick ended the boy whose name she cannot remember.

Maybe there, because she sees herself taking pictures, posed portraits, like the one of her great-great-grandad, except he isn't, of course, because her mum, this mum, the only one she has known, is not her real mum, and he is not her real great-

great-grandad in his sepia waxed moustache and robes. Pictures of people in Congolese suits and Polish football shirts looking down the valley at the end of the bus route, trying to believe this place was their destiny.

. . .

'That is Liam all over. No mention of Tony in that article. No credit to anyone else. What, do they think he's carving them tattoos on himself? He is a piece of work.'

Dee Dee's free hand rests on the magazine. Nico, the new Vietnamese boy with the fringe, is doing her nails. They are at the front of her cousin Lily's salon. Her aunties, Gracie and Marcia, sit under the dryers through the back. Lily has resurrected the old fittings since she took the place on.

Dee Dee was in a video which used dryers like these when she was singing. It had a kind of fifties cold-war feel. Aliens were beamed to earth through the dryers. They looked like crocodiles, or people wearing crocodile heads. The whole thing was intended to look cheap. It was post-modern, apparently. Dee Dee appeared briefly, pretending to scream as the crocodile women walked down the street. She'd sung backing vocals they used on the twelve-inch and ended up as an extra in the video. It was when she was about to pack it in. She remembered standing waiting to give her details in order to get paid, stood in a draughty corridor of some warehouse on the edge of London. She could see Wembley Stadium over the traffic. There was a pile of crumpled prosthetic crocodile heads. She was getting the bus home, meeting the lads at the bus station, Goldie was probably going to give her a lift. She'd had enough, her band had split up, which hadn't been much of a band anyway, thrown together by the management company. She'd sacked her agent, the brief attention she'd got from being the girl who walked out of a chart act to sing backing for more 'authentic' bands had faded. Authentic, my arse, she thought, most of them. She'd got married, and although she didn't know it, was less than a year away from adopting her best friend's baby and getting divorced.

'Tony seems pleased,' Nico says.

'Tony's too soft.'

From where she sits she can just about see the small red neon sign that Tony had sent to America for. It says 'Tattoos' with a jagged arrow flashing underneath it. It hangs off the old snooker hall awning. Stan Ahmed owned all the buildings along this little stretch at one point, where Lascar runs into the Anvil Yards. His grandchildren and great-nieces and nephews pieced together what was left and were doing OK with the pub and the salon and tattooists and gym. Heads above water OK, not private hospital on the outskirts of Marbella, still on the run from the police OK like Stan.

Running a business, standing in front of the magistrates was one thing. They'd nod in that particular way when she gave her name, although even that was fading now with Stan and his brothers so long absent. Phoning the police to tell them about Goldie was something else. They wouldn't listen anyway. Alina is twenty-one years old. Dee Dee thinks of phoning Liam and watches faces go past on the street. There has been no word from

Goldie since that phone call, she has started to hope that nothing might come of it. There had been a few calls, years ago, when she took Alina in, just silence on the end of the line, not even breathing. But she knew he was safely out of the way then. In the faces in the street she looks for the Goldie from that photograph. God knows what he looks like now, then she realises that it was like he said on the phone, that he's never really gone, not really, always there in the shadows. She'll know him when she sees him that's for sure.

She wonders when Liam goes to see Tony, whether he goes during shop hours, or even in the season at all. There was a match this afternoon, of course. She thought of Liam, angry and pretending everything was OK in the days before a big game. By the morning of matchday he could barely speak, would sometimes throw up before leaving the house. She wonders if it's still like that. He must've got used to it by now.

She wants a cigarette. Nico works at her cuticle.

'I just think they should've mentioned him by name, that's all. Liam could've said, I want my tattooist acknowledged, they'd have put it in if he'd said.' She stops herself, 'It's our Tony's work, after all.'

Her aunties do not listen. Gracie looks to be asleep right now. Marcia flips through a TV magazine. She opens one eye, arches the painted brow.

'You seem very interested in what Liam's got to say for himself, Dee Dee, that's all I can think, love.'

. . .

Another iron town. Their club crest shows a fist which holds a girder with the word iron forged into it. The old badge showed a blast furnace and ironstone fossils. The town itself exists because of its steelworks. They play in claret and blue shirts, modelled on Aston Villa's, which for reasons that may now seem inexplicable, the people of Scunthorpe thought might bring them luck. Some say it was West Ham, though, another set of irons, echoing across the empty London docks, blowing bubbles over the car works at Dagenham. Liam has Hurst, Peters and Moore holding the Jules Rimet Trophy aloft tattooed on his right thigh. When the supporters pile out on the away car park in Anvil Yards, next to the yellow concrete of the bus station, the sun glints on the towers of scrap over by the canal, and they sing *Gyppos* and *What a fucking shithole*. Some of them take off their shirts. Their blond hair and white bellies move across the burning plain.

'Who are yer? Who are yer?'

'We are iron men, from the Iron Towns, come from the Anvil Yards, come from the Anvil Yards,' they reply from the Greenfield End.

Quieter, a low chant in the background, fewer people, they bang the corrugated iron at the back of the stand to create the sound of thunder, a storm coming,

'We are the Spider Boys, we are the Spider Boys, we are the Spider Boys . . .' into a sibilant hush.

The spider mythology did not begin with the building of the Spider House, that was just its height. The eighth James Greenfield joined the craze for zoo building in the 1930s. He had the arboretum landscaped and built the Spider House at its entrance. The visitors dwindled but it lingered on like much else in the Iron Towns. They still draped lights through the remaining arboretum trees every winter, decorated the branches with silver webs and plastic spiders.

The first mentions of the spider came with the Norman farmers, settlers. Young girls – it was always young girls, milkmaids and farmer's daughters – would report seeing the movements of long thin legs high up in the trees, curtains of silver thread draped the branches and hedgerows. The land was cursed in some way. Rumours and strange stories lingered on.

There is a game the children still play. Liam sees them through the rain-dashed tram windows, over the wall of the Ironport primary school. Girls and boys – always one girl, one boy – back to back with arms linked, four arms, four legs, staggering around, pulling each other this way and that, trying to catch their screaming, taunting mates.

The spiders had moved over the years, become subterranean. Liam remembers lying on the furry rug in front of his grandparents' coal fire. He could lie for ages, watching the shape of the flames, seeing mountains, dark tunnels, fathomless pit shafts he knew his grandad crawled through when Black Park was still open.

'There's summat down there, I don't care what they say.'

'What you going on about, Dad?'

'You watch what yome saying Eli, you'll scare the boy.' His nan's voice from the kitchen, the flames flickering blue-edged around the coals. He remembers the rough black finish on the scuttle handle. It still sits in a coal bucket in his grandad's out-house, lined with ancient dust.

'He takes some scaring.' His grandad ruffled his hair. 'All I'm saying is there's summat in it. There's none of you ever been down there, and a good thing too.'

'It's dangerous enough without talk of giant spiders. You know what you sound like?'

'I ain't saying what it is, whether it's the spider or what. Just sometimes you get the sense of summat else, that's all. I ain't even saying it's a bad thing, that it means any harm. Just that there's summat there. There's things people don't understand, can't explain, no matter how many degrees or bits of paper they've got, that's all I'm saying, so then they say there's nothing in it, it's just an old wives' tale, just to make thereselves look clever, everyone else seem stupid for thinking it.'

'You'll be telling us to say our prayers next.'

'You know what I think about that nonsense.'

That his grandad, who had dug coal from deep underground every day like his dad and his dad before that, who believed in Marxist dialectics and liked a pint of mild and a bet on a Saturday, a week in Llandudno and his October trip to the Prix de l'Arc de Triomphe, also believed a giant spider lived in the tunnels that dragged down the hills they lived on never struck Liam as that strange. You could hold plenty of different things in your head, he knew that even then. That you could be a good man who did bad things or a bad man who did good things, and that they might amount to much the same, was something he understood from somewhere deep within him, like the coal in the hillside.

. . .

The lad takes a touch, half-turns just inside the centre circle. Not here you don't. Liam is in. Takes the ball, man, everything. He hears the air leave the kid's body as he falls. First big cheer of the afternoon. Liam stays standing, above him, says nothing. The ref blows up. Calls Liam over and warns him, talks in a low, calm voice to him. Liam nods but doesn't listen. He would've booked him had it been any later than the second minute, that's for certain. It's a free shot this early in the match, the season. There's a voice chipping away at the ref. Liam stares straight ahead. The striker is on his feet, jogs forward, doesn't look at Liam. They stick the free kick straight down the middle. Liam is up, bodies bounce off him, heads it back towards the sun. Out they go. Out. Out. A deep-throated growl goes through the crowd. They sing his name.

. . .

That she is the great-aunt of the dreadlocked man who stands on the ladder, with wires trailing over his shoulder and down the other side of the bar, is something that fills her with wonder. She knows it's a trick of big families, this overlap of generations. They joke about it. She has not seen Nathan for a few years, she remembers a shy boy fiddling with an electronic game, half-hiding behind his mum, Natalie, Dee Dee's niece, though Dee Dee is four years younger. The joke doesn't seem that funny to her. As a kid she had great-aunts with silver hair that they always tied in buns, who could remember when they brought electricity to the villages up on the Welsh Ridge. Maybe she is those women now. Sitting in a high-backed chair, lips moving with no sound coming out, remembering times of darkness. She tries to work out what relation Lionel is to Nathan. Lionel is her uncle but not Natalie's, she doesn't think, can't remember for a moment.

'Thanks again, Lionel,' she says to him as he comes back in from the van. They sit at a table with a beaten copper top in the lounge in the net curtain light.

'Don't mention it love. I'm glad you've seen a bit of sense installing those cameras. We worry about yer, chick, living down here on yer own. It ain't safe, love. I wish I could say it was. It ain't the place it used to be.'

She doesn't know where else he thinks she could go.

Lionel sighs, sits back. He's enjoying this, this show of concern. The subtext is it ain't safe since your uncle Stan stopped keeping things in order down here and had to do a runner to Spain. 'When yer uncles was around,' she hears quite a bit from the drinkers in the bar, said in the same tone as 'When the works was open'. Nostalgia has replaced fear, a trick of time. There was a lot more to the collapse of the Anvil Yards than the demise of the Ahmed family.

Lionel is the last of his brothers still around. He runs a car yard and a security firm that won the contract to guard much of the abandoned works sites. He runs the men on the doors in the fancier pubs of Heathside and Hightown, sends someone to watch the pub doors on matchdays, even though Dee Dee never asks. He still sails close to the wind, but hasn't been in any trouble, except over VAT receipts, as far as she knows, for years. He prefers the quiet life these days, Sunday roasts up at the golf club and so on.

She can hear voices from the kitchen and thinks for a moment that Alina is talking to Nathan but he remains with his head through a missing ceiling panel and Dee Dee sees the other boy – when she came to think of men in their twenties as boys, she is not sure, finds her own ageing unbelievable in some way – who stands in his blue overalls smiling at something Alina must have said. She didn't even know she was in.

'I didn't know Alina was here,' she said and watches the boy as he nods and says something and smiles again. A lovely look-ing boy, tall, with clear, golden skin and long eyelashes she can see. This is good, will do Alina good, she thinks, to be flirted with by a handsome boy. Alina is too serious, although maybe there is plenty to be serious about.

Lionel dips his biscuit into his tea and there is a moment of quiet while Dee Dee decides to say anything or not.

'You seen Bobby?'

Lionel flinches at the mention of his son, knew it was coming though, and she can't tell how much that reaction is rehearsed or genuine. She does not have such a high opinion of her own family these days. There is custard cream smeared on Lionel's lip.

'I told him,' he says, 'I told him not to come back. He's upset his mother too much now, crossed the line. I don't know what's the matter with him. I've washed me hands of him, told him don't come back. He's had too many chances, should've been harder with him from the start.'

From the start of what, she's not sure. He doesn't ask her if she's seen him, which she hasn't, she was out on the morning Paul told Bobby he couldn't serve him at just turned eleven o'clock in the morning with Bobby all glassy eyed and looking for an argument and Bobby had smashed the glass in the bar door with the fire extinguisher. That had been a couple of months ago, but it would be nice to be asked.

'I look at you here, and Tony and Natalie with the salon now. None of yer had it that easy, one thing and another. He had everything he ever wanted and what do we get in return? Everything throwed back in our faces. No, I've told him.'

'What about if he got cleaned up?'

'He won't get cleaned up. I've told his mother, one day there'll be a phone call, a knock at the door, yer know. We've got to steel ourselves for it.'

'He's only a kid, Lionel.'

'Some people am no good.'

'Your own son,' she says quietly but Lionel is not listening.

He nods towards Nathan pulling the wire for the new cameras up through his dreadlocks.

'These two here, great workers. You couldn't meet a nicer lad than our Nathan. And this other kid's his mate. I was employing him over the Yards, security work, you know, and some stuff on the doors, but he's a fast learner, he's worth more than that. I've got him out with me on jobs some of the time now. You could trust these with your life. The kid, Tyrone, he's off the Peng, right, background you wouldn't believe, even for there, unbelievable. Yet, here he is, getting on with things. And then you've got our

Bobby. We spoilt him, Dee Dee, that's for sure. Hundred pound trainers for Christmas, remember? Florida and what have you. I told Gracie at the time, this is too much, he's out of control, this one. And then with the boxing, we should have held him back a bit more. He believed what people said about him. Would her listen? I've told him, don't come back this time.'

Words for their own sake, is what she thinks. Lionel's right about the spoiling. Bobby needed help and he got fancy trainers. But Bobby's not her problem, thank god. If he turns up here again and asks for a drink she'll let him have one. It was like digging at a scab, mentioning him to Lionel at all, like she wanted to hear the worst, his hypocrisy and blame. Maybe he was just being honest. They had spoiled him and now he wanted to forget about him. But just because Lionel's practised the words doesn't make them less true. He sold used cars for years, for god's sake, can't sound genuine even when he is being, charmed the magistrates and the tax man, has kept his detached house on Heathside, with stone lions and cameras at the entrance to the drive, after all. She wonders whoever said crime didn't pay.

The boy Tyrone is still smiling, looks daft in the sunlit doorway, his eyes following Alina hidden somewhere back in the kitchen. Dee Dee cannot begin to imagine what they are saying to each other, but doesn't need to, she supposes. She wonders whether to mention him to Alina later, decides not to. She's never teased her like that, never pried, tried not to show how much she worries, how much she has put in to being the girl's mother, this lovely, lonely girl, and sometimes thinks there is more than one way of spoiling a child, and for the briefest moment as the light shifts in

the room and they hear a cheer from the Anvil Yards carried on
the wind, that she has more in common with Lionel and Gracie
than she would like to admit, and so maybe perhaps should not
be so hard on them.

. . .

Dave 'Iron' Willis: Such has been Irontown's form
in the season's first few weeks that to get to
half-time goalless is some achievement. They've
certainly tightened up since the League Cup
mauling by Wolves, helped in good measure by the
return to the back four of veteran skipper Liam
Corwen. Dominant as ever in the air, he has even
nipped in front of the Scunthorpe strikers a
couple of times for clever interceptions and the
odd foray into midfield. He has been ably supported
by Devon Samuels. No spring chickens, though,
these two, and in this heat — it's like a furnace
out there on the pitch for both sets of Irons —
the worry for the home team, without much threat
going forward, must be whether they might wilt in
the second half . . .

. . .

The sun has come through the frosted windows of the gents' and
there's a hot, thick smell of pissed beer. The porcelain still radiates
cool, though, and Joey is enjoying this moment, the relief for

one thing, he cannot make it through a game any more without needing to go, and Liam's performance out there, and he reads 'Dudley' over again in light blue lettering tattooed into the white urinal slab, even thinks of Liam's tattoos without shuddering, when he hears the groans from above his head and knows that they've let one in.

He does not know what had made him feel so cheerful in the first place, pisses down his leg and onto his shoe in trying to finish, not knowing he hadn't finished, and wanting to get to the clamour upstairs. He struggles out the door, the sounds of anguish coming louder, and there's the sound of a few thousand people all saying no at the same time and the square of blue sky at the top of the steps. He walks up into the light to the sound of another collective howl and sees the ball sitting there in the Irontown net and their winger, the quick one, running away to the corner and their supporters. The keeper lies outstretched and looks at the ball. Liam walks back towards the goal, twenty yards from it. Devon Samuels is just behind him with his hands on his knees.

He's missed goals before, Joey, of course, having a piss or wait-ing for a pint. He cannot remember ever missing two in the same trip. His dad's seat is empty. Les Martin leans across to him as Joey slumps down. He smells of extra strong mints. He is one of those blokes who takes a perverse delight in the team's failings. If Liam is at fault in some way, he never quite comes out and says it, just has that glint in his eye. He owns a tool hire place in Lowtown, lives in Heathside somewhere, is worth a bob or two.

'First from a corner, free header, back post, one of their centre halves up, nobody near him. Keeper should've come but never. Next, we kick-off, give the ball back to them, ball over the top, we've pushed up too far, kid runs after it, linesman don't put his flag up, but he was probably on, two-nothing. Two in, what, thirty seconds?'

'Took it well,' a voice comes from behind.

Les turns, 'He did, he did, I'll give him that.'

'I've seen it all now,' Joey says.

'Well, except yer never did.'

'What?'

'See it.'

Joey looks down at Liam. He thinks for a moment that he will gladly never watch another game of football in his life if Liam packs it in. For Joey, there is something about Liam's size that has always made him vulnerable. He remembers watching him in the playground, blond hair bouncing head and shoulders above the other kids. Liam claps his hands and says something to Kyran, the young kid they've got at fullback.

He looks across the low barrier into the director's box, no one sitting there except Steve Stringer, who must live in this stand, scurrying in and out of his little office next to the toilets, trying to make ends meet, helping Ally get players in, players out, and Ally treating him like he treats everyone else, like he's there to serve the great Ally Barr. Steve had been a ballboy with Liam, but never in any of the youth teams, just a kid who hung around the ground doing odd jobs, taking the post and the like. His old man used to work at Greenfields, used to drink in the Salamander. Joey used to enjoy having a pint with him. That was before he had to stop going in the pub after the mess with Dee Dee and the girl. Liam was a stupid boy, giving her up. He raises his hand and Steve waves back, the worry etched permanently on his face. Joey reminds himself to ask him how his dad is at full-time. Probably not good news, not here, the whole place is cursed, Joey thinks.

'Surprised you're here, Les, not off on another cruise or whatever,' he says and keeps his eyes on Liam as he gets up to head the ball, thinks of how many hours throwing balls up for him to attack just like that.

'What, and miss all this?'

.　.　.

Goldie holds the knife at a shallow angle to the steel. He loves the sound that the sharpening makes, builds a rhythm with it, sees his shape in the canal's green water. The sound comes back off the factory walls that form the opposite bank. The wall bulges where the water must have got in and Goldie wonders how safe it is, when the wall will come down. Tree branches grow from it, long rust streaks pattern the brick. But he feels good all the same, away from anyone, time a bit to think, no one will have followed him here. He sharpens the blade with a flourish and it glints in the sun. He hears a murmur and then a shout from the ground, a ripple of applause. He would hear a chant in his cell sometimes, from the Villa or West Brom, depending on who was at home and which way the wind was blowing. Sometimes just a great shout, voices all mixed together as one, some roar of joy or anguished moan. It's strange that he used to like to hear it, it made him feel less alone, that and the sounds of traffic outside or of work going on, like the clang of scaffolding poles, to make him think of a world outside. But then when he was out, like when he'd lay awake and look at the fuzzy yellow light outside the blind when he lived with Nadine, he'd listen out for those sounds and think of his cell and almost feel better and able to sleep. Maybe he should head over to the ground, he thinks, when he's done his knives. He is a free man, he can do whatever he likes, and he smiles as he thinks this, something about it not quite right, a thought in his head asking, when are you ever free of anything? He is bare-chested. When he thinks the carving knife is sharp enough he pauses for a moment, holds the blade to his skin until there's the shallowest cut and a neat line of blood, touches his fingers to it and then puts them to his lips. There is another shout from the Anvil Yards. The thought hardens in his mind, sharp and clean like the cut. When are we ever free of anything?

. . .

The ball takes a crazy bounce on the baked pitch, loops over Kyran's head, and he's too far upfield anyway, trying to force it, nothing doing. Liam is across to it. It's the last minute and he's beating their forwards to the ball, he wants people to see this. Wins it. Sticks it high up into the empty East Stand.

There's no time for the throw-in. He hears the whistle for full-time, the cheers from the away end and a smattering of boos from elsewhere, lets his run wind down in the direction of the ball and kicks out at the old wooden advertising board. The clatter of it echoes back across the pitch. Something moves in the cool shade at the back of the stand. Liam stares for a moment. The linesman, assistant, whatever he's called these days, walks towards him to shake his hand. Liam's seen cats up there, leap suddenly through the missing panels at the back, or slink down the crumbling steps, a fox once. They used to get kids sneaking in, but that seems to have died off.

'Played Liam.'

'Yeah, some use, eh?'

He begins to limp back across the pitch, then he turns and looks back once more. It was a man, the shape of a man running away. Liam shakes his head. If the bloke paid nothing, he's still been robbed.

. . .

Tony lays out photocopies of paintings by Zurbarán, proud faces in dark shade.

'It's their faces, their faces you want,' he says.

And it is, but it's something else as well.

Zidane slices it on purpose, hits it with fade like a golf shot. This is the World Cup final. Buffon, the best goalkeeper in the world stands in front of him. People crowd around televisions in Papeete and Tripoli, Basse-Terre and Dire Dawa, Mamoudzou and Asmara. Millions of people watch one man. Seen from above the earth must throb with the glare of those millions of television screens. Liam thought he'd mis-hit it, in the moment, leaping forwards from his chair by the side of a Finnish lake. Then something in Zidane's face as he turned away made him realise. He was in utter control. Millions of people. He'd even made the ball clip the bar on purpose, Liam reckoned, just for the lovely drama of it as it fell those inches behind the line and bounced back out of the goal again. If you had power like that you would go nuts. Perhaps that's what happened later when he flattened Materazzi. Maybe. And Liam wants that too, feels both acts, the penalty and head-butt, to be the same thing. Or maybe the shape Zidane's body forms as he volleys the goal at Hampden Park, another Hampden night, Di Stéfano there in the crowd, looking on. Zidane will take some thought. Zidane you could think about for ever. His face on that wall in Marseilles.

'Chiaroscuro,' Tony says. 'Light and shade.'

'Yeah, you're right about the faces, and maybe do that on another one. Pirlo's got a beard now and we can't do him till he stops playing, anyway.'

'Zidane though.'

'Yeah, but what I really want from this is that moment when everything stops, you know?'

What he wants is that stillness, the ball in mid-air, following a gentle arc, the keeper the only thing moving, tumbling away from it. That still moment of grace, that's what he wants.

There was a split-second in the play-off final, nothing more than a split-second, when Mark Fala stopped his foot and stunned the ball softly above the thick Wembley grass, when Liam thought they had that moment. His stomach flips over. The keeper flinches and doesn't move. Time does not stand still. The ball arcs into the keeper's hands. He catches it. Catches the penalty, and he is already moving, and so is Liam, or trying to, turning one last time on this thick, spongy surface, and his legs won't work properly. And the keeper has already taken his strides and launches a kick – he's alongside Mark who just stands there, a yard or two past the penalty spot, could even then have stood in front of the keeper and stopped him kicking it. And the ball meets its own shadow yards into the Irontown half and bounces once and then a second time, in that channel that Geoff Hurst ran down for the last goal in the World Cup final. They think it's all over, again and again. That kid, he's thinking of him as a kid because he's slight and fast but he's older than Liam, is on to it and even though he's running with the ball at his feet now, Liam is going backwards, the kid is running away from him, and is into the box and now he's sliding it past Big Al in goal, who never plays again either, same as Mark Fala, retires back to his pub in Carrickfergus, a man who is too old and slow to fall on this one last shot and the ball is there in the net. They were 3-1 up what seems like hours ago now, have lost 4-3. The ref blows the whistle. Liam hears it through the roar. He can see he's blowing for the goal and he's blowing up for time. No more time. It's over. They have lost. Mark Fala stands just past the penalty spot. Liam hits the ground. He cannot get up. He tells himself he will never get up again. But even in this feeling he knows there will be more games, more seasons. He is young and the days stretch out in front of him.

Fal – Liam never called him that, always Mark, the older lads called it him – has already started to walk off, separate from the others, shrugs off Big Al's arm as he tries to console him.

'Head up, son, eh?'

He walks round the pitch on the pale gravel, Mark walks like a young man at the end of a long journey.

. . .

You cannot understate the fact that it is Germany, of course. When the men Panenka grew up listening to said 'the war' they meant the second one. The ball that floats through the air, a conjuring trick, a joke, is an act of the deepest resistance. Resistance against what? A lack of imagination, perhaps, against too great a seriousness, an absence of humour? Is it a last defiant act of the Prague Spring? If there is a message in it, it must be not to take life too seriously. We realise it does not matter whether the penalty goes in or not. It is the gesture, the joke that matters. But thinking about it all is part of the joke, because it is to take it seriously, far too seriously, grown men playing games, chasing a ball, other men looking on. The joke is either on the penalty taker or on the goalkeeper, or on us all, but the joke is there. The joke is in the way the ball pops up, floats lightly in the air, the way a child's balloon might drift in front of a tank.

It did not just appear in Panenka's head, just like that, fully formed, even if he was the first to do it. It came from somewhere, not just from Prague, from the memories of the old Empire, buried deep in the minds of coaches like Jezˇek and Venglosˇ, back to Béla Guttmann, in the movements of players like Masopust and Puskás and Sindelar, layer upon layer, back and back, on pitches in Prague and Ostrava and Budapest and

Vienna, in countries which no longer even exist. Panenka's kick as a dream of Mitteleuropa, a stray idea from another vanished world.

. . .

Autumn in the Iron Towns, rust coloured, a slow drip-drip from a cracked pipe. The place leans in on itself, subsides, walls fall slowly and roofs sag, a slow motion catastrophe, a slow motion coup. Had it happened overnight, not across forty years, there would be soldiers on the streets, helicopters to drop relief packages all the way up the valley. Instead, it is quiet, moss and rust grow on factory gates. There is a long slow drift into silence.

One day, perhaps not so long in coming, the human world will be elsewhere. A few mossed over stones will remain, strange metal relics, chemical traces through the ground. There will be the myth of great ruined cities in the north and west of the islands, like the rumour of the giant spider, explorers will hack their way up narrow rivers, searching for a few lost tribes.

. . .

And these are men of great joy too. Do not forget that.

England v. Rest of the World, 23 October, 1963. A celebration. They play Eusébio and Denis Law as inside-forwards. Di Stéfano gets the number 9 shirt, the captaincy too, even at thirty-eight.

The only forty-five minutes Eusébio and Di Stéfano play as

teammates is goalless. Eusébio comes off at half-time for Puskás, a gentleman's agreement. There is a chance when Eusébio runs a diagonal, left-to-right, outside-in, and takes the ball on his right foot, fifteen yards out, turns the defender, but drives it with his left into Gordon Banks. Di Stéfano tries to get up alongside him before he shoots, can't make the distance, but then it is his dropping deep that has made the space for Eusébio.

He is the master of time and space, people move to his will, even now, this late in the day.

.   .   .

Liam cannot move. He lies on the bed. He has spoken to Jari, to Greta, sat and watched Jari playing with a set of wooden trains on the laptop screen. He lies still. He holds that picture of Jari in his head, Greta stands at the door and looks out at the lake. The light is falling now. He imagines the bed to be there at the lodge. He has that sense of sleeping close to water. He feels the flicker of light off the lake, believes he can smell pine woods. In a moment he will get up, walk into the living room, join Greta for a glass of wine and look at the water.

He buys two pricey bottles of Sauvignon Blanc from the Heath Vintners, the posh off-licence. George Best drank white wine near the end, that's what he's thinking as he chooses it. He is not near the end. His dad gave him a lift back to the house.

'Well played, son,' he said, when Liam struggled out, already stiffening up, 'see you tomorrow.' Liam groaned inside. Both his sisters and their families are here tomorrow. They are having

Sunday roast at his parents'. He will be expected to kick a ball about with his nephews and nieces.

He will never sleep in his house again, of that he is certain. When he is sure that his dad's car has turned the corner towards Black Park he walks to the row of shops at Heathside and then takes the long way back to the hotel. He considers buying a can to drink on the way but it is Saturday, early evening, there are people around. Someone sounds a car horn and he hears laughter from within as it goes past him too fast. A man walking hand-in-hand with his wife nods to him. They look happy, off to a meal at the Italian here. Liam wants to hide, could've called a cab, he thinks, too late, halfway to Meeting House Lane already. The pedestrians thin out as he comes down the hill, there's the occasional roar of a car that booms through the empty streets. The helicopter is up somewhere.

He thinks of rising, Sunday mornings. He and Jari run at the lakeside. The boy's hand is small in his, grips hot and tight. The boy laughs, 'Faster, Daddy.' Liam quickens his step and the boy half-flies along the track. They are barefoot. Their feet skim the packed earth, they feel the cool of the water on their left, the light comes through the trees and flickers, light then shade, light then shade, like old film run fast. Along the path they see the jetty, a blue boat against it. Greta stands on the veranda, waves and smiles as she sees them come through the woods.

Finland is a dream to him now. That was him. That was a life he had, somehow.

He lies on the bed alone and runs through the woods with his son.

. . .

'Albion, Albion, Albion . . .' The song echoes off the dark brick of Chain Street at the away end.

'Albion . . .'

Albion: the White Land.

'. . . Albion!'

The giants sing this as they approach Brutus' feast on the cliffs. The island has vanquished invaders since it became an island. Seas shift, land rises and falls, nothing lasts for ever.

The invaders are war hardened, Trojan refugees, delighted to find this empty white land. Brutus nods at Corineus. It must be done. The giants have grown soft in their isolation, despite their clamour and noise. They do not feel so much like giants, their arms and legs and heads scattered across the fields, their plump white bellies slit open.

They put Gogmagog in a cage. The bars twist to his shape but do not break, brand his flesh. He cannot move his head to look away from the ruin, from the feasting and celebration. They joke that they might keep him as their pet, tame him, lead him round on a collar. Brutus nods at Corineus again. He tips the cage over the cliff and Gogmagog is dashed on the rocks below.

'Albion, Albion, Albion, Albion, Alb-i-on.'

. . .

'Does he not want you in this morning, love?'

Alina walks into the kitchen, she wears a thin cardigan over her nightie. Her hair falls in her face. Groggy, she looks like she's had a night out, Dee Dee thinks, but Alina never goes out.

'No, he's opening a bit later he says, never anybody there before eleven.'

Alina works in Rob's record shop at the Lowtown indoor market, another of Dee Dee's cousins. He sells vinyl, reggae and metal and dance twelve-inches, scrapes by like everyone else. Dee Dee's voice locked in a groove on a record somewhere in the Lowton Bull Ring.

'Kettle's boiled,' Dee Dee says. 'Do you want some toast?'

'I'll do it, Mum.'

'Sit down.' There is suddenly not enough space for them here, with the leaves of the table drawn out. Dee Dee moves her widening hips through the space between the fridge and the back of the chair, feels Alina a head and shoulders above her. She thinks of her still as a gawky schoolgirl all arms and legs, and now she is this lovely long-limbed young woman. She thinks of Sonia, the way she could move hardly at all when she danced but everyone would still look at her, want to be her or be with her. Alina sits without saying anything else, pushes her hair back over her ear. She wears earrings with teardrop scales that shimmer in the light through the window.

'I like your earrings.'

'Thanks. They were yours, I think.'

Dee Dee puts her hand across the table to hold Alina's hair back herself. She cannot place this jewellery at all. They look proper silver on the undersides, a peacock blue inlaid on the other side, meant to be feathers or fishscales.

'I got them from one of the boxes upstairs.'

Always messing with things, this girl, poking into drawers and boxes, ever since as a sticky-handed toddler she found a photo of Sonia as a chubby little girl and pointed at it.

'Look, it's Lina,' she had said, 'it's Lina.'

'Might have been Nana's,' Dee Dee says and puts milk in the tea, gives herself a sugar, cannot get the energy this morning, barely dragged herself to let Roni in, banging on the door early, nearly half-seven, like the place needed such a thorough clean after a heavy Friday, when they had barely had half a dozen in all night, if they took a hundred quid they'd been lucky. This cannot go on.

'What about, you know, anything else coming up?'

'I don't know, Mum. What like?'

Dee Dee doesn't answer, puts the bread back down in the toaster, she can never get that setting right, doesn't know what to say. Twenty-one years old, no boyfriend, barely any friends it seems to her now. What happened to Donna? she wants to ask her. Do you not see Taylor any more, love? Nothing in response, not much anyway; seems happy enough in herself, but it didn't seem much of a life to Dee Dee, living in the rooms above a pub, bits of part-time work in your cousins' and uncles' – not even your actual cousins and uncles – shops and market stalls, not even doing much with her art now from what Dee Dee can see. When she finished college, Dee Dee thought Alina would do something else. She could've gone to university, something. The years start to drift.

'Just, thinking about the future, you know.'

'By the time you was my age you was married,' Alina says in

a neutral tone. Dee Dee isn't sure if she is taking the piss or not, chooses to give her the benefit of the doubt.

'Nearly divorced,' Dee Dee replies in the same flat tone, looks at her. There'd been some big blow-ups as a teenager, some big rows, but that was to be expected, just the two of them together under one roof, needing one another. Never, not once, any 'You're not my real mum.' Not once. The opposite, really. 'I don't care, I'm glad what happened,' she said once, when she was eleven, twelve, just going up to secondary school, 'otherwise we wouldn't have been together.'

'Don't say that, Alina, don't say that. Your mum loved you very much,' she said to her even as she held her tight. Maybe that was when they started to move apart. Maybe Dee Dee had pushed her away, for her own good she thought.

And she wasn't even sure it was true. Sonia had not wanted her, only as a little trophy, a little doll. When she cried as a baby, Goldie had been better with her, shushing her and letting her sleep on his chest.

'She needs changing,' Dee Dee had said to her one afternoon, early on, Sonia moping about saying she felt fat. Dee Dee looked after Bobby and Tony, plenty of other younger cousins.

'She'll get a rash, Son.'

'You do it then, if you know so much about it.'

And she had. Old style nappies with safety pins because that was what Sonia's mum knew. Dee Dee soon changed that when she got the chance.

'And what's all that rope doing in the yard?'

Alina has coils of rope sitting inside the back gate, too heavy to lift anywhere. Dee Dee has no idea where it's from or how she got it there, the kind they used to tie things on ships with.

'Where's it from, even?'

'It's for a project.'

'What project? For who? An art thing?'

'Yeah, an art thing.'

'Roni says it'll attract rats.'

'Roni's bloody obsessed.'

'Says she can't put her bleach down properly.'

They both smile at this, at least, look at each other for the first time that morning.

'What art thing?'

'Just something, I don't know . . .' Alina's voice tails off, then, 'Tyrone's collecting it in the van for me,'

'Oh Tyrone is, is he?' Should she ask, who is Tyrone and pretend not to know? Dee Dee tries to think on her feet, not as quick as she once was, she realises, understands that there's still a smile on her face that she should probably try to lose. The rope is an utter mystery.

There's the smell of burning, then a coil of smoke before the alarm goes off. She can never get this toaster right. The smoke rises from the grill and is drawn up behind the half-open blind, drifts across the ceiling.

Dee Dee swears, pushes the window open, grabs a tea towel to threaten the smoke alarm with. Alina scrapes her chair back, gets up.

'Is the water on? I wanted a shower before I go,' makes her escape, moves like the smoke through the kitchen door.

. . .

Like Zidane, Pirlo's expression does not change, not one flicker from start to finish. If there is anything, there is just the tiniest hint of self-admonishment. It's the face of a man who has been out and come back home and realised that he has forgotten to post the letter he'd meant to. He is wearied. He looks like he wants to sit on his arse and think about Dante. The English players chase the air between Pirlo and the ball. He passes it into the gaps between the players, it's simple, he says.

Hart is on his back, like some great insect trying to right itself, Gregor Samsa in a red goalkeeper's shirt. Maybe it's all some joke that swirls back to Prague. Still, Pirlo's face stays the same.

. . .

She tried it with wool before, had not taken the scale into account. Spent half a day deeper than she'd ever been into the works, part of Lysaght's, Greenfields itself, Alina is not sure of the demarcation line, the railway tracks maybe, heavy iron wagons sat in the sidings, grass growing in tufts around the wheels, tall thin reeds with yellow flowers that she does not know the name of grew between the wooden slats. She stopped to photograph them. There was the long wall of one of the sheds in the background, and the contrast with sun on the hillside beyond, a corner of the cemetery fairly indistinct at this distance, an angel's wings just about visible. So she had something to show for the day, they'd come out well. She wanted to do something with the colour, deepen it, heighten it. She didn't even have the language for this stuff. The material was too big, she thought. It would take a life-time to learn how to do it, how to say anything of what she wanted. There was a lot to learn. The scale, for one thing. She spent a couple of hours trailing the wool through what had once been rolling mills, the sound of pigeons from the roof, she was shat on twice. As she walked she thought she should record their sounds, the splatter of wings and shit, the vibrating murmur in their throat as they slept. Just the sounds, maybe pictures with it. This was more of a complete piece. Ariadne, she'd call it. And it was strange, because she never got scared in there, never, although she knew she probably should, but that day she had the feeling that every turn she took she would come face to face with the monster, some monster or other, anyhow. No one who came over here was up to any good.

It was wrong for the space. It wasn't a maze, not this part, this wide abandoned factory floor. The wool did not work. She'd wanted to suggest frailty, of course. You could barely see it in the pictures, just a slight thread, but then maybe it was good, maybe that was the point. When she started to think in this way every-thing just went in circles and she'd ask herself what was the point of it all, tell herself to get out of there. It was why she always took photos, there was always a fall back, and in the imaginary conversation she had in her head of what she was doing in there she would say taking photographs because it was clear, to anyone who looked at the place for more than a few seconds, really looked at it, that surely this was something worth capturing. But the Ariadne thing kept playing on her mind. Hence the ropes.

'You should watch yourself, wandering about them factories all on your own,' that was the first thing he said to her, she thinks, but he had a smile on his face as he said it and it was like he was setting her a question, like how would he know about what she did, where she went. Afterwards, she thought she should've been more freaked out than she was, his earring glinted in the sun.

'I'm taking photographs,' is what she said.

'What for college or something?'

'For meself. I was at art college, so sort of, but I've packed it in. This is my own thing.'

'But you do need to be careful. For real. There's people living over there, I swear. There was a kid in a tent last summer. You get all sorts. And the animals, a whole pack of dogs, foxes everywhere, skinny little wild cats. One of our lads said he saw a tarantula over there, it come up out of a pipe by the old docks. It's the blokes who end up over there you need to watch out for, though, obviously.'

She laughed. 'A tarantula?'

'That's what he said. Escaped from the Spider House, or left over from the days of the docks. Things would hide in ships.'

'They'd hide in ships, not canal barges come from Birmingham. People really believe them spider stories.'

'I didn't say it was true. But the people thing is. And you should be careful. You ever play that spider game, when you were a kid? Hey, where did you go to school?'

'The Ironport,' she said, 'then Lowtown.'

He was from the Pengwern.

'I'm off the Peng,' is what he said, ruefully, defensively. He started naming people he thought she might know and she didn't know any of them.

'But you're Nathan's cousin, right?'

'Yeah, second cousin, really.' That would do. Sometimes it was useful to be an Ahmed.

'I used to train with Bobby sometimes,' he said this sadly too.

'Do you ever see him now?'

'Funnily enough, over the Yards sometimes. I think he might sleep over there himself some nights. I don't know. I told Lionel. He wasn't so sure.'

'My mum looks out for him. I'll tell her. You tell him he can come here if he needs anything.'

'I don't know for sure, but he's sometimes around there, round and about. If he sees the car or the uniform then he runs off, even if he sees it's me. I'll give him sandwiches or something if he stops. Not money, because you know where that goes. He don't need money, though he acts like he does.'

She texted him the picture of the angel's wings, the one with sun and shadow, and he texted straight back. She asked him if he'd help her move the rope. He said no problem, and how about getting a pizza or something afterwards.

. . .

The second painting hanging in the Hightown Town Council chamber is from the same aspect, looks down the valley from the hills. They say de Loutherbourg painted it on his way to or from

the Bedlam works but it is not attributed, hangs on the opposite
wall to the other painting.

It is night lit as day by the furnaces which bloom along the
rivers. The Samson Foundry is there, the Watkins Cylinder Works,
the fires which form the first incarnation of Greenfields. Bridges
span the rivers. Canal mania has hit and barges throng the cut
and the half-built Ironport docks. Smaller fires illuminate the
shanty town of navvies from Ireland and the Black Country who
live in shacks and tents in the mud. There is winding gear on the
hilltops. The shallow coal is already gone, buildings sag down the
hillsides with the ground dug out from under them. There are
people everywhere in the valley bottom, tiny swarming black
figures, ants on a burning log.

. . .

The Quakers is the old Quaker Burial Ground halfway to Burnt
Village. They built their factories here in the valley, built the
village for their workers to live in. It's where people go to drink
when they've got nowhere else left. Saturday teatimes Mark Fala
heads up there to give alms to the destitute. Matchdays are still
hard for him. If he ever loses it again it will be a matchday. But
he feels calm today. Liam has started, he knows that. He listened
to the radio quietly for a while this afternoon. He pictures Ally
standing naked in the showers, talking at Liam, 'You are not a
footballer, son, do you hear me? You are a fucking warrior, a
fucking gladiator. You go out in that second half and dominate
that cunt, you understand me, son?'

93

For ages after Mark and Liam would put that voice on, try to get that wild look in their eyes. They would laugh about it, but the truth was they believed it too. That talk did the trick as well, Mark remembers, an away game at Port Vale or somewhere. Some old cunt playing for one last contract, to pay his mortgage, and Liam giving it all back to him, kicking lumps off him, taking an elbow and giving one back, grinning at the bloke and then taking the ball off him, shutting him up, dominating him. That was Liam: a fucking gladiator. He can see the floodlight pylons from here as he climbs the lane past the last houses and gets the feeling that sometimes comes, that he could be there right now, sitting in that dressing room, unlacing his boots, joking with Liam, or sat staring at the tiles, beaten. He doesn't know today's score. Burton Albion. They've started the season well, Irontown haven't. It doesn't matter. In the wheel of the days, there's always another match coming. Until there isn't. Even then, look at Ally, at Archie Hill, old Ted Groves who does the kit. Mark could've stayed for ever. He knows he has to shut out these thoughts. He'll have a can with the others in the Quakers if it's calm there, you can never predict. He doesn't drink that much these days, though, barely at all, contrary to what people think. Nothing compared with what he did. Let them think it, it suits him, means people leave him alone. If ever reporters come and bang on the door, track him down for some story of one of England's great lost football talents, he pretends to be so pissed as not to be able to speak. They can write what they want.

He puts a foot on the low wall. You have to be careful here. He is usually fine, it's usually just drink in here, the lifers.

Crackheads and the like don't climb the hill, not this late in the year. The drinkers enjoy a sunset, appreciate the autumn colours. Gravestones lean at angles against the wall. Drummer Pete salutes him, his belly bare and red and a can of cider resting on it.

'All right, Mark. Here he is look. Told yer he'd be here.'

A couple lie sleeping up the slope from where Pete reclines. A bloke called Jigsaw pisses loudly against the far wall. Stevie from Oxton stands a little way from Pete, his face to the sun, the last wisp of a roll-up tucked in the corner of his mouth. Mark pulls a couple of the Superkings from the pack in his pocket and presses them into his cracked hand. Stevie smiles at him, his eyes not quite there, whispers a thanks. When he's had a big session his voice goes.

Mark passes Pete a couple of cans, lays the bottle of sherry down on the tough grass. The ground here is uneven, the drinkers lie in little hollows where the graves subside.

'Cheers, Mark. Good to see yer. You are a saint.'

He cracks open a can himself, takes a sip, lights a cigarette.

'Not many here today,' Mark says.

'Some of 'em gone down the Assembly Rooms, there's a way in round the back.' Pete shrugs. 'We'll have to head indoors soon.'

'We could head down the caves again, or the old shaft at Black Park.' Stevie talks into the golden light and no one answers.

Mark enjoys the quiet, pulls long on the cigarette until his head buzzes. He has the odd one in the week, then a couple on a Saturday night. He is a man of moderation.

Tomorrow he will rise early as always. He will make the same

walk up the hill, past the burial ground. He has often gone past
and seen the shapes of bodies huddled against the stone walls.
Pete and Jigsaw and Stevie sleep up here as late into the year as
they can, come down with the first frost. If you're only drinking,
you can go on a long time.

He will walk the hill to the cemetery and the crem, has to
climb the gate sometimes when he's very early, clean his parents'
graves with a roll of toilet paper, flowers if he can, walk round to
the rose garden and sit for a while near Sonia's plaque. His weeks
follow a careful pattern.

When Mark looks past Jigsaw, holding a fresh can out for him
as he stumbles up the hill, he sees there are others, huddled by
the bottom wall. He makes out Bobby Ahmed's wild hair. Dee
Dee's nephew gone awry. He is not a boy for a nice steady drink
on a late summer's afternoon. Mark has a screwdriver in his back
pocket, not that it would do any good against Bobby. Mark is
not a fucking warrior. Bobby was a kick-boxing champ until he
went off the rails.

'Bobby Ahmed,' Mark says.

'Fucking headcase,' Pete says. 'It's all right, he won't come over
if we're all here. Won't start nothing, anyway.'

Mark is dubious.

'Who's that with him?'

'Fuck knows.'

The figure beside Bobby crouches, wears a hood. He raises
his hand and it looks as if Bobby will pull him up but instead he
just takes whatever he has been passed and sticks it in his pocket.
So Bobby's on the hard stuff now then, he reckons. So many dif-

ferent ways to kill the pain. There is something in the shape the
figure makes against the wall that causes Mark to pause.

Jigsaw opens his can, tilts it towards the two men in a gesture
of cheers.

'Leave it, Jig, fuck's sake,' Pete says, 'leave 'em to it, let's have a
bit of peace.'

The hooded figure stands, climbs the wall, and heads along the
path which runs down below the village and arcs back towards
the Anvil Yards, an ancient drover's track that winds down to the
old market where the rivers meet, through the ruins of Lysaght's
and Watkins Cylinder Works. Mark takes that way home sometimes, along the canal. He will not do so tonight. He looks at the
shape of the man running away.

Bobby Ahmed strides towards them. There is a sudden charge
to the air. Mark tenses, remains half hidden behind Stevie. He is
not a fucking gladiator.

Bobby nods at each in turn. 'All right, gents. Give us a can, eh.'

'Here you go, Bobby, cheers.' Mark holds a drink out towards
him. Bobby takes it, looks at each of them in turn.

He clinks his can against Jigsaw's, looks at Mark.

'What you up to Bobby?' Jigsaw says. Bobby sucks his teeth,
this is not a question he likes. Pete says 'fucking hell,' under his
breath, still lying back on the grass, a hand over his eyes against
the low sun.

'You should think about what you're up to yourselves, boys,
you should.' His eyes stay on Mark. 'Get yourselves indoors,
maybe. Storm coming, I reckon. Storm coming.'

'We'll get ourselves in then Bobby, cheers.'

He turns and strides to go over the wall and the direction from which Mark came.

'Storm coming,' he says again.

'Fucking headcase,' Pete says when Bobby is at a safe distance.

'He might have just meant the weather,' Jigsaw says to no one in particular.

Mark sits down, lights another cigarette, plans a route home which means he won't run into Bobby. He will not go anywhere for a while. When it starts to rain the world is safer. He thinks of the shape of the running man.

. . .

Corineus took his axe to the King's throat, son of Brutus or not he would have his way. He had wrestled giants, would not be denied.

'You must marry my daughter,' Corineus said in the blade's gleaming light.

So Gwendolen became queen, bore Locrinus a son. Corineus was pleased, watched his grandson play in the reflection of his polished axe as his own days grew short, dreamed of killing giants and of the Trojan sun he would never see again. But Locrinus loved another, Estrildis, the most beautiful woman of the islands. He hid her in caves and in shadowy clearings and loved her there out of view of the world. With Estrildis, Locrinus had a daughter, Habren, hidden away in the dark woods and as beautiful as her mother.

When Corineus died, Locrinus abandoned Gwendolen,

took Estrildis as his new queen. But Gwendolen sought out the wild men of the south and west, brought an army to Locrinus' lands. They fought a war along muddy riverbanks and Gwendolen fired an iron arrow across the water into Locrinus' heart.

Gwendolen had Estrildis and Habren bound tight with chain at their ankles and wrists and then cast down the river to the sea, watched as their hair twisted in the current and slid under the brown water, saw the willow trees bow their heads, set the crown on her own head.

. . .

Gary Newbon: When Mark Fala puts the ball down on the spot you go over and say something to him. Can you remember what you said?

Liam Corwen: I know what I said. Listen, he'd been messing around when he took penalties since, well since I'd ever known him. In training, anyway. In matches he'd usually just stick it in the corner, but I knew he had it on his mind. We used to watch the same videos over and over as kids. They'd been his dad's. They'd not long bought a video when he died so we only had a few tapes, George Best and whatnot, over and over again. That chipped penalty was on one of them. Panenka, for Czechoslovakia, you know? Mark always loved that sort of thing. I knew what was on his mind. I just said to him, 'Don't f—in' chip it.'

Gary Newbon: And what did he say to that?

Liam Corwen: Nothing. I think I might have made his
mind up for him, to be honest. Maybe. I wish I
hadn't said it now. He sort of waved me away,
the way he always knew best, you know? The more
I think of it now, it all had to do with his dad,
all of it, of course it did. His mum as well, of
course. Maybe that was worse, I don't know. He
never talked about it.

Gary Newbon: His parents were dead?

Liam Corwen: Died when he was a kid. You know the
story. What's that saying? The straw that broke
the camel's back or whatever, the penalty, that
is. He saw his dad get killed, he was there for
some reason, at the works the day it happened.
Jesus. His mother couldn't cope with it all after,
not really. I mean, who would? It hit us all bad
when she went, to be honest, so god knows how it
must have affected him. Like I say, he never talked
about it.

Gary Newbon: Something I've noticed.

Liam Corwen: What?

Gary Newbon: You always refer to him in the past
tense. As if Mark Fala is also . . .

Liam Corwen: He's dead to me, to a good many others
as well. It was his choice. I think he died when
he last kicked a football, the day of that penalty
miss. He's dead to us.

Gary Newbon: You never see him now? You've never been
in contact since he stopped playing?

Liam Corwen: I saw him at another funeral not long

after. A friend of ours who died on the day of
the game, the play-off. You know all this. There
was enough of it in the papers. He don't want the
contact. He wants to be left alone. There are days
I don't blame him. Can we stop talking about this
now?

He should never have agreed to the documentary in the first
place, thought it would disappear, but they still show it every
now and again, late at night after the football highlights. It's on
Youtube, anyway. He has tried not to read the comments. He
agreed to take part when he was in Finland, thought he was rid
of the place, never coming back. As he asks to stop the interview
and puts his hand to his face, they play footage of that goal against
Stockport as Liam says these last words, the one they always seem
to show, the one Mark scored on his eighteenth birthday. Wayne
Coombs wins a header under his own bar at a corner and the
ball goes up in the air and drops near the edge of the box. Mark
nips in front of their midfielder who is watching the ball, about
to hit it, and heads it over him, runs the other side of him and
takes it on his thigh, bounces it once, twice, three times on his
right leg as he runs, with a player having two kicks at him, they
called it the M'bou, Mark and Liam, after the Cameroon player
who ran with it down the line against Argentina in the Miracle
in Milan. Liam has it tattooed on his left ankle, he has Benjamin
Massing taking out Claudio Caniggia in the same match on his
right. Sometimes he thinks the tattoos are just some kind of
coded message to Mark. That he'll see a photo of Liam, his body
adorned, and the world will make sense.

And the Stockport fullback tries the Massing trick, throws his whole body at Mark, who lets the ball drop to his left foot, still midway inside his own half, and Mark twists and the bloke goes hurtling past him and crashes into his own player instead, and now Mark takes off. He runs straight up the middle of the pitch with the ball at his feet, defenders surging back and clipping his heels and falling away, they cannot catch him, running full pelt, he looks like a boy on a beach, and then twenty yards out or so, he gets it away from his feet for the first time, looks like he's miscontrolled it, and there's another defender sliding in from his right now, but he's got his head up and he clips the ball, no back lift, over the sliding challenge and over the keeper too, and the ball arcs perfectly into the net and he wheels away. You can see Liam on the edge of the screen, he was on the bench that day and Ally had got him warming up, he runs on the narrow track between the East Stand and the pitch, arms aloft towards the Greenfield End, going crazy. People always forget they lost that game 3-2, won the league though, and that's what mattered.

. . .

He is the eagle. There is low, hard autumn sun for the derby. The stadium is a bowl of light, rightly named, the white-shirted crowd shine. When Eusébio rises to meet the ball he sees his shadow ripple across the pitch and he is the eagle, of course. He hears this in Guttmann's voice, but Guttmann has been gone two years now, yet his voice lingers on, whispering doubts, except not in Eusébio. For a moment he is not sure that this voice has not arrived with the ringing in the ears he got from the clatter of the Sporting keeper as he beat him to the ball's bounce off the hard surface and zigzagged his legs to clip it past the brim of the keeper's hat and have it bounce away from the direction he'd run and into the corner of the net. He takes the ball down and arches his back, head up, his eyes in their matchday squint, eagle eyes. The keepers wear hats like workers at the docks. Torres. Where is Torres? His arms reach, swim him through the light and past defenders, propel him, wings. He looks for Torres and races his own shadow across the grass.

. . .

She finds a length of broken iron pipe. Rust bubbles foam down one side. Goldie '89 is painted in an unidentifiable media (correction fluid?). The G and o are formed in thick sweeps, the lettering fades until the '89 appears in thin scratched strokes. It gives the impression of a boy in a hurry, a careless boy. The hairs rise on Alina's neck.

She takes the pipe from the outside wall of Lisbon House, an abandoned block of flats near where they used to all hang about. It's up the road from Stevedore House, where the Falas had lived, where that photo she loves had been taken. It's there she was headed for, to see if she could get onto the roof, when she stops to take a look around Lisbon House. Then she sees the lettering on the pipe, the kind of thing she'd been searching for all along. She stands and looks at it for a long time, prises it free with the iron cutters she bought from the place in Lascar that sells stolen bikes and the equipment with which to steal them.

It's the sort of place her dad would've appreciated from what she can tell.

She keeps it in a box with some other stuff at the back of Tony's studio. If her mum sees it, she might get the pipe wrapped around her head.

.   .   .

Saturday teatime Mark likes to turn the telly on, sometimes he can face *Final Score*, sometimes not. The telly was a bit of company, his mum used to say. Not enough for her, it turned out. He likes quizzes. Right now a couple from Leicester are being shown around houses in Tenerife. They don't seem very happy with the situation, red-faced and looking as though they are being short-changed against a hard blue sky. He presses the tea bag to the side of the cup, adds a sugar and watches it spread and dissolve like a galaxy flaring and dying millions of miles away. He has his routines. The apartment is close to a water park. The Corwens all went to Tenerife one year not long after Christmas, during the season, of course. Liam missed a week of school and a Mercian Cup game. Freddie Rogers, their old coach at Lascar Boys Club got in a mood about it, tried to drop Liam for the next game, but then Joey Corwen got involved. Mark remembers watching from the minibus window as Liam's dad pushed his bronzed head into Freddie's bobble hat, 'You leave him out then I'll take him up to Cowton Sports, don't you worry about that, you ungrateful cunt.'

It was always a bit like that, like Liam was doing them a favour.

He started next match, of course, and all the others. Freddie was a good coach though, a bit soft with them maybe, still lived in the same house with gnomes in the front yard, roses and canes of runner beans in the summer, rode his mobility scooter up to the row of shops at the Ironport.

'Yer fit?' Freddie asks him if he sees him, same as he used to greet him as a fourteen-year-old out on the old Heath junior pitches.

'I am, Fred. You?'

'What's it look like? I see your mate's up to no good again.'

There had been letters about Liam and the Wolves supporters in the *Chronicle*. Ally has promised an investigation. Liam can do whatever he likes, just as he always has.

'What, Liam? I don't see him no more Fred, you know that.'

'No, that other one. Him who robbed the shop, got that girl killed.'

'What?'

'That one. I seen him in the Bull Ring the other day, up to no good, most likely, I thought.'

'No Fred, no, he ain't ever coming back round here, must've been somebody else.'

But as he says it he thinks of a crouching man, a running man. 'There's a storm coming,' is what Bobby Ahmed said.

Flies rise past the window. They are demolishing some old outhouses down near the docks wall, buildings gone the shape of cardboard boxes left in the rain. There is something in the afternoon paper about progress being made on the redevelopment plans, architect's drawings.

'I'll believe it when I see it,' is what Freddie Rogers mutters, on his way back from the new Ukrainian shop, when he sees these pictures of landscaped gardens between flats and offices with shiny windows, no men on mobility scooters or clutching oxygen masks or even straggling along with sticks and walking frames in these drawings, uniform couples and families, none of them old, or poor, not one too black, or too white for that matter, not one shuffling along with one shoe on and a football boot on the other foot, not one sprawled with a can on that neatly trimmed grass, no one sitting with their shirt off having a smoke, or dragging their kids and stepkids along with bags of shopping hanging off the pushchair with a dodgy wheel, and none of them reflected in any of the glass, these vampires.

When they knock the buildings down the flies come this way on the wind, rats scatter in all directions.

'What are you thinking?' asks the young woman in the summer dress on television, who looks not unlike one of those figures in the drawing, of the couple from Leicester who look not unlike some of the people not present in the picture. Perhaps that's where they'll all get moved to, Tenerife.

'What are you thinking?'

They stare at palm trees and lizard-backed mountains. If they don't like the place they shouldn't move. That life is very long, is what Mark thinks. He sips his tea, still too hot, like he does every afternoon. He waits for it to cool, for the couple to make up their mind and his afternoon quiz to start. You need routines. People always say life's too short. He thinks they're wrong. A fly taps the window glass. There are creatures that only live for a day, for a few hours. They have no memories, no sense of themselves at all, or if they do it's all present, all happening right now, an endlessly running moment, so that in a sense they live for ever, like the way they say fish think, which he does not fully believe. The couple from Leicester say they expected more wow factor. Outside the flies rise.

.   .   .

A list of the proposed redevelopments of the Greenfield Ironworks and the surrounding areas of the Anvil Yards since British Steel finally ended production in 1984:

A shopping centre.

A J.R.R. Tolkien-inspired theme park (this in the days before Middle-Earth was outsourced to New Zealand. There was a story that a trip Tolkien made to the Iron Towns, west from Birmingham or Oxford, inspired his vision of Mordor. But travel the lanes that weave across the Heath, or go on the back roads through Far Valley or the Welsh Ridge and you could just as easily be in The Shire).

A site for the World Student Games and/or Commonwealth Games.

Another shopping centre.

A King Arthur-inspired theme park (a 1960s New Age paperback linked the valley with the journeys of the Knights of the Round Table. There was a plan to use one of the Lascar docks as the lake, from which the sword would emerge every afternoon).

A Japanese car plant (before the Japanese economy went the way of the Iron Towns).

A new home for the BBC.

A mega-casino and attendant hotel development. (Quickly nicknamed
Ironvegas, this idea is unique in that part of it was actually built. The
hotel in which Liam currently lives is the only building that was
completed before permission was halted and the money ran out. The
project revived the idea of using a dock as the lake, for a giant lap-
dancing venue called Guinevere's. A topless lady of the lake was set to
emerge each evening.)

Another shopping centre.

Arcadia: an eco-development which meant emptying out anything that
was left and letting nature take its course, introducing deer, eagles,
even wolves in one version of the plan. Chernobyl-chic.

An airport and giant freight terminal. (In one set of plans called London
Iron Town. The developers tried the old Eusébio trick.)

A privately run complex of super-prisons.

A Chinese-owned steelworks with surrounding factories supplying the
People's Army (in spite of terrible feng-shui, it was the absence of any
skilled workers that put an end to this plan. The whole thing has now
gone on so long that there are plenty of people who were in their teens
when the Anvil Yards began to rust, now approaching retirement age,
who have never worked).

There are arguments about who owns the land, contamination,
decontamination, compensation, what to do with the businesses
that simply refuse to die, not to mention the people who live
there and refuse to move, viewed by developers in the way that
divers look at molluscs on the hulk of the *Titanic*. Then there
is the issue with UNESCO placing the Greenfield Ironworks,

the Samson Foundry, the Watkins Cylinder Factory, Lysaght's, the East Stand and half the docks on their World Heritage Sites list. Soldiers in blue helmets, Bengali, Armenian, Dutch, might arrive to halt any dynamiting.

. . .

Mark Fala did not go to school that morning. There were days when his mum said not to bother, he helped carry her shopping bags or took wet clothes up to the washing line on the roof. Or he would spend the whole day on the uneven wasteland that doubled as Wembley, Anfield, the Azteca, and drill his tennis ball against the flats' end wall and take the rebound anywhere on his body, on the full, and drop the ball dead to do the same thing all over again.

That morning she asks him to take two empty pop bottles back for the deposit, and to drop his dad's sandwiches at work for him. He has left them sitting in the foil in which she wrapped them last night next to the sink, distracted by something out of the window in the blue dawn light.

His dad hauls a chain, backlit by a furnace which burns somewhere deep in the works. He sees him, sees Mark standing there outside in the yard, his foot on his ball, an empty pop bottle in each hand, a thin plastic bag holding the sandwiches hangs from his wrist. They both smile. His dad goes to raise an arm. Mark thinks it is to motion him to the gates, or wave, or tell him to wait, when something happens to the chain.

His dad jumps backwards and then the bucket that swings above the moulds, that his dad is set to pour, wobbles and spills.

Here is the molten metal, so white hot that it burns a shape into Mark's eyes that he is not sure he ever really blinks away. And it pours, liquid and heavy, not into the mould, but onto Antony Fala. The movements are slapstick, innocent, a broken chain, a spilled bucket, a fall-guy. Mark sees his dad crumple, his body withers, the way a match does if you leave it alight and wait for it to burn your fingertips. There are screams, shouts. Men run. A bell starts to ring over the clanging sounds from elsewhere in the factory. Mark remembers later that there was a magpie chuckling, hopping across a pile of scrap metal in the yard. The magpie flies away as the men run through the gates. When he thinks of this later, he believes that it is his dad's soul leaving his body and jumping into that of the bird. He puts silver foil pellets on his window ledge to see if the magpies will come.

'The boy, look, the boy.'

'What?'

'His boy, Fala's boy, in the yard.'

'Oh, Jesus.'

'Come here, son, come here.'

'Get him away from here.'

This is Mark Fala, eleven years old. High clouds move over the Anvil Yards. Mark stands with his foot on his ball, a bottle in either hand, the sandwiches his dad will never eat hanging from his wrist and he looks past the running, shouting men and sees the blackened shape on the floor. The empty mould sits on the stopped conveyor, a broken chain swings back and forth above it. Mark does not remember anything about what comes next, days, weeks. He kicks his ball against the end wall.

. . .

'I found a johnny in the toilets this morning, Dee Dee.'

'What?'

'Has it been that long that you've forgot what one is? A condom, a johnny, in the bogs.'

Dee Dee pauses to consider this.

'Used?'

'I wouldn't say otherwise, would I?'

'I wouldn't have thought they'd got that much life in them.'

Dee Dee is suddenly pleased by this news, that she might be running somewhere that inspires enough passion for a quickie in a toilet cubicle. She thinks for a minute about who was drinking in the lounge last night.

'Which toilets?' she asks. Roni holds her mug of tea in both hands. Her pyjamaed legs are folded beneath her.

'The ladies,' she says, 'in the bar.'

'In the bar?' Dee Dee says.

'In the bar, behind the cistern. I fetched it out with the mop.'

'The only people we had in the bar last night was Manjit Kohli and them from the bakery.'

The bakery is the last factory open in the Anvil Yards, sliced bread on an industrial scale, Sikh men backlit by yellow sodium at all hours of the day and night.

Roni shrugs.

'Life in the old dogs yet, Dee Dee.'

'Am yer having me on?'

'I swear to god. Behind the tank in one of the ladies cubicles.

Disgusting, really, they could put it in the bin.'

'Well,' Dee Dee says, pauses for effect, doesn't look at Roni, 'I had it in the bogs here once.'

Roni spits a mouthful of tea onto the yard, swears. 'What? Who with?'

'Who with? Who'd yer think? Liam. Who else would it have been? Who with?!'

'I don't know what to say.'

'In the lounge, mind. We had standards. I did, anyway.'

. . .

He rises from the French mud, where he lay bootless.

Leônidas rises, this mud man, as if a ghost of the middle passage torn from the seabed, and then skips and dances with the ball through the hacking legs. Defenders move like magnets repelled.

This European dream of Brazilian football is born in Strasbourg. Men think of that goal, some of them in their motley workers' caps, as they trudge away from the river, as their trains slowly pick up speed, heading south and west, when they evacuate the city, empty it completely, when the Germans come across the Rhine. Another iron town, with its factories and cranes and its port so many miles inland.

Wenger grew up there, in a pub stained brown with tobacco smoke, in a town stained grey from chimney smoke. Liam tells himself the pub was called the King of Sparta. He doesn't even know if pubs have names in France.

Leônidas's footsteps, which barely mark the ground, become

those of Vava and Didi and Garrincha and Pelé and Jahrinio and Zico and Eder and Socrates and Ronaldinho, a whole string of little Juninhos, and Ronaldo and Neymar and on and on into the future.

I am the resurrection and I am the life, runs the text in the shape of Leônidas's dash for the goal, which winds along Liam's spine towards Ronaldo as Christ the Redeemer.

'Biblical quotations,' says the journalist, a woman in her twenties, into her recorder, her dark hair cut into a harsh fringe. She looks at him and her fingers almost brush his flesh.

'Nah, The Stone Roses,' he says, then wishes he hadn't and had just held her stare. The words were Tony's idea. The words do not mean anything, but the swaying run through the mud, the goal that brings the sun out in Strasbourg, the one that Leônidas scores without a boot on his foot, to make it Brazil 5, Poland 4, they win 6-5, that is real. He wonders if the boots remain buried. Some corner of a foreign field.

Except he watched it later, after the tattoo, some bleached-out newsreel resurrected on the internet, and the mud isn't there, not really, and the sun shines and it is so, well, deflating, and lacks all of the grandeur that they have invested in it, words or not, this dark figure rising from European mud etched halfway up his back.

'And what does it mean?' she asks him, and he is struck that no one English would ever ask this kind of question with this earnestness, no one he has ever met, anyway.

'Leônidas was the King of Sparta,' he says, 'leader of the three hundred, hero of Thermopylae.' And she nods but looks confused, not sure if he is serious, or if this is just one big English joke, and this time he holds her gaze, smiling, with a kind of half-mocking look. Of course it isn't serious. Of course it is. He knows she is staying in the hotel. He cannot play golf, has no share prices to check, just the afternoons to fill stuck inside the room's four walls, inside his own head.

· · ·

And if you're the Baggies,
or the Wolves,
or them sheep shagging bastards,
then you ain't no friend of mine.
All together now,
My old man . . .

They do not sing about us, these other clubs, Liam thinks from the dugout, his feet up on the breeze block, concentrating on the pock marks the players' studs have made and the sheen of mud and the white line in front of him as the lights become stronger. He will not get on today. The game drifts along rudderless. Needles of rain come suddenly in the lights. He hears the clatter of seats behind him as people stand to leave before the end. He cannot understand this, begins to lift his head and turn to glare at the punters behind, but what's the point? He wears a snood. Dee Dee and Sonia had them once, luminous green and orange. His is Eton Blue. He sees Sonia's eyes waiting for him through the rain. They saw each other once at a bus shelter on the Heath, like a mossy cave with the rain beating on it, down by the Goat Wood where the witches meet.

And those other clubs do not sing about the Iron Towns, do not even consider them worth acknowledging, not even Wrexham he doesn't think, not even Newport, unless you count 'Stand up if you hate England.'

'We need some new songs,' he says.

Shaunie McLaughlin nods his head, now neither of them are starting. Ally's got a lad in on loan from Cheltenham Town, looks half-decent.

'New songs,' Shaunie repeats and nods like this is wisdom of great import. Ally must have told him to listen to everything Liam says. That's all the kid needs, Liam thinks, wipes his nose on his snood.

. . .

Caller: I mean, you lot all talk about how Liam
    Corwen is a great player, a great servant to
    this club. Listen, when he got in the team we was
    fifteenth in the old second division or whatever
    it was called then. He's played for twenty years
    and in that time we've had relegations, all them
    money worries and nothing but trouble. Them
    years he was away, we had the Trophy final, we
    had the play-offs again. They was the best years
    of the last twenty. Then he come back. What's he
    come back for? He's on the biggest contract, the
    highest wages. Bleeding the club dry, that's what
    people like him am doing. That Julius Williams,
    Devon Samuels, the same. Listen, my old man worked
    on the railways. They used to have a name for

folks who'd bring bad luck, straight from the Old
Testament. He's a Jonah, Liam Corwen. Throw him
overboard now, before it's too late.

Dave 'Iron' Willis: Graham, Graham, you cannot
be seriously saying that the problems faced by
Irontown Football Club are caused by Liam Corwen?
He's a club legend. The guy bleeds Eton Blue.

Caller: Legend? I've told yer what he is. And it's
not just him to blame, no. I'll tell yer what,
though. He is plain bad luck.

Joey turns the radio off and sits in the car outside the shops. They used to say pay no attention to the table until October was out. They might win a few and be in the play-off places come the new year. He knows this will not happen.

They are a cancer, these phone-ins. Joey does not use the term lightly. Liam wasn't even getting a game. Maybe if Ally picked him for more than one game out of three, if Ally picked the same back four two games running, in fact where was Ally in all this moaning? That bloke could swim through honey, nothing stuck to him.

Cancer the crab, he thinks of pincers taking hold, of never letting go. It's why the disease is so named, pub quiz knowledge. He thinks of young doctors, consultants, peering at pictures of Liz's insides between rounds of golf or skiing trips, or whatever they do, these men from a different world, their hands on your wife, cutting your wife, laying her down on their cold slabs.

They would pore over the shapes and patterns that come from Liz's insides like maps of some strange empire, discuss strategy, absentee generals. Not for too long, though, had tee-off times to meet and the like. Mr Ali is not here on Friday afternoons. Dr Roberts isn't in until tomorrow. The arms, pincers, tentacles stretch and writhe inside her body. Some terrible, invisible war raging. And then thank you doctor, thank you doctor, thank you . . .

The nurses were better, the porters. At least they spoke to you like you were another human being, like if you saw them in the street or at the football or whatever they'd smile and say hello.

Liz wants to move and who can blame her. She'd wanted to go when the kids were young. He hadn't wanted to move Liam, already showing a bit of promise, hadn't thought the whole place would close down, just showed what he knew. They say they stay for his old man now, so Liz can do his ironing, clean the house, take his meals round. But Joey knows it's really him they stay for. He tells himself he'll look at those brochures she put out, houses in Bridgnorth and Brecon, retirement villages on the Algarve and Costa Dorada, anywhere, anywhere but here.

'Cup of tea, love?'

'Yes please.'

What else to say?

Now it's over, she's better. They don't say better, but she's clear, and there's nothing to say to each other at all. If Liam visited once in those months without being reminded, without still just sitting himself down and his tea done for him, then Joey was being kind.

Cup of tea, love, cup of tea, love, cup of tea . . .

. . .

These noises would destroy most men, that's what Goldie tells himself these first few weeks. He'd adjusted to prison noises over time, the breathing of other men close by, shouts down tiled corridors, a low, constant hum of strip-lights. The twitches and pain in your temples at the sharp movements or sudden sounds of other men who might do you real damage, given half a chance. With time, with the days, that sense eases, but only somewhat. If he thinks about it all, perhaps that feeling has always been with him, way before prison days, that knowledge of the harm you might inflict, that might be done to you, always there, the steady hum at the temples, the sound of windowless rooms and boys' shouts down tiled corridors.

Noises and the dark fill his mind. The first night he hears an owl hoot and imagines the rustle of wings. There are bars at the window. The desk drawers are stuffed full of reams of typed paper, fading text and digits in purple and grey. The figures make an indentation on the paper, each one a little hammer blow. Rats splash in the narrow canal under the window. The men left the place as if everyone would be back in work tomorrow, thirty years and more now. No one is coming back.

He has five hundred pounds in dirty notes done up in red elastic bands that the postmen use and little plastic change bags. Some of it from the back of Nadine's underwear drawer; some from the biscuit tin in the cupboard in her mum's kitchen, first places anyone would look. It was money to go away with. They were going to book something for the bank holiday week,

Nadine, her mum and the girls. That has passed now. Summer is over. He was tired of trying to look after another man's kids and not doing very well at it. He has not done a good job of anything since climbing through those skylights into warehouses stuffed full with treasure all those years ago.

'Here comes Spider-Man,' Stan Ahmed had said to him, clapped him on his back, so hard as to knock him over, just to let him know who was boss. He thought the name might stick but it never did.

This morning he sits on a step in a doorway that opens onto the canal towpath. The gap between the tall buildings makes a ravine that the water runs through, iron rings and hooks jut from the brickwork, rust stains trailing from them. He is safe here, he thinks. No one comes this far into the works, not even people up to no good. He looks at the blue swirl of the lion's mane on the signs which warn of security guards and dogs. They walk the perimeters from a Portakabin office over by the Ironport, sometimes they drive around the buildings in small white vans. The roads are subsiding, potholed, soon they'll need diggers, caterpillar tracks, bulldozers. One day they'll flatten the place but not yet. This will do for now.

When he stands his trousers fall down over his arse. He was always skinny, now his hips jut out and his jeans hang from them. When he came out the second time, after he'd gone back in for robbing and whatnot, like what was he expected to do now, to keep going, put food in his empty belly while they expected him to carry on in one scheme or the other, cleaning the kitchens at the college, chopping onions and taking scraps out to the bins, giving him a knife. He remembers the shock of seeing soft-faced white boys on the bus with their trousers falling down to show their pants. Everyone wants to be a bad boy now.

He is safe as he can be here, he thinks. No one comes this far into the world of cobwebs and typed paper and telephone dials, back through time and space. The money will run out. His trousers will fall down. Winter will come. He thought phoning Dee Dee would spur him on, make him do something. It got him here. He used to dream about Dee Dee and Sonia together, wanking as quiet as he could under scratchy blankets, still does sometimes. He wishes he hadn't phoned now, let them all know. He'd like to see Liam, he thinks, to see Mark. There are days he thinks he'd like to meet them with a knife, they just cut him off, not one message or card or anything like that. Something will come to him, he thinks, something is out there waiting for him.

.   .   .

'Hey,' a voice calls from the dark entrance to the old Assembly Rooms, a figure leans forward off the cardboard that patterns the steps. Mark has got too casual. He steps off the pavement into the gutter, rests his boot's worn-down studs on the high kerb, doesn't want to run or look too startled, his heart going.

A hand reaches out at him from the gloom.

'Hey, geezer, all right?'

It's Bobby Ahmed grinning at him, not quite looking at him. Still, Bobby must be the only person in the whole of the Iron Towns not to call Mark by name. It irritates him for a moment.

Geezer. No one says that within a hundred miles radius, more.

They came to see Bobby fight here when he was a kid, no more than a little boy really, before he switched to kick-boxing and steroids and weed, and whatever else he is doing now, boys boxing against clubs from the Welsh valleys or the Black Country. *Iron Towns, Iron Towns, Iron Towns* would echo from the back of the hall. He went to one once with the team where there were blokes eating steaks watching kids batter each other's heads in. *Kill him, Bobby*, they would shout.

'Penny for the guy, blood?'

Bobby's open hand reaches out to him, cracked and dirty. Mark thinks he must have slept on the steps, it's not much after first light, a thick dew on the world, cold first thing in a morning now but the sun still shines in the afternoons. Bobby's mum and dad live in a mansion somewhere up by the Heathside, he must still have his bedroom there. Just go home, Bobby, he wants to say.

It was a mistake to stand down the kerb like this with Bobby standing over him, no one else around, this the turning that the bread lorries use for the bakery and be careful not to step back and get flattened, Mark thinks, and somewhere wonders at his own capacity for survival. But then there's Bobby's soft face and the way he doesn't really look at him. The idea that he really would hand some money over to him, although he's done it in the past, of course.

'Where's your guy?'

'What?'

'You ain't got no guy, Bobby.'

He sees that Bobby is surprised that he uses his name, wonders if he can actually see anything, looking like a blind beggar, some roadside penitent from a painting of centuries past, dressed in a ragged Nike track suit.

'You can't ask for money with no guy, mate.'

Bobby giggles like a little boy. Mark feels a stab of pity and then disgust. He has a handful of change in his pocket. He is going to the back hatch at the bakery to buy a warm misshaped loaf, teacakes if they've got any.

'It's trick or treat they go for now, Bobby, any road. You should try that instead, mate.'

Bobby nods and smiles, his shoulders tremble with mirth and he laughs again. The punch comes quick, so fast that Mark is out on the wet pavement before he even realises he has been hit. Bobby had nothing in his hand, he will think later, when he tries to convince himself he's been hit by a brick, by some gargoyle tumbling off one of the ruins, but no, it's Bobby's fist all right, hard and fast and the last ability to leave him.

Mark covers up in the gutter, waits for more blows. Instead there's an iron grip on his shoulder and lips that brush his ear.

'I am the fucking guy,' Bobby says, steps over him, hasn't even bothered to pick up the change that jangles from Mark's pocket.

He lies on the wet stones for a bit, his head getting bigger and then smaller, the street rising and falling. The running man was Goldie, a thought that comes with the throb in his head, like a vision across the years.

A bread van slows as it goes past him, the sound of the tyres on the tarmac like that of a tide coming in, going out, he moves so they don't think he's dead, but the van doesn't stop.

. . .

Stanley Matthews, Duncan Edwards, Billy Wright. Men from Hanley and Dudley and Ironbridge. Princes of Mercia, like Offa, like Kenelm. They run together around the Highbury pitch at England training, conscious of the photographer's gaze. They match each other's stride. Legs built on cobbles, by racing up slag heaps and terraces. Stanley Matthews runs on Blackpool sands. It's one reason why he plays until he's fifty. Duncan Edwards wears a jumper to build up a sweat, the two older men wear shirts open at the neck, day-trippers at the seaside. Older men: Matthews is forty-two, in his last year with the England team. There's a happiness and confidence and determination in their look.

Billy Wright's dad worked in a foundry, big Duncan's too. Matthews's was a barber and pro boxer; his own son plays tennis, wins the Boys championship at Wimbledon just five years hence, they say he's the new Fred Perry. But this photo offers nothing of what is to come. Look at the big young man in the middle of the three. Ten months after the picture is taken he is dead, twenty-one. Later, Duncan Edwards's dad leaves his foundry job, works at the cemetery where his son is buried, tends the flowers and the verges and the graves.

. . .

Liam sometimes went to watch the Villa on his own, midweek or on a Sunday, when they hadn't got a game. This in the years when it went wrong for them, Irontown, for him, with the team struggling, with Mark gone, no chance of an England call ever coming again, just ridicule, in fact, because Taylor had been sacked and everyone said the players he'd picked had been no good. And the big money and the TV came now and they'd missed out on it all thanks to a fluffed penalty, a loss of heart, loss of nerve. When he played away from home now Liam was singled out with braying donkey noises, even though he held that defence together, and that's what Ally whispered in his ear, and Ally kept him going. It was a kind of big man syndrome, everyone wanting to have a pop at him. His dad kept quiet, like he thought he had it coming. Maybe he did.

'If they're making a noise, son, you're doing something right. They are scared of you, terrified. You just carry on as you are,' Ally would stand naked in the middle of the dressing room, telling them that Liam is the best defender he's ever worked with.

Sometimes their opponents – places like Peterborough and Doncaster – would sing 'Where's Mark Fala gone?' to the tune of 'Where's your caravan?' but it never really took off, and the Iron Towns support would drown it out with his name, over and over, like he'd gone nowhere at all. It was Liam they really liked to taunt, sensing a wound, sensing blood.

He'd pull a cap down tight, bury his face in an old scarf, lose himself in the crowd round Villa Park, in the red brick and the rain. There was a cup match he went away to, Sheffield United, Bramall Lane in the snow, when Yorke chipped a penalty just like Mark had tried.

You needed an iron will to do it, to carry it off.

Yorke runs up as if to strike it, does not shorten his stride, but instead digs his foot underneath it, like a pitching wedge or something and hits it with back-spin, almost too hard, so it dips just under the cross bar and into the net and he runs off to the side of the goal, laughing.

Back then people fixated on Yorke's smile, like it was all a joke, which it was of course, but they'd patronise him and say he played with a smile on his face, like none of it mattered, like you didn't need an iron will to pull that off, to come from where he had come from and end up where he did, that's what Liam thought. Everyone missed the point. He might have had a happy smile but he had balls of fucking iron.

Then they ended up with Liverpool in the semi-final. Liam went to that too. They got undone by Robbie Fowler, who flitted in and out of the Villa area like he wore an invisible cloak. It was at Old Trafford, that semi-final, in the time before they played them all at Wembley. He wouldn't have gone to Wembley, was glad when they pulled the place down. He stood and looked at the Busby Babes' stopped clock before the match. He wished he had Mark to talk to, Dee Dee as well, too late now. Most clocks keep ticking.

. . .

He can hear horses' hooves. It must be a Friday, Goldie thinks, and is caught somewhere between now and then, because it is Friday, and there really is the sound of horses' hooves echoing through the estate.

They used to call the Pengwern the Lost Valley or The

Island. There was a little iron bridge that went over the cut, the Navvy they used to call it, the Chain Navigation, and led into Lysaght's, where the men had worked, and apart from the road that ran down from Lowtown, that was the only way on and off the place without a coracle. The gate at the bridge was rusted shut now, of course. There was the gasworks on one side, towers of scrap and the river itself on the other, so the Peng had always been a little world to itself.

They used to ride pony traps all around the estate on Friday afternoons. The ponies came off the back field next to the river. The traps were customised, seats from old cars, rigs from the fairground, all from the scrapyards that petered out into the back field. All the kids who never bothered with school used to meet down the stables early afternoon and sort out who was riding with who, a kind of rough democracy, common owner-ship to it all. A mate of his called Tommy Knock used to take him out. Goldie was scared of horses. This was in the days before he started to hang around with Liam and Mark, Dee Dee and Sonia, before he got into all that stuff with the Ahmeds. He should've just stayed here, he thinks, not for the first time in his life, looks at the grass that grows out of the gutter, up the middle of the road in places. There were people when he was growing up who'd never even been into Hightown. He wasn't sure his mum ever had. He could've stayed here, headed out in the dark for ware-houses packed with treasure, ridden around in a carriage like a prince on a Friday afternoon.

It looks the same, the houses anyway, more or less. There are grilles here up at the windows and doors at the end house where the Sadlers used to live, a family where it was the women who used to go to prison, forward thinking, thieving even when everyone else was still trudging over the bridge to start their shift. Nana Sadler was an old flame of Stan Ahmed's, would fence stuff down at the row of garages. They called her the Black Cat, perhaps because of her ability to get away with things, but also because of her luck at the bingo, at the horses. She'd been a bookie's runner as a girl, left from the pubs and the factory gates to take messages to the Carter boys who waited at the Hightown station. There is nothing left of the Sadlers. He wonders what is behind the green metal shutters. With eyes half-closed they look like windows on a doll's house, or on postcards of happy places in the mountains in countries far from here. There is the odd blue brick among the red.

The hooves get louder, closer, there is a whooping shout from somewhere and then a flashing movement from the end of the street and a young brown horse comes trotting down the middle of the road and he sees the trap make a clean arc around the bend behind it. He steps onto the pavement and tugs at his hood and when he looks again, swears to god that it is Tommy Knock's freckled face above that of the horse. Red freckles on Tommy, white freckles on the horse's face, a mop of red hair on both. Tommy holds the reins three-quarters taut in his hands. A young girl sits next to him, leaning back and laughing, pale faced, with black hair tied up on her head, wearing clothes too thin for the weather.

And then they are gone, and he listens to the sound bouncing off the Sadlers' empty house and he puts his hands on the low wall and takes a gulp of air to steady himself.

He will have had kids, Tommy, of course he will have. He probably still lives down there on Stream Crescent, out the other end of the road, past the shops or whatever is left of them, past Goldie's old house. Where would he have gone? The towers of scrap are all still there. It was Tommy's son, must have been.

His legs will not move as he wants them to, will not go one step more in the direction he wants to go. He listens to the hooves as they fade and the boy drives the trap on the old circuit, Goldie can tell from the sounds, down to the road that runs parallel with the cut, where you could really get a speed up before having to slow into the corner, unless you wanted to end up in the drink. In summer, they'd have races after tea as the sky turned a darker blue. Lads would come to race cars there on Sunday nights. There is just a faint clip-clop now in the distance, that far corner, and Goldie turns his back and walks up the road back towards the Lowtown turning. He'll come back another time, another day, when he feels a bit better, a bit more up to it.

He has not seen his mother since she used to get the early morning bus to Birmingham, visiting orders in her handbag, wearing her best clothes and trying not to catch anyone's eye, but all that faded, and they have not spoken since he moved in with Nadine, wrote the address carefully in a Christmas card that he sent her much too late. Strange, how they'd got through the hardest part, she could've just disowned him, never spoken to him again, but she didn't, then everything faded away after he'd been released, like she thought he should still be inside. Maybe

that had been easier for her. A few days won't make any difference now.

. . .

In the photograph Tony has laid out on the desk for him, there is
a man running, telephone wires stretched above him. Abundant
green leaves explode at the roadside. In the foreground another
man, shirtless, wearing a beret, turns and smiles, a rifle held down
at his side. He seems to look back at the man in mid-stride who
stares nowhere in particular, down the road and out of shot. But
it is not the running man at whom he smiles but the severed
head that sits in the road like an unkicked football, eyes half-
open, a snail's trail of blood behind it.

'Fucking hell,' Liam says. He realises the shock is in not seeing
the head at first. Or that you see it – it is right there in the middle
of the picture, it is what is being photographed – but don't reg-
ister it. And that is what the running man does too. The longer
that Liam looks at the picture the more he believes that the running man has not seen the head. It is the man in the foreground
who makes us see it, grinning back at it. The other man runs
down the road, towards something, away from something, both,
maybe that isn't important. This is just another picture from some
unknown African war. Liam wonders briefly about the men, the
boys who straggle in a line by the tree. That everyone in this
picture is now dead. Another image forms, another photo he
must have seen once or something half-registered from the telly.
It is one of the men today, maybe the man that grins and holds

his gun down, older but not that much, another roadside. The man rides a wobbly bicycle, rings a bell. An icebox is balanced on the handlebars and leaks across his shorts. In the box he keeps cold beers, bottles of pop, river fish, whatever he can buy and sell. Sometimes at night he dreams that he opens the icebox and finds a severed head.

'Just think about the shape of the figures,' Tony says. Liam shuffles the cuttings and sketchbook pages on the desk. Running men across all of them. The door bell rings and Tony steps away to pull back the curtain which separates this small space at the back of the shop, which he insists on calling his studio, which has the table at which they sit and an old green velour comfy chair that Liam thinks used to be in Dee Dee's nana's front room and a rattling fridge which leaks water against the back door. The door and window are barred and look out onto the yard. A bag of rubbish has burst across the uneven concrete, chicken bones and batter, and Liam thinks of the foxes, how there are so many more of them each year and how only that morning he'd seen one sitting out on the path that ran along the old railway line under the hotel window and how the colour of the path with no rain is the same as that in the picture. He wonders what the fox might do, confronted with a head on the path in the Anvil Yards. How it might accept it, unquestioning, circle it and lap at the bloody trail or whether it would become spooked by the heavy lidded eyes and hide.

More men running. This time Liam recognises the face in the picture a while before he realises who it is, half-listening to the muffled voices at the front of the shop. The young man's face is almost hidden behind the bulk of an older man, bearded and fierce, who leads the run.

'Run so I can throw a goal net over you all,' was a line Freddie Rogers used to use when he had them training at Lascar Boys. Liam uses it himself, now, when he sometimes trains the kids or leads a warm-up. It is how these men run, how the camera has caught them, beads of sweat and a gob of spit glint in the sunlight, their feet arch or leave the ground completely as they run slightly askance to the white touchline. Behind them the spindle and mesh of a half-finished football stand rises. There is a distant worker in a yellow hard-hat. Beyond that are mountains, with snow on top although these players shine with sweat and water bottles dot the pitch.

Luis. It is Luis, Liam is sure. The slender black boy, half-hidden behind the bearded man. He pulls the picture closer to him. It has been torn hastily from a magazine and the desk lamp catches the page's gloss.

. . . a team of nomads that have so far played matches across Central Asia. They take their ground with them, the club erects a temporary stadium the week before a match in a feat of impressive engineering, dismantles it after the game and moves on. The club have played local sides in front of thousands in the middle of the Gobi Desert, on the Mongolian plains and in the shadow of banks of . . .

The threat of bans from FIFA dooes not seem to have bothered these trans-national mercenaries. The club employs players from several African countries, Brazil and Eastern Europe. 'It's the future of football,' says the club founder and president Yousuf Khan, a petrochemical bil-

lionaire with influence in several Central Asian states, in his strangely Midlands-inflected English (learned in spells at Business School in Oxford and, oddly, Birmingham, he says). 'Certainly the future of football here.' His ambition is to play one of the great European clubs somewhere out in the Gobi Desert. To paraphrase what Kevin Costner's character is told in Field of Dreams, *'If you build it, they will come.'*

There is a crash from the front of the shop, glass breaking, a shout. Liam jumps, spills tea across the pictures and bends to get under the rows of pictures hanging low from the washing lines. Not for the first time he is too big for a room, so that by the time he has struggled around the chair and got to the doorway, the shop's front door is swinging shut.

'What's going on?' Liam asks and Tony waves him away from the broken glass. A display case is smashed.

'I'll get a brush. Watch that glass is still hanging.' Tony reaches up to bolt the door and says 'Fuckin' Bobby.'

There is blood on the glass still in the case, a foam of spit where Bobby had gobbed past Tony's ear, more blood spots on the chequered lino floor.

'What, your Bobby? What's he done that for?'

'He ain't our Bobby no more. He wants me to do his face. I've told him no faces. He only comes in when he's drunk or off his head on summat else. Do me face, he says to me. I've told him not to bother me with his crap and I get this.'

'You better watch that blood, Tone.'

'Eh? Oh. I'll get some gloves on, stand back.'

As they work they remember Bobby as young boy, big and round faced, a cheeky boy whose big crazy hair the grown-ups would ruffle and give him a pound for an ice cream. Liam watched him up close at the gym a couple of times, so quick, and with something in him, jagged and clever. He watched him fight a boy from up in Cowton, quite fancied before he got in with Bobby, at the Hightown Town Hall, how Bobby sliced down all the angles so the boy was cornered, big punches to the body and angled kicks to the head. Bobby left the boy standing for his own amusement, a cat with an injured bird. The ref stepped in and the crowd booed.

'Kill him, Bobby, kill him.' He remembers a voice from some-where at the back of the room. It was Gracie, Bobby's own mother. Liam knew the plea in that voice; how people look at you and want you to do what they can't, feel you've betrayed them if you can't do it either. He is glad his own mother has stopped coming to watch him. She is not speaking to him since he didn't turn up for that Sunday roast. He needs to find a way to make amends, feels he's been trying to do that to people one way or another half of his life. He'll send her some flowers or something.

He sweeps up the pieces of glass from the floor, fills the bucket for the mop and Tony removes the big jagged edges from the display case, broken heart designs and pictures of sailors' girls beneath.

'We used to look after him Tuesday nights upstairs at the pub, me and Dee Dee. For years, really, when he was a little kid, two, three.'

'Tuesday nights was when they went to the bingo,'Tony says.

'That's right.'

'Where was I?'

'What?'

'I wonder where I was, if you babysat Bobby.'

'I don't know.You're, what, seven years older than him. Maybe yer mum never went. Maybe Natalie or somebody had yer.'

'That's my point, though. Nobody can remember, even me. But we can all remember where Bobby was.'

Liam is not sure where this is going.

'What yer saying, Tone? Who'd yer rather be? Yerself or Bobby? Look at the state he's in.'

'Killed by love, eh, all that attention.'

'He ain't dead, though, is he? Maybe he'll sort himself out.'

With this Tony makes a sort of noise in his throat, like he won't even grace that with an answer. Bobby is only going in one direction. He has cleared the glass from the case, wrapped it in a towel.

'I'll make another cup of tea.'

'What's he want, any road?'

'What?'

'On his face?'

'Eh, oh, tonight it was a spider and a web he wanted. Round his bad eye down onto his cheek, had it all planned out.'

'Man of tradition, see. Couldn't yer just do it for him?'

The same noise from Tony.

'I'll phone Lionel tomorrow. He'll know someone who can do it cheap, I hope. The son smashes it and the dad patches it up, eh?'

'I don't know. Lionel's done his fair share of smashing things up, I reckon.'

Liam pulls a couple of notes from his wallet.

'Here, have this towards it.'

Tony goes to wave it away.

'Go on,' Liam says, 'put it on me account.'

. . .

The leaves sweep down Meeting House Lane with the gusts that come now, bonfire weather, great pyres going up on the wasteground at Cowton and by the Peng scrapyards, kids dressed as witches and spiders roaming the streets and demanding money and sweets. There's the sound of fireworks every night, whistles in the dark, the crack of bangers up the hillsides, barking dogs. It makes it sounds like there's life, but there's no one in the pub. Dee. Dee is scared to look at the books, pays Roni out of petty cash, then her own purse, prays there's enough in the bank for Paul. God knows what she's going to do for the Christmas boxes. At least Lionel hasn't invoiced for the cameras.

Mark stands at the hatch, shifts from foot to foot, in need of his overcoat today, although he's worn it all summer anyway.

'My god Mark what have you done to yer face? Who's done that to you?'

He is shocked by her shock, has spent a week or more living with it, staring into the mirror at an eye that would not open, bathing it in warm salt water, something remembered, he thinks, from his mum. It had been swollen tight at first, then slowly turned purple until a jaundiced yellow spread across that half of his face and the eye opened a crack. There's a lump still on his cheek, which he wondered if he'd broken, but there's not much pain, a numbness to it, a tingling in the morning. He thought of walking to A&E at the Bethel, the colour of the leaves changing over the Heath. He's OK as long as he remembers to chew up the side and he doesn't eat so much anyway. He has reduced his life. But he's been staring in the mirror and thinking about how stupid he's been and then trying to tell himself how lucky as well, could have been much worse, the white of his eye has begun to show again, criss-crossed with blood, much worse, in an attempt to ward off demons.

He nearly says he walked into a door. He remembers how Sonia turned up with a black eye once and no one did anything about it, Goldie with scratch marks all down his face, mind. She'd been dancing with some boy from the posh houses up by the Heath. They split up for a few weeks, Dee Dee indignant about it, warning Goldie to steer clear.

'Admit it, though, she was asking for it,' Liam had said to him while they sat waiting for the minibus to training, he remembers it now, same time of year and the pitches strewn with big yellow leaves old Ted got them to rake up down at the training ground, and he hadn't said anything at all, just put his back into the work.

'Fell off the pavement,' he says, a variation on a theme, 'when I run into your Bobby the other day.'

'And he did that to yer?!'

Mark shrugs, 'You should see what he looks like, eh.'

He turns to her, with his good eye and his half-closed one.

She can't remember the last time she'd seen his face, not properly, not without him looking down at the ground, shuffling about, eyes always somewhere else. She knows he hasn't seen a doctor, decides not to even bother with that line.

'Fucking hell, Mark.' Tears come quickly to her eyes and she leans through the hatch. He is just a step too far away, the counter a bit too wide and she is left on tiptoe with one arm rubbing his shoulder and her hair falling out of its clip between them. They both smile at the position they are in.

'Do you want to come in Mark? Do you want a cup of tea? Something to eat?' He has never been in the pub, never been in a room with her since a couple of times when he came to see her when she first took Alina, when she and Liam still lived together and he knew Liam was at training, and he knew Liam was leaving her, the first year he stopped playing and the club were trying to persuade him to come back, threatening all sorts on the one hand, trying to get him in the Bethel on the other.

'I don't need a psychiatrist, Dee Dee, I don't need doctors, nothing, I just need to stop playing football,' is what he said to her, looking out of the leaded windows onto the hills, like they'd trespassed into some other country, which they had in a way, he supposed. He spent a lot of time trying to sneak back, to get home, that's what he thinks. He had needed a psychiatrist, needed some help at least, they were right on that score.

'No Dee Dee, thanks, you're all right. I'll let you know if I need anything.'

She is crying, trying not to, sniffs, feels the anger rising at the same time.

'Hang on there a minute. I'll get you something.'

He nearly says that he thinks he saw Goldie, but the certainty left him when the headache eased, why should he worry her over nothing, a phantom, a ghost? He tries to forget what Freddie Rogers said to him. He has scared her enough with his face, with the ghost of her cousin, too many ghosts all still alive, trick or treat, he thinks, and what is he?

She expects him to disappear, but there he is standing in a pattern of leaves in the autumn light, an autumn pattern across his face. She gives him a bottle of whisky and two packs of Co-Codamol. She worries afterwards that he'll take them all in one go.

.   .   .

Bladud was a leper, cured by the waters of the willow streams, and a good king too. He could speak to the dead as well as to the living, to Maddan, his father, Gwendolen, his mother, and Corineus his father's father. He lit fires that burned his whole life, that heated the baths that he built to wash away the evils of the world.

He had a son named Leir. To entertain him, Bladud had red kite feathers collected from the fields, stitched them into a great set of wings, did not heed the dead voices in his ear, and launched himself from the highest treetop.

The boy laughed to see that his father could fly and Bladud swooped through the clouds and flew for a while without a care, saw the green island, the white island, spread out beneath him, and then tumbled and fell, as men must do, and was dashed into pieces on the city that grew beneath him.

'The boy, look, the boy.'

'What?'

'Bladud's boy there in the yard.'

A magpie hopped across the stones and strewn body and called something to Leir that he could not understand, spent his whole life wondering, and he watched as it flew over the ruins, over the island, and on out of sight.

. . .

On the coach journey up to Hartlepool, a six-pointer in the December gloom, Liam watches the man commonly agreed to be the world's second best footballer chase a ball across a field in Stockholm. Sometimes he watches all three goals and waits until Ronaldo disappears under a pile of gambolling teammates, under the whole of Portugal, laughing and cheering and crying with joy. Sometimes he pauses it after the second goal, the real killer punch, the young man stood off by the near-post where he finished his run, his hair still perfectly in place, banging his chest, bellowing, and then opens the images Greta has sent that week, in an email with no heading or text at all, just attachments, pictures and video of their little boy, one swift exit left from Greta's bottom half in a long skirt and barefoot in one of the clips which he has now played twenty times or more. He touches the screen. When did we start stroking these things? He can't remember. Jari ran his hands across the old television set at his grandad's in an effort to find a cartoon. There he is, running with the mud between his toes. These films from the last weeks at the lake house before they boarded it up for winter. They had been back at the house in town for weeks now, darkness settling in.

When it gets too much he turns back to Ronaldo. Liam is conscious of telling himself that it is too much, aware somehow outside himself of playing the role of the heartbroken, absent father, feels his throat tighten. This is no state, he tells himself, at the same time aware that he tells himself, this is no state to be in, as if he could choose something else, some other way of being Liam Corwen, iron man from the Iron Towns, football man, tough and classy defender, heartbroken absent dad, failed husband. Ronaldo accelerates over the halfway line, after the ball, with all the movements of a man who knows what is coming, what is written, as though he has scored this goal a hundred thousand times before, knows he will outpace these chasing defenders even with the ball at his feet, knows how the keeper will come towards the near-post and how he will hit it low and hard across him into the far corner, none of his showmanship here, until the ball sits softly in the net, and he turns to the side of the goal and waits for the world to catch up.

'I am here!' is what Ronaldo shouts, bangs his chest, 'I am here! I am here!'

Liam has started six matches in a row now. Unprecedented in these later years, he tells himself in a voice that is not his own, some highlights-reel voice-over. Everything hurts. He cannot get his hip comfortable on this seat, shifts himself again, these long coach rides are a problem themselves, past Wakefield, Doncaster, Beverley, in the English rain.

'Unbelievable,' Devon has moved down the aisle, stands and looks at the screen, 'He ain't human.'

Liam shakes his head, eyes wide, in a kind of mock-awe that he really means.

'Think of all the things they might try to stop him.'

'Force him wide . . .'

'There is no stopping him.'

'. . . get bodies between him and the goal, that's all, bodies.'

'They can try and kick him if they catch him, look, but he's six foot odd, built like a cruiserweight.'

'Bodies, that's all it is, all you've got. Sit deep is all you can do. Chasing the game, Sweden are fucked.'

Their voices sound strange to Liam, amphibian, muffled by the coach seats and drowned in the sound of spray. There is the odd thumping beat from the other players' headphones up and down the coach. It strikes him that the build-up to games has become quieter and quieter over the years. The young lads barely say anything. And it wasn't just their age, even Ally, Archie Hill, spoke in calm, measured tones these days, most of the time, that is. Liam prefers a bit of sound and fury. When he first got in the team they still had headcases like Wayne Coombs in the side who would shout 'Who wants it? Who fucking wants it?' and stare unfocussed into your eyes and carry that on right into the tunnel. They had Kevin Burns playing Iron Maiden on one of those twin-tape decks. And the thing was, these were better players than the ones they had now would ever hope to be. When Liam first got in the first team squad there was a card school up the back of the coach that preferred these long trips to the north-east to get the pot built up. He and Mark would pass mix-tapes back and forth – not Iron Maiden – and listen to their Walkmans, sometimes a headphone each, the way Dee Dee and Sonia did. They'd never do that anywhere other than the sanctuary of the coach. Liam glances backwards now and sees Kyran stroke his phone, not attached to him by wire, but a pair of goldie-looking headphones sat like a crown on his head.

The coaches have not changed, the sort that would take them to Weston or Rhyl or Alton Towers when they were kids, the kind with ashtrays that pulled out from the headrest in front, with plastic covers on the seats or else plastic fake-leather that his grandad would organise from the Miners' Welfare to take them each October, a real adventure, over land and sea, to Longchamp and the Prix de l'Arc de Triomphe, sick bags and rare cigar smoke, tots of whisky in hip flasks. He thought the Arc was the race, not the monument. Dee Dee caught him out with it and laughed. They went to Paris for a weekend once. He fancies a drink right now, which is not a great sign three hours before kick-off. He read that McGrath played pissed a few times, Tony Adams too. Had decent games. He is not them.

They are sealed inside this coach. The young lads are sealed inside their headphones, all of them locked inside their own heads. They wait quietly in rooms. His hotel room. The dressing room. Until out they spill when that bell goes, spat out onto the scrap of green, silent no more, hidden no more, exposed. He used to dream recurrently of playing naked.

Devon walks back up the coach aisle. He is playing well. Devon is keeping him in the team, truth be told, but he doesn't care. They work well together, fit each other, though neither of them is getting any quicker. Devon moves soft on his feet for a big

man, he treads like an astronaut negotiating a space station corridor, uncertain of the gravity. There are signs for Scarborough and
Darlington. There are ferries to Norway up here somewhere. He
imagines continuing. He could hitch lifts through the forests, the
tundra, cross borders, ride into Lapinlahti in the snow, look up at
a lighted window, a man come home.

'I am here!' Ronaldo shouts, 'I am here!' and it seems to Liam,
at least right now at this moment, heading through rainy England,
half a continent distant from his wife and son – that it is maybe
all most of us ever, ever want to say.

'I am here! I am here!'

.　.　.

Goldie's old man had twenty kids. A bloke told him that once
in the back room of The Magpie, an old pub with sagging walls
that sat just outside the Greenfield East Gates. He's sure the pub
has gone now, the man too, who he remembers toothless, his
lips puckered over a barley wine and half a mild. Those men
have gone, he thinks to himself, twenty years gone by and more,
because he was a kid when he heard that, tilting the pool table
in the back room to get a free game when no one was looking,
Tuesday, Wednesday afternoons when he should've been at
school. Men in daytime pubs knew him, knew who he was and
where he came from. The bloke that day must have assumed he
never saw his dad, never knew him, but he was wrong on that
score. He would come by and stay a few days every year when
he was a kid, must have stopped when he was nine or ten or

so. He took him fishing a couple of times, right up onto the Welsh Ridge one time to an old run-down farm, 'To see a man about a dog,' he had said, and it was true that dogs had barked all through the yard and in pens out against the hill, and for ages Goldie thought he was getting a dog and it was years later that he heard it as a saying, and understood, too late by then to do anything about it, too late always to catch on to things. His old man had grown up on farms, worked on them, and on the roads, when they built the motorways, was never at home in the towns. It's strange to think he might still be alive, but Goldie guesses he would've heard somehow if he'd died, maybe not, people slipped through the cracks, into the shadows. He never had twenty kids anyway, but a few, here and there.

But it's true he has half-brothers, half-sisters somewhere, twenty years older than him, some of them, older, in their sixties, dying off themselves now, most likely. His own flesh and blood. He used to think he should try and get in touch with them, track them down like you see on the telly. When he was with Nadine, she'd pointed a bus driver out to him, on the number 7, similar age, lighter skinned than Nadine, but the same cheekbones high up his face.

'That's my brother,' she'd said.

'What? Your brother don't work on the buses.'

'Half, half-brother. Me dad's babby with that Denise, who-ever, fat Irish cow. Lives in Erdington, don't speak to us.' She'd given the finger to the bus as it sat in traffic. The driver wore dark glasses and sat looking at the lights. Nadine had stepped out into the road and Goldie could picture her hammering on the bus doors with her hard little fists, mouthing off, spitting up the window as the bus edged along, people looking and then looking away, but he was saved from this by the lights going green and the bus pulling across the junction.

'He's normally on the 11,' she'd said, and then they must've got distracted because he can't ever remember talking about it again. No idea what his name was. But then, he didn't know the names of his relations either. Ann had a son, Michael, who everyone knew as Snowball because he had a patch of white hair big as a fist above his right ear, even from when he was a little kid. He was killed that year there was the big feud between the Oxo and Cowton, kicked to death in a back field. Snowball had run with the Bullet Krew, before they were even called that, just young kids messing about. They only became the Bullet Krew after Goldie went inside. He'd hear stories. The Bullet Krew only came after everything fell apart with the Ahmeds. Not that Stan Ahmed ever had anything to do with Cowton or the Oxo. 'Leave 'em to it,' he'd say, 'Scottish Jamaican cunts. There's no one you can speak to up there. They'm all nine years old, running round with razors.' Which had some truth in it. No hierarchy. The Ahmeds were a family, a clan, and they'd only come to the fore with Stan and his brothers, taken over from the Carter family, the ones they said had stolen the FA Cup in Birmingham and buried it somewhere on the Heath and got the Anvil Yards cursed by a gypsy because of it, who'd ruled the roost since way back in the days of the Peaky Blinders and the Iron Towns Sloggers fighting it out at the Heath races. The gangs had come down from Glasgow in the thirties as well but they ran out steam after the war when Oxton and Cowton went up.

Funny thing was, everything had reversed now, from what Goldie heard. The Bullet Krew had old men his age sitting up there, looking down the valley. When everything collapsed they'd taken over. All the drugs came in and out of Cowton. Lowtown, the Ironport and the Anvil Yards, were just full of empty buildings with holes kicked through them and kids running wild. But now there were real Somalis and Bengalis in Lascar again and power was going to come back down the valley. It would come to whoever was most desperate and then seep away from them like blood running down a drain. It was a whole secret history, he thought to himself, the kind that never gets written down or anything like that, or if it does, they just get it all wrong. Because the Ahmeds grew rich and lazy and moved away, other groups moved in. You cannot have a vacuum. Nothing stands still. Because the works closed everyone started killing themselves in as many ways you could think of, and some you couldn't. It was cause and effect.

The gangs were the opposite of the works, the opposite of working for a living. Thousands and thousands of people poured through those gates when the works were open, banging metal, crawling through mine tunnels under the hills, all for nothing if you asked him, all for lungs full of black dust and a few days at the seaside. A handful sat in back rooms with people like Stan Ahmed. It was a way of setting yourself apart. And they'd been right, of course, because nobody worked now, and everyone was on the hustle, on the make, and desperate too. They were pioneers. The gangs had always know that working was a waste of time. Everyone was a gangster now.

And here he was, a gang of one, just like his old man, like

everyone else these days. But without as many kids, he laughed to himself. Just one, he thinks to himself, one little girl. A man should have a daughter.

. . .

'He is here! He is fucking here!' Devon grabs Liam's head and pulls it into his chest. Liam sits, slumped forward, in his shorts, with his socks rolled down and shin pads untaped, pushes his matted hair into Devon and kisses him as Devon pulls away to point at Liam again.

'He is here! He is here!' Devon bangs his own chest now and moves towards the showers. Liam wants him to stay here, to savour the moment, everyone grinning, laughing, Ally talking thirty to the dozen to someone. There has been some talk of him taking an ice bath after a game, Devon and Julius too, the over-thirties, but steam curls through this dressing room now, pipes hiss, mud splatters the floor. The classified results plays from somewhere, patrician English voice, like every Saturday teatime he has ever known. They are announced as a late result.

He scored when time was up. A late, late free kick down the left, Kyran somehow skipping along the heavy pitch. He didn't even want to go up for it. They were lucky to get the point, luckier still with a clean sheet after getting the runaround for ninety-odd minutes, a chasing, he wasn't sure he could move. But there was Archie waving him up there from the touchline.

He got fouled, thought he was blocked off, stumbled at the back post and then there was the ball, a shit free kick which had barely risen off the ground, through a thicket of players who all missed it, body after body in front of him until there it was, and because he was tumbling, falling, he headed it, not eighteen inches off the ground, down into the wet turf, and it skidded inside the post at some pace and he saw it go in and heard the whistle and nestled his face into the soft pitch as they all leapt on top of him. Pandemonium. He saw a pair of black brogues come running past, a bloke had leapt the hoarding and onto the pitch in the rain, trailing an Irontown flag. In the melee, he could hear Devon shouting, 'He is here! He is here!'

When he got to his feet, groggy, he hadn't realised the ref had blown for time, and walked with his fist clenched and raised towards the hundred or so Irontown supporters behind the goal, all going crazy in the rain, up and down the old terrace, the Baa Baa boys starting a conga, the bloke who'd run on the pitch, old enough to know better and red-faced drunk, clinging to an orange-coated steward.

Big Archie hauls him up, slaps him on the back, tells him to speak to the radio. He doesn't want to leave the dressing-room warmth, steps on the toes of his socks to pull them off so to walk barefoot across the wet floor, mud between his toes. He pulls on a too small T-shirt that someone else has sweated in to dip his head out of the door and speak to Dave Willis who grins at him with crooked teeth, thrusts what looks to be his phone up at Liam. He is aware of steam coming off him.

'We can hear, Liam, how much you all enjoyed that victory.'

It is true. The commotion inside comes through the thin walls. Devon still going on. 'Stop that fucking swearing, but,' he hears Ally say and hope it isn't picked up, some fuck-up to take the edge off the warm glow. Dave Willis and his crooked grin.

'Well, last-minute winner, last touch, I think. Away from home. Clean sheet as well, rode our luck a bit, maybe, but we deserve some. Delighted.'

'Relief as well, I guess. Had you not scored, the way the results have gone would have put you in the bottom two tonight. As it is, eighteenth. The only way is up?'

'Of course. Listen. We know we're better than the table suggests. So do the people who turn up every week. With this group of players we know we can achieve more. I'm just delighted for everyone tonight, the supporters who come up here to stand in the rain, it's a long way, everyone.'

'Liam,' Dave Willis leans forward, puts his hand on his shoulder. When Liam left for Finland Dave wrote a piece in the *Chronicle* which said end of a chapter long unfulfilled, basically saying what a disappointment Liam had turned out to be. Still spoke to him like they were good mates, seemed quite a nice bloke really, always cheerful, asked Liam if he fancied doing a book with him, to which Liam had said no, he didn't believe in books. 'I know it's a team game but a word on your defensive partner, Devon Samuels. He's playing well for an old-stager.'

There it is, a barb about his age. He is six years older than Devon.

'Immense, a rock. He's great to play with, reads the game so well.'

'And you must be delighted with your goal.'

'Well, yeah, of course. I was shocked it come to me really.

Shocked to be up there. I thought I'd been fouled, got summat on it, yer know. Not bad for an old-stager, I suppose.' He smiles now, pleased with himself. Dave doesn't.

'Well said, Liam. You're still breathing heavy, what a battle today. We'll let you get back in the dressing room and have a well-earned sit down.'

Dave presses something on the phone, looks grey in the tunnel strip-lights.

'Well played, Liam,' he says in his everyday voice, a lower pitch than for the radio. Liam says thanks but he is already halfway back through the door.

And last in the showers until the water cools, same as it's been all these years. The shouts and the bangs die down but the feeling remains.

Julius flashes his phone at him as they board the coach, he feels his own phone beep in the pocket of his blazer, under the Irontown badge. He sees his name, Corwen 90+6 mins. A goal in the time beyond time. You just never know. He settles into his seat, lets his phone ring away in his pocket, closes his eyes, holds on to this feeling of early Saturday night. Ally says they're stopping for a fish supper on the way home. Old school, old school. Kyran asks if they do chicken. They move through the English dark. Wet snow falls gently on fast tarmac and metal.

. . .

In a small room in the museum in Dudley are Duncan Edwards's things, caps, shirts, medals and cups. A screen plays flickering images of the '57 cup final on a loop, a strange choice in many ways, it's his last appearance at Wembley. Peter McParland flattens Ray Wood, smashes his cheek and wins the game for the Villa, a curse on them ever since in the cup. They say it was the only time Big Duncan lost his temper on the pitch.

This shrine is in a small room in a building of red Victorian brick, the relics are neighbours to dinosaur footprints and paint-ings of furnaces long since put out. The caps used to be held in a glass case in the foyer of Dudley Baths. You could look at them and sip a hot chocolate from the machine, the smell of chlorine and shouts of kids everywhere. This place is a quieter tomb. On a shelf there is a coffee set, Ottoman style, stamped 'Red Star Belgrade', never used.

. . .

. . . will complete the draw for the Third Round of the FA Cup.

They are the first team out of the hat. Here in the hotel where the players are gathered to watch the draw, not everyone is sitting down or even listening yet. Liam leans towards the screen and concentrates, sees the hands swirl the balls in the glass bowl. They are the same balls they used to use at the bingo. He remembers sitting with a bottle of vimto or dandelion & burdock if he went to the Miners' Welfare when his nan was alive, the clack of the bingo balls and the tray they'd be placed in when drawn.

. . . Irontown . . .

He has only ever played in the Third Round twice, the years they were in the second division, first division, Championship, whatever you want to call it, it had the same name for a hundred years and now they change it every five minutes. The year they lost the play-off final, they got beaten by Crewe in a replay, extra-time. Their cup record had been terrible since the twenties, apart from that one run in the fifty-seven and a couple of seasons when Ally first took over. Liam made his debut in a First Round match when he was sixteen, Ally threw him on wide on the left, the only time he ever played there apart from his seconds with England, getting beaten by Leigh Railwaymen's Institute, non-leaguers. He remembers them all sat in the dressing room with their heads down afterwards, Ally standing in the middle of them all, naked, telling them all what a waste of space they were apart from Liam, exempt from all blame, and the older blokes looking at him under their eyebrows and him thinking that he was in for a kicking if he joined first team training again. And he was, but he kicked them back.

There are voices shushing each other in the seats behind. It had been his idea to get people together, players who live close enough, a few families and hangers-on, Sunday night out, there are sausage rolls on plates on a side table, they sit in one of the conference rooms in the hotel with sofas and chairs laid out in front of the telly. Amir thought it was a good idea, would bring a bit of cash in at the bar. The camera pans to Ally, who has been invited to the draw, they're making a big deal of it, trying to revive the cup, which is dying, like all things.

. . . will play . . .

He knows, wills it, as he watches the hand retrieve the ball, that it's a big one.

'Come on,' he hears himself say.

It used to be Monday dinnertimes. He remembers hopping over the school wall and across the garage roofs to get to Mark's where his mum let them listen to it on the radio, in the kitchen, and she made them cheese on toast. There were those years when they got to the quarter-finals, lost to Liverpool, then to Everton, and nothing since.

. . . Number twenty-six . . . Manchester United . . .

They are on their feet. Liam has his fists clenched above his head, someone is banging him on the back, there are whoops and cheers around the room, people lifting their heads from the carvery table and their meal deals to ask what all the fuss is about, the sound of thirty ring tones all going at once.

They'll switch it, Liam thinks, as he goes to each player in turn, clasps their hand and then pulls them into a bear hug, like he willed that ball out of the pot. They'll switch it for the money and we'll get to play at Old Trafford, either that or we'll have the telly here. He can see Steve Stringer at the back of the room, talking on the phone, a smile in his grey face for once, heading out into the corridor. Liam puts his thumb up to him. This season, you just never knew, what with the Hartlepool game and now this, win a couple more and their game in hand and they were mid-table, fringe of the play-offs, some kind of miracle against United, some kind of backs to the wall draw in the mud and then a replay, cannot even dare to dream of a win, and the telly again, you just never knew. He looks around at the shining eyes. There is life yet, is what he thinks. He'll be marking Van Persie. Fucking hell.

Ally is talking on the telly, too noisy to hear him. They must have finished the rest of the draw. He hears a voice say, 'Possibly the tie of the round, certainly the most drenched in cup folklore is Irontown versus Manchester United, a repeat of a famous tie played there by the Busby Babes nearly sixty years ago . . .'

Dave Willis, by the plate of sausage rolls, is talking into his phone with another one clamped to his ear.

Liam sees Amir, asks for some champagne, when he looks back at him, says, 'Well, that cheap fizz you put out for the weddings,' and Amir grins and says he'll find some good stuff and put it on Liam's room.

He sits down with a bottle of beer in a chair next to Devon and the Irish lads and Kyran who cannot stop saying, 'Man United, man, Man United, man,' over and over, where they have settled in the lounge bar. They've put the big screen on in here now and switched Sky Sports on and they've got Ted Groves on the phone, Ted, who is standing with Steve Stringer near the bar, Steve holding the phone to Ted's ear, who is being interviewed about the game in '57, a match that Liam knows his dad was at too, as a kid, down the front of the Greenfield End, the record crowd, fifty-six thousand and Liam thinks of old records books, sat poring over numbers and results and memorising whole lists of matches and scorers and attendances like some kind of cat-echism. He thinks of Mark, wonders if he is sitting there in that same kitchen now, listening to it on the radio with his toast. It's possible. One day he'll go round there and just bang on the door. Maybe he'll take him a ticket round for this match.

All things are possible, he thinks.

. . .

Like Bonnie and Clyde or something is how they took off. Goldie had bought these magazines for ages, years, still never got the full collection, which concentrated on a particular criminal or crime. Bonnie and Clyde were one of the editions. Then there were those kids in that film *Badlands*, which Dee Dee made them watch, and Liam took the piss out of all the way through. He remembered thinking that if he was going on a killing spree then Liam Corwen might well end up first in line and that was sort of how the events of that afternoon started. He'd talked about it so much since, that the language he used, even in his head, was touched with other people's view of the world, therapists and the prison chaplain and social workers and the like. It wasn't even his story, not any more.

After Mark had missed the penalty, after they had shown Liam lying on the pitch, his face pressed into the grass, after they showed them both crying, and the commentator said, 'You have to feel for these Irontown boys. They have given everything,' the whole pub swooning over them, Sonia looking at Liam lying there on the grass and going to hug Dee Dee, he had to do something.

They'd always had this thing between them, egging each other on.

'I don't believe you've got it in you, Goldie, I don't,' Sonia would say, that kind of thing. Well, he called her bluff this time.

'Goldie, you're not OK to drive,' Dee Dee said, came out to the street, her make-up all run across her face with the tears. Goldie imagined Liam's big homecoming that night.

'He's all right, Dee Dee, honest,' Sonia had jumped in, and she was pissed, an unlit cigarette hanging out of her mouth, did not even smoke. Alina was sitting there in the back of the car, always a calm baby, assured. God knows who she got that from.

So they headed off across the Heath and they didn't even say anything to each other, perhaps they must have talked about it before, he had certainly described the place to her, he was sure now, but there was something making him think that Stan Ahmed would not be very pleased if he found out, still, he didn't need to find out, and this was Sonia's voice in his head now.

Just on the last stretch of Anvil Yards, past the South Gate at Greenfields and almost at the turn in the road near where Lionel's car yard was, there was a paper shop, a paki shop as they would call it and then have Dee Dee go 'Eh, eh, none of that,' and have Liam stare at them, anyway, there was a shop on its own just before the road turned towards the Heath, always this old woman just sitting there on her own behind the till. Goldie and Sonia had worked it up into some story that the place made a fortune. It was a shithole. There was nothing on the shelves. No one went in there, no people to go in, Greenfields had been shut ten years by then and the South Gate was rusted shut.

He pulled up in front of the shop, there were parking spaces out in front, no one around. They never said anything to each other, knew what they were going to do from previous conversations. There was a baseball bat, well rounders bat, that he kept in the car and he knew that would do, picked it up from between his feet and opened the car door, intending to leave it open, so he could jump back in and make their getaway.

Then Sonia jumped out of the car as well. 'Let me do it, Goldie,' she said, grinning drunk, had dropped the cigarette. So they left both doors open. Alina was sat in her car seat in the back, listening to that Prince tape they always played. He would swear now that they were only in there for what twenty seconds, thirty maybe.

He walked in with the bat and, sure enough, it was the old woman behind the till, pointing the bat at her head and she was up off her seat and back against the wall without a sound, something like a whimper, maybe. It was Sonia who pulled the till drawer out, found a some fifty pound notes hidden under there, so maybe there was something in the idea the place wasn't quite right. They thought they'd hit the big time, one big massive rush, and out of the shop they went, laughing and shouting, so fucking easy, and into the car, and he remembers swinging out so hard into the road that they almost ended up in a hedge then and that would have saved Sonia's life and that was something he often thought about because he was no way in control of the car and it was just luck, plain luck, that they didn't crash then. The other thing was that at the trial they said that it was all Goldie, that Sonia had not even been in the shop, that it was Goldie who had ripped open the till drawer and found those fifties, although they never mentioned the fifties either, said all they robbed was fourteen pound ninety, which was what they took in change and threw it onto the back seat next to Alina and it went rolling around the car floor.

The woman only spoke Tamil. The shop was Sri Lankan. His solicitor said it must have been misinterpreted, the business of

Sonia and the till, Sonia wanting to do it in the first place, leaving her daughter in the car while she robbed the shop. In court it was just him. His solicitor shrugged.

Sonia took the money and it was Sonia who was laughing as they drove away, her legs kicking the dashboard, and then screaming at him to get away, to drive faster, when they heard the siren, Alina crying in the back now, 'Oh God, Goldie, Oh God,' Sonia said over and over then. She'd even done up her seat belt. This bad girl. If she'd left that off she might even still be here and the whole world different, that's what he thinks.

. . .

Liam never answers his phone, never has, and with the way it was ringing for two days after the cup draw, he thinks that if people want to find him they know where he is, so the message is a couple of days old at least, maybe more than that. A mortgage advisor keeps ringing him and he assumed it was another of their calls. They want to know if he's thought about leverage options, whatever they are. He could rent the place out, he supposes, but he could ask Devon about that kind of thing. When he hears her voice he stops, stands at the window, looks across the Anvil Yards towards the pub, realises he's doing that as she speaks.

'Hello Liam, it's Dee Dee, I'm sorry for ringing you and I know you're probably busy,' she has been smoking, he can tell from the huskiness in her voice, smoking or drinking or crying or something, no good for her asthma, or her singing, but then, she didn't sing any more. He wonders if someone is dead. 'You're

probably not going to want to hear this either. I saw Mark today.
You should see the state of his face, someone's set about him.
His face is a right state. Look, I think he's doing OK generally.
But I just wondered, I don't know, if you could check on him or
something.'

There's a pause, the sound of Dee Dee listening to her own
voice, her own silence.

'Anyway, I hope you're OK. I hope the results get better soon,
they're not very happy in the pub, maybe they'll drink more.
Listen, I'm rambling, and there is something else, Liam. There is
something else. If you could call me back that would be great.'

He is leaning against the window glass. He can see the cranes
just about, the top of the flats, but he can't make out which block
is which from this distance, across time and space. From the hotel
roof he'd be able to see the pub. He has thought a few times that
he should ask Amir if he could change rooms every now and
again, get a different view. He leaves his head against the glass,
breathes onto it.

Her voice, he always loved her voice, singing, talking, whatever. She used to read poems out loud, lyrics, half-singing, half-
talking. There is something else, she said. There is something else.

. . .

He is dressed as Father Christmas when Greta phones him, the
day before they are meant to arrive, to say they aren't coming.
It was all arranged, they would get here on the 20th and stay
until the 29th. He had it all written down on a pad of hotel

stationery. Ally told him not to worry about Boxing Day, to be ready for Shrewsbury on the 21st, for York on the following Saturday, to keep himself fit for United. Things are on the up. His mum has got the rooms ready at the house, made Jari's bed for him, although Liam knows that the boy would sleep with them, although maybe not, so much will have changed in six months, the seventh or so of his son's whole life that he has just missed, and he tries not to think about it. Probably not with both of them in the same bed either, more like in the summer when Liam slept in a chair at the side of the bed with Greta and Jari in it, and he would hold the boy's foot or hand, apart from that one night they went for a meal in Heathside and things had felt good, but then they'd argued afterwards about something which he now can't remember at all.

'You can't do this to me, Greta, to us.'

'It is too much, Liam. I am sorry, I am sorry. I should have said something earlier. It is too much for Jari. He is settled and happy. He is looking forward to Christmas here.'

'Without his dad.'

'You are not here, Liam.'

'It's not right.'

'We did not leave anywhere. We belong here.'

He hadn't asked her about coming back to England, had just assumed that was what they'd do. They weren't really living together when he agreed to come home, things had already gone wrong. He couldn't work her out. He tries not to think of his beautiful son. She is right that they belong there. He thinks of the cold hitting his face when they got out of the car at the shops near the lake once, the wind coming across the frozen water and the dark forest beyond it, straight from the Arctic, winds from places from storybooks, from Lapland, from Siberia; or the procession to the church that time, Jari strapped to him and under his coat, the baby's face poking out from under a fur-lined hood, the crunch of snow under their boots, the line of candles, Greta holding his arm.

'What about all his stuff that's here, his presents and things? It's too late for the post.'

'He does not need plastic robots, Liam. He needs a father.'

He is dressed as Father Christmas and sits on the edge of the bed he slept in as a boy. He wonders how he might tell his parents. They want to see their grandson. Just say it straight out, he supposes. They aren't coming. He guesses Greta will never come here now. Part of him can't blame her. He never told her he was coming back.

He has seen the way she watched the streets as they drove through the Iron Towns, a place she could not believe existed. England was a disappointment to her, she had thought of it as a land of kings and queens, country cottages and hedgerows and winding lanes. And it is that. But what she saw was the rust and the people, his people, shuffling up the Anvil Yards pavements.

She'd visited Russia as a student during the days of the collapse, she'd say the names of the towns to him, show him photos, Baikalsk and Vydrino, and a place called Asbest, named for asbestos, the worst place on earth she'd said, and then shown him photos from her dissertation, and there was something in the look in people's faces, he wanted to tell her that he knew them, these people. The worst place on earth, she said. But that couldn't be true. They joked about it in his parents' kitchen one time, one of the few visits. It was the Jubilee. Spitfires had flown up the valley. There was Union Jack bunting strung up and down the street. She held up a jar of instant coffee and a carton of sterilised milk.

'But the war is over, Liam. What's more, you won.'

'There's always a war,' is all he said, joking, not sure what that meant, like something his grandad would mutter, but certain there was something hard and true underneath it all.

He sits on the edge of the bed with the phone in his hands. A horn sounds from outside. Devon is collecting him. He and some of the others are taking presents to the children's ward at the Bethel. He opens the window, shouts, 'Hang on a minute,' goes downstairs and takes a couple of black bin bags from the kitchen drawer, pushes Jari's presents into them, heads outside and motions to Devon to open the boot. He wonders if he might even look at flights to Helsinki, there is time still for that, just. He has always been a man for the grand gesture.

· · ·

The same routine every morning. She opens the bar doors dead on eleven. It used to be that a straggle of old men would be waiting out on the pavement, hats on, their morning shopping done and a bag of potatoes or sausages wrapped in paper in their hands. Those men had gone now, but you still got the odd early morning drinker. She can remember weekday mornings with men stood shoulder to shoulder in the bar, the days of the old livestock market, or at the shift-change at Greenfields. Not much this morning except hard shadows in low winter sun. There is a swirl of grit across the road they put down with the meagre snow, the bottom of Meeting House Lane is a brown puddle, the shape of the buildings murky on its surface. She likes these mornings best of all, quiet with the sun as it angles across the road. She latches the door open to air the bar, considers a cigarette on the step, queen of all she surveys. It isn't cold, winter still not here, not really, in spite of the snow flurry. Instead, she heads back behind the bar and through the darkened lounge to the doors. She doesn't know why she still opens up so early. Perhaps hopeful of some stray Christmas shoppers, men on the roads finishing up for the holidays maybe, a few up from the bakery. Court was sitting today, so it's possible she'd get a few of them in from there.

The lock makes a solid click as it slides back with the key, and it's as she does this, and moves her hand up towards the bolt, that maybe a shape catches the corner of her eye that she remembers an old man, a tramp of the old sort with a piece of rope tied round his middle holding his clothes together that used to come to the hatch for her nana to give him tobacco and papers and a bottle of something. He had a great beard, grey and white, tobacco stained, and he'd take off his hat, a battered version of the ones the men wore to market, and scratch at the skin peeling from his head. They had a name for him. She can't remember it. A stray line comes into her head, *My many-coated man*. The rest of that stays at the edge of her memory, something just out of reach.

'Got something for me dog, Dee Dee?' she thinks of Mark.

And then of Goldie. 'Yer dad's here Goldie.' She remembers Sonia, after some argument they'd had, saying it in reference to the old tramp at the off sales hatch, but no, it couldn't have been him, because he was a memory from years before that, when Dee Dee toddled about behind her nana through the daytime pub and her mum and dad were still here. With the same meaning, though, one of the ragged old men in the bar. 'Yer dad's here Goldie.' Sonia said it with a smirk, she had that streak in her, Sonia, and they must have had a row. Goldie didn't see his dad, it was said to hurt him, to dig into him. His face would flinch with pain but it was a kind of habit. They'd have a row about nothing in particular, the way she looked at some bloke, or where he'd been the night before, both jealous like that, needing to cling to one another, to someone. They were an accident waiting to happen, the old saying. Then the accident happened.

And there he is in front of her. She turns back from the lounge doors, touches the frosted glass in the window and then stands in mid-step. He is there in front of her, sitting on one of the heavy wrought iron chairs, the shape of him part reflected in the hammered copper table at which he sits. There he is from across the years.

'All right, Dee Dee,' he says.

All right?

All right?

All right?

She feels everything fall away from her. And she thinks of that idea of your life flashing before your eyes and has never believed it, never believed in any of that stuff, she has seen people die, but that is what happens now, even as she thinks that all that stuff is rubbish. She sees herself toddling after her nana and hears the sound of glasses and singing and voices in the bar, the glamour of blue smoke and pub chandeliers, the warm press of drinking, dancing crowds, tiny rooms off hospital wards, where she was told she'd have to say goodbye to her daddy, to her mum.

She sees him as she first saw him, as she first saw Liam and Mark, all the swagger and laughter and dead certainty that life owed them all something. It owed them something, all right. A kick in the guts for being so sure of themselves. And then another and another. More than that. He has crawled from the wreckage of his life and everyone else's. She wants this to stop, to turn back to the doors and he will not be there, sitting with two coats on, her own many-coated man. His face wears the years. He is dirty. There is a smell coming off him. She sees the knife on the table top.

'Get me a drink please, Dee Dee,' he says in that voice that was always a bit too soft, a country lilt or lisp that did not match his hard, sharp edges, leans back on the chair like a king restored to his throne.

. . .

Liam sits on the tram, pulls stray white strands of beard from his chin. There were a couple of kids on the ward who might not make it to Christmas Day. He'd watched Kyran sit at one boy's bedside, holding his hand, reading him a story. He'd underestimated Kyran, just a young lad himself, growing a beard now which somehow made him look even younger, a boy who'd gone to the Ironport school, same as Liam, grew up on Cowton, this latest great hope of the Iron Towns. He held the boy's hand, who lay very still in the bed, just his eyes watching Kyran as he read a story about Rudolph lost in the snow on Christmas Eve, trying to get back home so that he could pull the sleigh. When he finished the story the boy's eyes started to close. Kyran leaned over and kissed the top of his head. Liam thought he might not hold it together, watched the nurses coming past with tinsel in their hair, and the kids in their dressing gowns, smiles on their faces, Kyran walking towards him now, and told himself he better had.

'Ho, Ho, Ho,' he boomed down the ward, felt the ripple of excitement, felt his own son's toys in the sack over his shoulder.

Outside in the car, after Liam had changed in the toilets and stuffed his Santa suit into one of the torn bin bags, Kyran sat in the passenger seat with his head against the glove compartment. Devon had his hand on the lad's back. Liam motioned to Devon that he had somewhere to get to, headed towards the tram stop.

. . .

The boy Merlin tells of times to come, times that have gone, of better days, and days of rage. He says the streams and valleys will boil with blood, tells of a red dragon and a white in endless struggle. That lion cubs will become fishes, that silver will flow from cows' hooves, that the hills will be hollowed and their black insides burned. He tells of kings that will come and go, of war and plague and famine, of how Arthur will die on a riverbank, his insides leaking into the mud, and how they will set him off downstream in a coracle, to his island of apple blossom, to sleep and wait. He tells of life enduring, in the rocks and the trees, of people biding time out in lost valleys, of dispersing and re-forming, of things changed, transformed, but enduring still, of death by fire and death by water. All things come again, he says.

. . .

There is the deep tick of the clock. It hangs high in the lounge. Someone comes from the museum to wind it every third week, then Dee Dee gets up on the stepladder when they've gone to push it forward a few more minutes.

Anvil Yards, England, it says, and it is too loud for this empty room, for her head, and she needs to think. She pours him a brandy, gets him a little bottle of coke, remembers he and Sonia drank that for a while when they came back from the holiday they had in Majorca, when her uncle had given Goldie a load of money for god knows what, and she hadn't wanted to ask.

'Do you want ice?' she says.

'Yes please, Dee Dee,' he says, 'and get one for yourself,' and he smiles faintly and she feels her legs go a bit, and says, 'Fuckin' hell, Goldie,' but she pours the drink just the same, and does herself a glass of water from the tap, and thinks that if she had any sense at all she'd have had a panic button fitted, or something, Lionel had even mentioned it. From here at the bar she hears a footstep on the loose floorboards upstairs, prays for a moment that maybe

Tyrone has stayed over, something she was expecting to happen soon enough, but she can tell from the movement that it is Alina and her legs go again, just a bit. Nowhere to go but back here, to the table that Roni has rubbed a shine into. *Nowhere to run to baby, nowhere to hide.* She thinks to herself that this is how people go, with old songs playing through their heads, and what they might do on Tuesday, and what they might do in twenty years' time, and how there are always thoughts of a happy ending right up until the end and maybe even beyond, because there is the knife on the table and what else has he come back for after all these years other than damage, more damage.

'I wanna see her, Dee Dee.'

'You can't.'

'I stayed away, Dee Dee, I kept away.'

'And now you're back,' she says.

'And now I'm back.'

When he reaches for the drink she thinks he's going for the knife and her heart stops, she can feel it actually stop, and he takes the bottle and pours some coke into the brandy and it fizzes and the ice cracks and she is back in the world again and her heart thumps and the clock ticks. It is a proper brandy glass, fresh ice. She has wet herself, she can feel it under her, not too much, and she shifts in the chair with a small puddle to sit in, glad to be still breathing, a crackle to her breath like that of the ice.

'Fuckin' hell, Goldie,' she says again and he lifts the glass towards his lips and she can see that his hand shakes, and it gives her a bit of hope.

'Cheers,' he says.

. . .

Liam watches the pub doors from the tram shelter, and then from under the sign at Tony's shop, a flickering arrow that says 'tattoos', and Liam stood under it thinks it would make a great photo if they do any more magazine stuff. There is no one on the street, not a soul. The winter has not been cold but he shivers now, looks at the pub doors and then at his watch, a few minutes past already and the pub not open.

It was a ritual, opening up, he used to help Dee Dee with her nana, when he and Dee Dee were first together. After the cleaning and whatever needed doing in the cellar, the walk down to the post office for change, or the counting of tomato juice bottles and the like in their green crates, the filling of the ice machine, the placing out of beer towels and mats and ashtrays, in those days, a last dust over of the tables. All this in the same order, depending on which day of the week, like on a Thursday, for instance, the shifting of empty barrels and unbolting the cellar hatch and waiting for the drays.

There was a ritual to observe, all through the day, from half-seven when you let the cleaners in, to a last check of the locks at half-eleven, a nip of something warm from the shelf and the kettle on. He remembers that Dee Dee's nana would set the clock to the one at the Lowtown market and then push it a couple of minutes forward. When the market one rusted to a standstill, she'd phone the speaking clock and do the same thing using that. These same things each morning, every morning.

It's not like Dee Dee to be late, he thinks, but then wonders really how many times he's seen her in these years. Since they split up, perhaps only a dozen times, if that, twenty years gone by. To have someone in your head, there and not there, all those years, that's how they all live, he supposes.

He can see a light on in the lounge, thinks of the old chandeliers and flock wallpaper and wood and brass, and then realises the bar might be open. Perhaps they only open the bar in the daytime now, it's not like they've got any punters, god knows how the place stays open.

So he crosses the road and walks towards the pub and he swears he can see someone at the bar, people sat at a table, through the frosted glass of the only window with the curtains half-drawn back.

. . .

He wears the years on his face, the pain, she can see that. Something, maybe that she can see the lad she once used to flirt with and then deny, and she thought she has hated all these years, makes her pause.

'She's my daughter, Dee Dee, and I kept away.'

Because he did. And why did he have to anyway? She could've written to him, sent him photos of Alina growing up. There was nothing from the courts about not doing that. She managed to get some message to him inside, though, through her uncles, Stan was still here then, maybe she never had any choice. Don't come near, don't come back to the Iron Towns ever again, or you're a dead man.

She sees his face now and the years on it, the face of a man with just the thoughts of what he has done, and she thinks that a few words of comfort would not have gone amiss. A visit might have taken something out of his eyes, something that she sees now, a shadow across them.

And maybe for Alina, to have known her dad, at least a bit, and not just through old photographs or worse, through newspaper clippings that she knows she has pored over at the Hightown library. He pulled her out of the river, after all.

Dee Dee does not speak. His hand does not move towards the knife.

'I saved her, Dee Dee. I pulled her out that car, out of the water.'

And something inside her, like the weather shifting, because she wants to say, but you put her in there in the first place, and you left Sonia in there, and she knows deep inside herself, like the way she feels when she opens the cellar door and sees the wooden steps drop into the dark, that there will always be a part of her, hidden and unspoken even to herself almost all of the time, that wishes he'd done the opposite and it appals her, scares her, the layers beneath. So all she says is, 'I know Goldie, I know.'

She jokes to Alina that she wears the years on her hips, and here they are on his face, and on Mark's face, she thinks, these coats they have wrapped themselves in, these lost boys. It's a secret joke to herself, a solace, that Alina really is her daughter and that she wears her on her hips, like all mothers. She gave up so much. Maybe it is on all their faces, in all their eyes. She doesn't look in the mirror so often these days.

And she sees his eyes change now, like the way they see the light across the valley here in summer and things that are there are suddenly gone and the hills appear out of the haze, and his face does look lighter, just for a moment, as if a terrible weight has shifted and eased and then settled again as his eyes fix back to their stare.

She moves her hand onto the table and touches his. There are scars on his fingers, knife cuts and scabs. He is cold. He does not know what to do now and neither does she and she feels calmer for a moment, can hear her own breathing with just the trace of a rattle in it, because she can see it is no longer in him, perhaps never was, not really, an unlucky boy is all, out of his depth.

They could have stood up in that water, something that stuck with her from what the papers wrote afterwards. He'd only taken the car to show off, jealous of Liam and Mark, is what Dee Dee thinks, she was sure at the time, some inkling. Liam hadn't let Dee Dee go to the match, he was a big one for luck back then, all superstitions and ritual to be followed. She never went to away games so she wouldn't go to Wembley. His parents went, of course. So she helped out here in the pub where they set a screen up in the lounge and then there was some problem with it and Lionel rigged up a bedsheet on the wall on which to project the match, right there under the ticking clock. Then when Mark missed that penalty and then the goal went in at the other end, Goldie was off, stamping around, he'd never even liked football, but he was angry now, and the next thing they got was the phone call.

'I want to see her, Dee Dee.'

'I understand,' is what she says, and then, 'Not like this though, Goldie, eh?' and gestures towards him, at his dirty clothes and his exhausted face, this many-coated man.

'No,' he says, 'no.'

· · ·

The bar door is ajar, Liam opens it, smells the mopped tiles and the traces of beer underneath. He steps inside and for a moment, just stands there because this is harder than he imagined. There's something else, Liam, she'd said. He is wearing a roll-neck jumper because she hates his tattoos, he knows this, she always said to him, don't get any more now, after those first few, and then after that she had no say anyway. He thinks he can hear voices in the other room.

'Hello?' he says. 'Hello, Dee Dee?'

They used to come and sit here in the cool of the bar some-times, with all the old timers, the clack of dominoes and the telly playing quietly off to the side, sit and hold hands and look at the smoke coil up towards the ceiling. He hears a commotion, the thump of a chair going over and a little cry, like a whimper or something and he can tell it's Dee Dee's voice but no sound he ever heard from her, not even when they would ride out to that clearing in the woods or when they bought that house up the hill and would wander through those rooms naked, a curse on that place he is sure now, and he thinks that he is disturbing something here, and does not want to see her, does not want to see her like that, as if you might find her with a boyfriend at this time of the morning with the door open, and as he thinks this he walks through the open hatch at the bar and off the tiles and onto the lino with the swirls where someone has mopped, still drying, and he sees them in a mirror etched with a picture of the old Chain brewery, two figures standing facing each other. Her hair has never changed. He loved her hair and her voice and he sees her shape in the mirror and this other figure half turned to him that he doesn't know, with an old coat on and the smell and he thinks for a minute that it is Mark, but then thinks it can't be, and something in his head is not making sense, which is when he sees the knife.

He shouts, is not sure what, into the mirror, and then again as he turns through the doorway into the lounge. There is still the bar between them and he sees the man's hand go for the table and hears Dee Dee scream and run towards the hatch.

And he tries to vault the bar, his hands firm on it, but there are too many matches locked in his knees for that, too great a distance run, and it's more of a scramble, this, kicks a tray of drying glasses, which smash, and he comes over the bar towards the man with the knife in his hand head first, not with his feet, as he thought to, and sees the blade and thinks, this is it, and that he should've grabbed a glass, too late.

Goldie –

. . .

He is not dead, not dead, but changed.

At low tide the men on the cliff-top sleep in their tents. The giants and parts of giants lie strewn across the rocks and shingle down to the foam of the receding sea. Gogmagog, what's left of him, severed head and a severed arm pulling it along, drags himself across a ribbon of rough sand, assembles limbs on the rocks as the rain comes down, a spray comes in. He pieces together arms and legs from his comrades and his own head like a crown atop them, and scuttles along the cliff-base like a monstrous crab.

Up the wet rock he goes in the rain, a sea fret coming in to hide him, just the shape of legs working through the mist. The creature moves through the grey morning, through the green island, the white island, looks for a quiet hollow hill in which to rest, to wait.

.   .   .

– it is Goldie, the way he moves in this big coat like the way he used to dance that Liam always envied, even now his movement smooth across the floor and the knife is going away from him and not towards him. Goldie turns and gets to the lounge doors, rattles the bolt, and Liam has his hands up to grab him, is coming at him, but there is the knife held out in front of Goldie, and Liam stops, and in that moment of indecision Goldie has the door open, flings it open so the patterned glass shatters at Liam's feet, and he is away down the road and Liam starts after him and is through the door and onto the pavement and would catch him no problem but for Dee Dee's screams. So with Goldie halfway down the road he turns back to see her hanging onto the bar as if it's a raft.

There's something else, she had said to him, there's something else.

· · ·

Oh I wish I was you Billy Meredith
I wish I was you, I envy you, indeed I do.

When he lifts the cup they sing his name. You cannot see the crowd's end, they fill the square and the streets beyond, the gaps between the grand brick buildings. They lean from windows, edge along tree branches in the far distance, throw their caps in the air and cheer and sing. He lifts the cup and they sing his name.

Oh I wish I was you
Indeed I do
Indeed I do.

And he lifts the cup and thinks but you are me. I am you and you are me. They have come from their factories and mills and docks and he has come from the deep black underground and into the light.

He would feed the ponies in the mine, feel their wet noses on his hand, the clink of chains, crawl down those tunnels and dream of the green fields above, the path of the ball across it, the arc of it across a bright sky. Those crosses he hit to Sandy Turnbull, the goal in the final, how he let it run across his body to strike it, to whip his foot through it with the force of all his dreams, all that came from the blackness, from his brothers too, of course, but the force of it, the whip of it so no one would stop it, that came from the very depths. And when it went in, and when he lifts the cup now, it's like that moment you see the daylight when you're coming from deep below, that surge inside yourself. It's the same for them, he can see that, his dark eyes like there is still coal dust on them, star dust.

Oh I wish I was you Billy Meredith
I wish I was you, I envy you, indeed I do.

And I am you and you are me, he thinks, *though there be many members yet there is one body*, Corinthians, he remembers the preacher on a Sunday, the green hill, and they cheer as he raises the cup.

.   .   .

Steve Stringer hears footsteps come out of Chain Street and along under the grandstand, sees a figure running, his overcoat flapping open, what he thinks could be a knife in his hand. He hears the man breathing, heavy, running full pelt, the slap of the soles of his shoes offers percussion to the echoing steps. Steve gets just a glimpse and he is gone. He stays here, rests his cup of tea on the scaffolding pole, looks up and down the street for a pursuer. He sees nothing but a fox nosing around at some bins at the far end of the street. It is quiet. This place, he thinks, shakes his head, thinks of the curse for a moment and wonders if he should contact anyone about the running man, maybe not, probably not a knife anyway, he couldn't be sure, and why break this new sense of optimism? This is the first month he can remember for years when he hasn't been talking to the bank about how to pay the wages. The posters are in a pile in the corner of his office, to be pasted up on the corrugated iron at the Greenfield End later today. He'd checked the design of those from 1957, gone for the same look:

Football Association Challenge Cup
3rd Round Tie,
Sunday January 5th 2pm ko
Irontown FC v. Manchester United

There are banners that say *SOLD OUT* to paste up over them and add to the effect. The phone rings in his office, unusual these days, people usually call his mobile. Might be the FA themselves, he thinks, as he looks up and down the empty street.

'Discrepancy?' he says, when he hears out the voice on the other end of the line, thinks he can hear steps again in the street below, not so much worried as a sense of unease rising within him, 'What do you mean, a discrepancy?'

. . .

He has his arms around her at the bar and she sobs into his chest. He kisses the top of her head, not sure what to do.

'It's OK,' he says, 'it's OK. He's not going to hurt you.'

She has her arms against his chest and it feels good to hold her like this, and he knows he should not be thinking of this right now, looks at the upturned table and chair and the threadbare carpet, hears the ticking clock, feels the palms of her hands on his chest and she pushes him away.

'What you come in like that for?' she says. 'You could've just phoned. I was talking to him,' she says. 'Why didn't you just phone back?' She hits him in the chest with the flat of her hands, 'Like any normal person,' she says, and thumps him again and starts to sob.

He hugs her to him again and she shakes as she cries.

'I'm sorry,' he says. 'He had a knife, Dee Dee, he had a knife. Jesus, what did you want me to do?' but softly, quietly into her hair, like he is telling her a story in the middle of the night because she has woken from a bad dream.

They stay like this, at the edge of the bar. In the mirror that reflects into the other room Liam sees a man come in wearing an ill-fitting suit. He stands at the bar for a while. Then he rings the little bell but they stand there and don't say anything. The man cannot see them in the mirror. Liam sees the man go to speak and then shake his head and turn and leave.

Then they sit and look at each other over the righted table, each with a cup of tea. Dee Dee has poured them each a brandy, she says, 'For the shock,' with the intention of making a joke, but knows she just sounds like her nana, who would often reach for a glass after closing, shock or no. 'Goldie never finished his,' she says, again in a voice completely neutral, drained of all colour, and Liam doesn't reply.

He tells her to ring the police and she says no and he doesn't know what else to say.

She has put the bolts back on but is conscious she wants them open again soon, to act like nothing at all has happened. While the kettle was on she hurried upstairs, changed her clothes as quick as she could, heard water running in the bathroom, and stood at the door,

'All right, love?' she called, then a moment of surging panic when there was no reply, her hand flat against the locked door, until she heard Alina's quiet singing and smiled. She wore her headphones in the bath, could never hold a tune.

The room is quiet and cold with the air coming through the door's broken window.

'So nothing before? Just the phone call. No contact, no turning up like that before?'

'Nothing between when he phoned and now. I mean, that's five months, I thought it was just talk, a mistake, you know, tried to put it out of my mind.'

'You need to phone the police, Dee Dee.'

'Maybe,' she says.

'Maybe Lionel or somebody . . .' he starts, but his words tail off.

Alina comes from upstairs, moves behind the bar, looks confused, her hair up in a towel.

'What's going on?'

'Just a bit of trouble, love.'

'Bobby again?' she says.

'No. No one we know.'

'Better phone Lionel,' Alina nods towards the broken glass, looks at Liam.

'Liam was just passing, love,' Dee Dee says. Alina nods at him as with the broken glass, moves back towards the stairs as quietly as she arrived.

'Bobby?' Liam looks at her.

Dee Dee nods, 'In here kicking up a fuss a while ago. He's in a bad way.'

'He did the same at Tony's,' Liam says. He needs to go. Seeing the girl has made him uneasy.

Dee Dee asks him about Greta and Jari and he's surprised she remembers their names. He tells her about not seeing them over Christmas, that he thinks that means a change, an ending. She just nods.

'That must be hard,' she says to him and he can't tell if her voice has changed or not. 'I'd phoned you about Mark,' she says. 'You could go and see him, Liam. It wouldn't kill you.'

'Has he said he wants to see me?'

'It'd be good for him, Liam. Might be good for you both.'

'No,' he says, 'he doesn't want to see me.'

When he stands up to leave it's awkward.

'Thanks, Liam, thanks,' she manages to say, although there's something about it that doesn't ring true to him, he's just saved her life and she wants to talk to him about Mark. They hug at the door with the broken glass. He goes to kiss her and she puts the palms of her hands on his chest again and pushes him away.

'It's a bit late for that, Liam, don't you think?' is all she says.

. . .

Billy Meredith sits in his good suit at the FA Tribunal. It's a much better cut, more expensive cloth, than the ones worn by the men who accuse him, these petty men, these rich men who know nothing and yet think they own the world. When they accuse him of those things, as if he'd have fixed those matches in the way they said, in full sight of everyone, he wishes he had the toothpick, so he could play it along his lips and show them what he thought of them. He would stroll down the wing chewing on it sometimes, and the crowd would laugh and sing his name.

Oh I wish I was you Billy Meredith
I wish I was you, I envy you, indeed I do.

It is a game, nothing more, and people should remember that. He shows how he feels instead with the look in his dark eyes. He knows all about contempt, how to give it and receive it. He knows they can see what he thinks of them, these rich men, these men who think they have the power, think they can buy the world. The people do not sing their names.

These men want to treat them like the pit ponies, stabled in the dark underground, and he wants to see the stars in the night sky, the sun on the fields. These ways of thinking are irreconcilable. It's what one of them says. And he has seen all this before. At Black Park as a boy, and at all the mines and factories and mills beyond. The whole country is a robbers' den. Well, the tables can be overturned. The world does not have to be the way it is.

They ban him and he comes back stronger, looks at them with his dark eyes and doesn't blink. (Cantona, years later, points at the three Federation officials, 'Idiot! Idiot! Idiot!', leaves France and starts out on a road that leads to Old Trafford.)

And when he lifts the cup again, for United this time, not City, the colours of the shirt matter little to these men and, it's true, that is the difference between them and the crowds.

The people sing his name over and over.

It is their own names they sing.

.   .   .

Christmas night. Liam sits on the bed that had been his as a child. His mum and dad have never altered his room, all these years. His sisters used to share the bigger bedroom and now that's made up as a spare room, but this room has stayed the same, as if some kind of shrine.

He has brought a bottle of beer upstairs with him, it's been too hard trying not to drink, been trying to hide it all day. He wonders if there's a way to get back to the hotel, gives that idea up, will sleep in this narrow bed, with his legs sticking out of the end like they always have since he was fourteen or so, and his dad will take him to the match tomorrow.

'I thought I'd told you to stay at home, son?' Ally said to him this morning, down at the Heath after he'd watched Jari wave at him on the computer screen, saying, 'Merry Christmas, Daddy' in English, looking happy, a few thousand miles away.

'They're not here, Ally. They never came. She wants to keep

him over there,' was what he said to him, nothing more, and trained on Christmas morning like they always had, ran around the field like a kid. Everyone else quick to get off and back home and Liam was last away, doing a proper warm-down.

'You OK, son?' Ally said to him, the last two in the showers and he'd just nodded.

'It must be hard,' and Liam nodded again and Ally went to say something more and then didn't, patted his shoulder as they came out into the damp car park with their wet hair.

He looks at the pictures on the walls, all taken from the football magazines he and Mark would pore over. Baresi, Maldini, Paul McGrath, Des Walker. There's an Italia '90 wall chart, filled in meticulously up until the semi-finals, then nothing, as if he didn't fill in the score Gazza's tears might cry their way back into his head. He used to look at these pictures and imagine himself as these men, in the way that all boys do with their heroes he supposes, but then he somehow stepped into the pages of the magazines, was somehow out there on the pitch, like he walked out of the real world at some point and now couldn't find a way back, became his own tattoo. There are pictures of these men on his walls, pictures of them on his body.

He should not be playing tomorrow. He could still have gone to Finland. God knows what to do about Dee Dee; Goldie's resurrection.

He reaches to the shelf, takes down one of his old football annuals to flip through, to distract himself. He remembers this one. *Ally Barr's All Time Anvil Yards XI*. The players must have played at the Anvil Yards at least once: *Lev Yashin, Djalma Santos,*

Luigi Allemandi, John Charles, Billy Wright, Duncan Edwards, Billy Meredith, Steve Bloomer, Eusébio, Alfredo di Stéfano, George Best. He and Mark would pick their own teams, riding in his dad's car on the way to games, or in the back of the minibus, students of the game. On the back leaf of the book is some writing in pencil.

DAD: Banks, Santos (D), Santos(N), Moore, Beckenbauer,
    Jairzinho, Edwards, Charlton (R), Pelé, Greaves, Best.
MARK: Schumacher, Josimar, Bossis, Olsen, Koeman, Laudrup,
    Baggio, Socrates, Van Basten, Maradona, Gullit.
LIAM: Shilton, Kaltz, Maldini, Baresi, McGrath, Matthäus,
    Gascoigne, Baggio, Dalglish, Maradona, Barnes.

If only everything could be contained by eleven names on a team-sheet, by the white lines around a pitch. He has lived his life as if it could, and look at the mess it's brought.

He hears his mum say downstairs, 'Where's our Liam?' in a voice that could not sound more tired or disappointed, hears his sisters and the kids getting ready to leave so Gary and Martin can have a drink at home. He wonders how they manage to keep their lives in such order. And she could be a bit more sympathetic, his mum, with him stuck here and exiled from his own family. He exiled himself, all right. But he treads carefully around his mum, kept his distance when she was ill. He can see in the look in her eyes, the mess she thinks he's made of things.

And Dee Dee. He saved her life, for god's sake, from a maniac with a knife, because that is all Goldie is now, perhaps all he ever was, not that she seemed very grateful. He wants that to be different. On the phone it had sounded like she needed him. He might go and see Lionel, tell him about Goldie, considers the police but thinks Lionel might know what to do. He wishes he did, that's for sure. He tries to think about the United match, the excitement building, and a quiet dread in his stomach that they might run riot, end up with eight, nine, ten, imagine. He should leave off the drink, that's for sure. He lies back on the bed and thinks of lifting the cup, the same dreams he had in this room as a kid, to stop himself thinking of anything else.

.   .   .

A man in a room dreaming dreams, bloated and reaching for the drink. He tells that joke so often, the one where he is in bed with Miss World and a couple of bottles of champagne, or is it one bottle and two Miss Worlds, and the waiter bringing room service, the fall guy, with his thinning hair and an odd button on his uniform sewn on by his wife, with his grey face and Manchester accent and season ticket for the Stretford End and pale blue eyes, who says, 'Oh George, where did it all go wrong?'

And they laugh their brittle laughs, on the television chat shows and in after-dinner smoke-filled rooms, but he understands as he says it, even as they laugh with him that these people are from a world that is not his.

Where did it all go wrong, George?

Whole iron towns warped with rust and time and pain.

.   .   .

Liam remembers the story that they picked Yorke off the beach, that he'd been a crab fisherman, would haul his lines up and down and do tricks with the ball for the tourists. There were Union flags that flapped in the harbour, under the Caribbean sun, people in yachts waiting for crab meat and cocktails and black people to fetch and carry for them, it was how they'd built an empire. Taylor could spot a player, in spite of what they said when he managed England, signed John Barnes from a London park pitch, so there was at least something to the story.

Then he did it again, like he'd perfected it this time, and it's unusual, because when you've done it once, why would you try it again, because at some point you'll mess it up.

At home against Arsenal, this, a full house at Villa Park, and he runs up with more purpose than the one before, like he's about to blast it into the corner, and this time opens his foot as he strikes it, might have toppled backwards as he hit it, balls of iron, so it hovers in the air, a couple of feet off the ground, and Seaman sits down, tries to get up, crumples, and the ball lands in the goal, and in Liam's head at least, stops dead. Sits there like a full stop at the end of a story.

Liam imagines watching this with Mark.

'You should've just done that,' he says to him.

'I should've just smashed it,' is what Mark – the Mark in his head – says back.

. . .

Geoff Stelling: And another goal at the Anvil Yards. Dave Willis is there for us.

Dave 'Iron' Willis: A third for Accrington Stanley.
Francis Jeffers, the original fox in the box,
strikes again. Very little seasonal cheer at the
Anvil Yards for the second year running for Liam
Corwen, sent off for a foul on Jeffers, who in
all honesty was giving the big man a runaround,
definitely getting the upper hand in the battle of
the former England internationals, and the red card
might have put Corwen out of his misery. That's the
tenth sending off of his career, incidentally. Looks
like Irontown will be in the relegation places
for the new year. They need to liven up their act
for the visit of Manchester United in the cup,
a wonderful distraction from the reality of the
league table, that's for sure . . .

. . .

He can tell something's up when he gets to training, thinks
for a moment that it's just the six-nil to Accrington, a feeling
of doom all around. The sending off was a joke, he barely
touched him. There's been an intensity in the last few weeks
since the cup draw, but with a few wins as well, and the sense,
if nothing more than that, that they might start to climb the
table, but the wheels fell off the wagon with the Boxing Day
match and there's something even about the way the cars
are parked haphazardly in the car park, as he walks across it
from the bus turnaround and up the wooden steps into the
prefab that moonlights as the canteen and gym and sometime
meeting room, that doesn't add up at all. Half a dozen of them

sit on plastic chairs not looking at each other.

'You heard?' Devon asks him.

'Who's dead?'

'We've been thrown out of the cup. Ally's been sacked.'

And he is halfway across the room, to the connecting doors that lead to the dressing rooms, before this registers.

'What?'

'He fucked up the paperwork for that First Round game. That kid we'd got in from Cheltenham, he'd played in the qualifiers for some non-league side, fucking August they start them games, never thought to say though, the kid must have forgot, not realised.'

'Thrown out the cup for that?'

'Ineligible player. It's in the rules.'

'He was shit an' all!'

Liam can't tell who says this but still replies, 'But better than you.'

'He probably forgot. He was a good player. Prick.' Kyran says towards the floor and the unidentified voice.

Liam stands in the doorway, 'No one's dead,' he says, 'no one died.' He does not know why he says this. The players look at the floor. He thinks of Boris Becker that time, another picture from his bedroom wall, summer distractions, when Becker lost for the first time at Wimbledon, 'I did not lose a war. No one died.'

No one ever gets sacked here. No one has made a decision for twenty years. Dorothea sits there drooling in the Atlantic sun, from what he understands, refuses to sell up, refuses to do anything, holds all the shares, the last in the dynasty. Steve Stringer fills out bits of paper, writes cheques and invoices, talks to the bank and the league.

'Who's sacked him?'

No one answers.

'Archie says there's a meeting in a bit, to wait here.'

'Where else we gonna go?'

'Archie didn't fucking sack him,'

'Archie's in charge for now.'

'Who said that?'

'Archie.'

'Better get changed anyway, lads,' is all Liam says, punches the wall in the dressing room when he gets in there, doesn't notice Julius sitting there in the corner until he's already done it and his knuckles are bleeding, staring into space, thinks, this whole place is fucking cursed.

'Archie said to go home,' Julius says, sitting there, staring into space with a towel wrapped around him, 'Have the day off. There'll be a meeting tomorrow.'

．．．

He pulled her out, saved her. Even the judge had mentioned it when he sentenced him. He pulled her out. There was the shock of hitting the water. It came in through the open window and he felt the shock of it, cold, as it hit his leg and the lurch of the car with the water entering so they went nose first into it and it felt like Alina was in a seat above them as well as behind them, at the angle now, but all of them sinking. The log flume at Alton

Towers, that's what he thought of, shocked by the water. Sonia's head had gone forward and thumped into the dashboard, she turned to him with her nose bleeding and they look at each other. He swears he can see the look on her face when he shuts his eyes. The back half of the car dropped into the water. Alina was quiet, had been crying, was quiet now, with the shock of the impact he guesses, and the car filling up, going under, the sound of the water sloshing up the sides of the culvert and then come running in through the car windows. She tries to hit him, scratches at his face, his eyes. Both of them still in their seats, water up to their waists. They would find his skin under her nails in the post-mortem. He grabs her wrists and she won't calm down. He can hear the siren. Alina begins to scream. The windscreen gives way with the brown water, there was a crack in it he knew he should've seen to. The glass and water hit him. He twists and reaches to the baby seat, has to pull himself with the water filling the car. They are jammed tight against the bank on Sonia's side. This is what kills her, when she's underwater she tries the door handle but it won't open. Goldie pulls Alina to him, through the gap between the headrests the sound of water pouring in. A splinter in his brain says they are going to die. He pulls him to her, ducks under the water, pushes her from him through the window now because the car is full of water, they are underwater now, and from somewhere, somewhere, some old action film or something he thinks later when he talks of it, and talks and talks, in counselling, and it is not all bullshit, it has not all wrecked his head, his mind is the shape of the crumpled car all right, but he knows, he understands that with the car full of water they can come out through the window, it shows his speed of thought, he thinks, and he saves his daughter's life that way, pushes her out and away from him through the window, has to take a hand off her to get himself through the gap wriggling and swallowing some of it, so that he's choking when he gets his head out, holding Alina away from him half on the steep grass bank that rises from the concrete and if the grass had not been so steep he might have been able to lay Alina down and go back and get Sonia, her belt still fastened, and it is here, still choking and holding Alina and not thinking she is dead, never thinking that until some minutes later, when he sees the policewoman walking away from him with the baby in her arms looking down at her and talking into her radio.

'Jesus, Rita, there's a babby.' He hears a man's voice, the policeman, and the sound of their boots on the lane. Sonia struggling, the water only just above her head, not quite filling the car, the water not that deep, she could've stood up in it.

She didn't stand up in it. He remembers looking at the water sloshing against steep banks and then back again towards the car roof that was still above the water, at an angle, sloping forward, and the water going more and more still. There was no movement at all. He looked at the banks, still thinking he'd see Sonia, not thinking anything, looking back at the still water and the still car.

'There's someone in the car,' he says to them.

That's what they talked about after, in the court, how calm he'd said this. He was trying not to panic.

. . .

Scotland against England is serious business. It is 5 April, 1902, and at Ibrox they have to walk past dead bodies to get back onto the pitch. There are arms and legs at angles they would never be in life. There are men behind the men in charge, always, men in suits in the dressing rooms who tell them to get back out there. They say if they don't play on there'll be more dead. They say this time and again through the years.

Steve Bloomer is captain that day, the first time, and he leads his men past the bodies and back out onto the pitch. It bothers him that he should have said no, respect the dead. They ferry people to hospital on makeshift stretchers as the match goes on. There is a black hole in the stand where the wood gave way; men of iron towns, laid out by the side of the Ibrox pitch. It will happen again, at regular intervals in the century ahead. The authorities decide to replay the match at Villa Park in the end. They give the gate receipts to the families, at least.

When he looks at great tides of people he always sees that black hole. There are people absent from every crowd.

. . .

Ally looks relieved, is what he looks. Jesus, Liam thinks. How terrible can managing this club be if you don't feel too bad about passing up a game against Man United, putting the final nail in the place's coffin with this last mess-up. Ally won't work again.

With the money and attention from the United match they would

have had a chance. Without it, now, out of the cup, near the bottom of
the league, struggling to pay the players, there is very little hope. The cup
draw was a miracle. To ask for another seems to be stretching the bounds
of reality. Although with this club you never know . . .

Dave Willis did a piece on Midlands Today last night. They found the most dilapidated corner of the car park to film in, both the factory wall and the Chain End looking like they might fall into the canal at any moment. There were kids jumping around in the background, giving the fingers, one of them was even wearing a United bobble hat. There are no kids in the Anvil Yards any more, god knows where they had come from, maybe the people from the telly had brought them with them.

Ally looks like a man who has slept sound in his bed all night. Fifty years in football, he's had, just over, signed for Celtic at fifteen, has managed Irontown for more than twenty of the last thirty years. When he became player-manager in 1984 the club was one place in the league better off than it is now, except what Ally will tell you is that he has never taken the club down. He would win promotion, leave for somewhere else with a bit of glamour, more money, then come back when Irontown had been relegated again. That was the pattern. Hail, hail.

He is thanking everyone. Last night in an interview he said he'd be off to Portugal for a bit of sunshine and golf, was looking forward to spending time with the grandkids.

'I've done nothing wrong,' he said, 'I'll sleep soundly in ma bed.'

Dave Willis tried to press him, wasn't it the manager's responsibility to check these things?

'It's the club's,' Ally said. 'We acted in good faith.' Then he was off, the camera lingered on the Mercedes come from Lionel Ahmed's garage which Liam guessed Lionel would be calling to get back. The club say they've sacked him, Ally says it's mutual.

He could speak to Lionel about Dee Dee. About the situation. What else to call it? The situation, the emergency, the trouble. He might have been describing the Iron Towns themselves, he knows. Thirty years of it, three hundred nearly, just times when you might not have noticed. Lionel might know what to do. He thinks of going to the police. She might thank him in the end. She might not.

They've got the heating on full blast for once, everyone crammed in the canteen, the carpet threadbare, there are framed photos of old players and matches on the walls, there's one of Ally on Archie Hill's shoulders with the Welsh Cup, from the days when Midlands sides could enter, Ally wrote to UEFA to try to allow them into Europe. Liam feels like his eyes might close. He is not a man who sleeps easy in his bed, any bed, any more. Ally is thanking Ted Groves, really hamming it up now. Ted and Ally have got tears in their eyes. Liam puts his head in his hands. He hears a camera whirring.

They've revived talk of the curse with this latest catastrophe, especially because it involves the cup. There are two versions that Liam knows of, probably more if you asked around. One is that when the team arrived back on the train from the old Crystal Palace after the last final they won, to be greeted by great crowds at Hightown Station, men in caps hanging from the castle walls, the Crusader stone, the trees at the arboretum, James Greenfield took the cup in his new car, his latest toy, the first to be seen on Iron Towns roads, and drove across the Heath. His driver slowed for an old gypsy woman, picking flowers at the roadside. It was a hot day and she called out to them to ask for a drink of water. They slowed and Greenfield laughed and told her to go and get a drink from the brook. She pointed at the cup, sitting next to him on the seat, and told him that it would never be seen in the Iron Towns again.

The other story involves the cup when it was stolen from Birmingham, when the Villa put it on display in a jewellers' shop. There was a rumour the Carter family took it, melted it down for coins in an Anvil Yards furnace. Another version has them burying it out on the Heath and forgetting where they left it, like that Saxon gold they say is somewhere, piles of coins stamped 'Offa Rex'. This forgetfulness has always seemed unlikely to Liam, from what he understands of the Carters, the Greenfields, the Ahmeds, well, some of them, and from what he understands of Saxon chieftains, for that matter. People who make money keep it, most of them, anyhow.

All football grounds have curses on them, it's just some of these curses work better than others, that's what he thinks, really. They could undo the curse by playing well.

Ally says Liam's name and eyes turn towards him. Ally is telling them all to pull together. Through the window Liam can see Steve Stringer on the phone. No one has made a decision at this club for years. Old Dorothea is almost a hundred, no family left. From the way that Steve is pacing up and down and the bags under his eyes, it seems to Liam that he's taken a stand about this and now regrets it. Who's going to want to come here? Big Archie has been named as caretaker, but he's not a manager. There's a rumour going round that they've asked Wayne Coombs, just been sacked by a club in Malta, back at his ex-wife's in Calon. That's all they fucking need. Liam moves to put his head back in his hands, realises it might not look good. Ally says his name again, talks about fighting spirit, the embodiment of the club.

Liam clenches his fist and nods his head to murmurs of support. Julius pats him hard on the back.

Steve Stringer is nuts letting Ally talk like this. Ted Groves is crying.

And then he's done. 'This club will go on,' he says, and they're already clapping, on their feet. 'and maybe we'll meet again, you never know, Happy New Year, everyone, Happy New Year,' and he's gone.

Out the door he goes and towards his car, ignores Steve who moves towards him and then gets the message, so hangs back and maybe he's even pretending to be on the phone, no one is going to want to talk to him except Dave Willis for the latest gossip. Liam can see brake lights from the cars out on the Heath road, they shine blurred through the dirty window and damp January air, through the leafless trees and then move around the corner and out of sight, it's where he came off the road, keep going half a mile and it's where Goldie drove into the river, there's a turn-off for the clearing where they used to go in summer, up there on the hill is where the people took that German parachutist and killed him and stuffed his body down an old mine shaft that no one still is meant to talk about, and there's the Goat Wood, where the witches still go on full-moon nights and the solstice, and it's already getting dark.

. . .

It starts to rain.

They missed the floods before Christmas, just a postponement against Torquay to show for them, as the weather skirted the Iron Towns, but now it comes hard and Liz and Joey watch the rain gutter down the steep Black Park hill.

'It's coming now,' Joey says, his nose almost touches the steering wheel. White water froths up out of the drains, comes in a wave down the kerbs, a pink child's wellington boot tumbles over and over.

'What was he thinking?' Liz says.

'Nothing, nothing.'

The light is falling, either that or the rain is coming even harder now, picked out in the streetlights. 'That's not true. Himself, of course, thinking of himself, as usual.'

Liz sighs.

'You warm enough, love?' he asks. He has the window open a crack to stop the windscreen steaming up.

'I'm OK.'

Eli is missing, out when he should be in, not for the first time. They have told him not to try the hill on his own any more, certainly not just with his stick. He refuses a walking frame, laughs when they suggest a scooter. All talk of him moving has long since gone. They'll have to carry him out, as the saying goes, unless the houses fall down or wash away first. It is possible.

The water has gathered at the bottom of the hill, meeting other water in brown swirls, a lagoon, cars pull in, hazard lights blink in the water.

'Well, I can't go through that,' Joey says. On the radio an excited woman's voice plays at low volume.

'There's boxes of stuff just floating along the road. What's this? Saris and communion dresses and flat caps,' she says.

The Lowtown Bull Ring is flooded. The radio says to avoid the area if possible.

'I've avoided it for twenty years,' Liz says, pleased with her joke.

A bus ploughs into the flood, headlights on full beam, sends up a plume of water. It is not a designated stop but the bus creeps carefully along the kerb, opens its doors. The driver leans half out of his cab. Sure enough, there on the platform is Eli. In the rain's din they can see but not hear the conversation, but can imagine, they get the gist.

'Don't get out in this, mate. Wait till it knocks off a bit.'

'I'm all right, what's the matter with yer? I'm all right.'

Eli teeters on the bus steps. A young woman's arm stretches out to help him. Joey jumps from the car, headfirst into the deluge, grits his teeth. There's his dad ankle-deep, the water rushing over his smart brown shoes, spreading up his trouser legs, neatly creased by Liz.

'What am yer doing?' Eli says. 'What yer playing at?'

'What do yer think?' Joey says and takes his elbow, half expects to feel it in his ribs.

The last time he did this was in the riots. Well, he did it all the time, but the last time he put himself in danger that they knew of.

'He puts himself in danger every time he inches down them stairs in his carpet slippers.' Liz says.

'Yer couldn't even get a stair-lift in here. Yer couldn't fit one,' Eli'd say right to the face of the occupational therapist come from social services, moving his teeth in agitation so the bottom set nearly came flying out, some girl young enough to be his great-grandaughter telling him otherwise about the lift, come to visit him at home and assess his needs, as they put it. Joey and Liz would smile and apologise with their eyes.

At least the riots were in the summer. He'd got the bus out towards the flyover to go and have a look at the trouble himself, a bonfire burning in the Tesco car park at four in the afternoon. Young lads tried to nick trainers at the shopping village. Joey could never get to the bottom of whether Eli had gone to tell them all to go home or whether he thought the revolution had come at last.

'Not even any proper trouble, just some young lads setting fires and the police watching 'em do it,' was Eli's only comment afterwards.

That night, some of the Bullet Krew attempted to burn down the police station, set squat and flat just off the Wrexham Road on the rise between Oxton and Cowton, but the flames didn't take, it was a night of soft drifting rain coming out of Wales, the last night. The men went home, the boys got their new shoes, people too tired to riot any more.

. . .

Dee Dee stands in her boots, the water darkens her jeans. A couple of empty barrels bob in the water and make hollow sounds on the cellar walls. The rain beats on the iron doors which rattle and threaten to fold in on themselves with the weight of the water. She tells herself not to breathe in, does anyway, concentrates for any smell of shit in the water. She needs Roni to descend. All she can smell is dead leaves, mulch, the usual damp cellar wall smell. She should be worried about the beer spoiling, she knows that, is not sure of the insurance procedures. This could mean the end, but the actual fact of the water sweeping through the Anvil Yards streets exhilarates her. She thinks of the language of survival, keeping your head above water, going under, holed below the water line, and the like. She imagines the door at the top of the steps swung shut, the water at her chin, her mouth, nose, ears. The temptation to let go, her hair floating in the water.

'Mum, what you doing? Come on.'

The door is open and the lights on. Alina stands at the top of the stairs with that rope in her hands, coiled round her slim body.

Alina floats down the river towards her. The child saves the parent in the end, she thinks, wishes for a moment she still tried to write songs.

. . .

The rain comes through the whole building. There is glass in the skylights and he is afraid they might give way with the force of the rain but it comes in everywhere else anyway. He's got a candle lit, eats a cold tin of beans with an old carpet wrapped round him. Goldie would never have thought he could've coped with something like this. The one time they went camping at school he walked back from the Heath himself, wanted his own bed, his mum. He wishes he had never left his room, imagines himself there now, the water washing time backwards.

There's a glow that comes from the motorway flyover that enters at the far end of the building. He can see the rain guttering down in the orange light, holds his hand to the candle and shivers, the fire escape stairs at the far end of the building dissolve in the rain. They were only held together by rust, he sees them peel off the wall and crumble and disappear without even making a sound. He wonders if it's the end of the world.

. . .

'Death by fire, death by water, death by fire, death by water,' Mark Fala stands at the window, rocks back and forth, looks out into the storm. Half the lights are out up the hill, so he is left with the sounds. He knows that when they found her there was mud and brick dust under her fingernails where she'd tried to claw herself out, stones in her pinafore dress, clothes her own mother wore.

The inquest was inconclusive. She might have slipped down the bank in the rain. It was possible. He almost went in himself a couple of times, when he used to go down there just to sit and think about things. He went there a lot during that last season, thought a lot about packing it all in right there. Not just the football, everything. You could see the back of his dad's old works from the bank, no one ever mentioned that at the inquest and he didn't feel any urgent need to say.

He told himself she didn't mean it. It was one thing to wish yourself dead. It was another thing to actually go ahead and do it. She wouldn't have left him. That was what everyone said. But then, they hadn't been there in the dark nights, had they? They hadn't heard her crying, or not crying, other noises, just shuffling from room to room in a small flat she said she wouldn't leave, even though he was earning the money then. Ally had got them with money coming in hand over fist. The older players loved it. What use was it to him? He used to ask sometimes, and they took it as some quirk or other, but he knew there was something wrong with him. They'd have put up with anything as long as he kept performing, as long as they kept winning.

He'd beckon with his hands for the ball, had never been one for saying much on the pitch, never one for saying that much anywhere, really.

'Give it to Mark, give it to him. Hit Mark's feet. Release him. Just fucking give it to him!' Liam's monologue coming from the other end of the pitch. At first the older players didn't want to be spoken to like that, not by Liam, big and cocky and decent player as he was, but still just a kid, and then they looked at Mark, and knew that he was right.

He'd always known. He'd chased around the flat as soon as he could walk with a little ball at his feet that the dog had chewed. His dad always liked to keep a dog. They had two scrappy puppies once that his dad called Jackie and Bobby. And he'd have the ball at his feet when they went down the shops and would play one-twos off the kerb before he even knew what a one-two was. His dad had been a good player, his mum's dad too. His mum had been a great one for dancing. His balance he got from her. She'd always had great balance, something else he was glad no one ever mentioned at the inquest. The bank was steep and it could be slippery in the rain, but still, it was hard to see her floundering about like that. She always walked with her head up. Not two pennies to rub together, as they used to say, not a pot to piss in, except maybe the last few months, years, with the pay-out for his dad's accident and the money Mark had started to get paid. He got offered adverts, a boot deal. Those other clubs came in for him. Everyone was mad to go to Italy then. Imagine, him on the same pitch as Van Basten, as Baggio. What was strange was that it almost happened, like with the Torino thing. There was talk of Lazio too. He was meant to get an agent. Liam's dad looked after it all for a while. A lot of good the money did her, anyway.

It suited everyone to think it was another accident, there was the mud under his mum's fingernails. She always kept her hands nice. He could sit now and conjure up the smell of the cream she used to use on them, there was probably some in the back of a drawer somewhere. He'd never thrown her things out. It suited them all, meant the priest could come round and sort out the funeral without any complications. Very good for everyone, they could all feel a bit better about themselves.

She couldn't swim. That was why she chose that way, he supposed. It was a while before they found her. Just under the surface, face down, bobbing against the wooden planks that held off the bank there, her skirt billowing out behind her. The police had taken a picture. He hadn't seen her until the hospital. Her body was all swollen up because of the water, three times the size she'd been in life. He'd been worried she'd got too thin. He'd got his build from her as well.

He knew well before he missed that penalty that he was going to walk away. In fact, missing it almost made him think he'd go back, even just for the start of the season, if only to shut everyone up.

What he thinks is that she changed her mind. That itself was unusual. Something else he got from her was that he knew his own mind, never had any doubts. That's why packing it in was a question of when and not if. He tried to drink himself to death. He thought that might be a solution, but it was harder than you might think. His heart wasn't in it maybe, he had never been that much of a drinker, would get drunk and pass out. You had to really give yourself over to it, like Stevie and Jigsaw and the others at the Quakers. You could admire their determination in a way. He wasn't joking. To achieve anything, you had to put some effort in, even if it was just leaving. He thinks she changed her mind, thought that what she wanted was to leave and then realised too late that she wanted to live, if only for him. In dreams she would come to him and ask for forgiveness and he would say it's OK, it's OK, Mum, don't cry. Maybe she just wanted to be with his dad, but he wasn't sure that any of them believed in that stuff, not really. You didn't go anywhere. You just stayed here in the Iron Towns.

He can't swim. It occurs to him that one day he might do the same as she did, but he doubts it now. He's come through dark days, hours, minutes, sometimes the world just reduced to nothing, but he has started to not feel so bad. He wonders if it is simply the fact of getting older. He couldn't play football now even if he wanted to. He can't drive. He has not had a girlfriend for twenty years, even back then just someone to hold hands with. He wasn't like Liam, like Goldie. He used to look at Sonia and imagine, dream about what it might be like. She had all sorts under her fingernails too, she had clawed for life too, but then Sonia had never wanted to die.

The wind changes and the rain drills against the window. When it comes at a certain angle, a wind out of the north-west, from out of the far mountains, the water gets in and patters the floor in his mother's room, sometimes the bed cover. He'll go and get some old sheets from the cupboard. Everything is still here. He thinks of it as her room. There's still some stuff of his dad's in the back of the wardrobe. His funeral suit, for one thing. Didn't need it, after all. He is not sure what clothes he was buried in. There was a kid who died, one of the ones they'd visit down at the children's ward at the Bethel, buried with one of Mark's shirts. The grave wasn't far from Sonia's plaque, just outside the garden of remembrance. Mark thought about it every time he went up there. When the wind blows from the other way, it brings his name on it. The way they still sing it. They need some new songs, is what he thinks.

.   .   .

With the game off, Liam sits and drinks in the hotel bar with Devon and Julius. The car parks are under water, both at the ground and the hotel. Devon and Julius are shipwrecked.

'So if the ball went over the stand, right, you had to scamper down these steps and open this door, like a hobbit door, right. There was three of 'em. One level with each penalty spot and another at halfway.'

'Scampering, that's a great word, scampering.' Julius grins at his bottle of beer.

'And each door opens onto the riverbank, right, except there ain't much bank just there. You know you could only get into the East Stand at either end of the ground, it's one of the reasons they closed it, right.'

'Health and safety considerations,' Devon says.

'Exactly. Anyway, you'd open this door and have to watch your step, what with studs on the concrete, to not end up in the drink, and then you'd put your head out and, I swear to God, there'd come this old bloke in a bobble hat rowing a little boat, a coracle it's called, this kind of boat, and he'd fish the ball out with a net and row it over to you to take back. I can't think of his name.'

'Someone needs to scamper to the bar.'

'I can't think of his name. This bloke was ancient, all bent over, thick glasses on, three coats in winter. Looked like he slept in the boat, but, get this, his old man had done the same job before him, right, before they even built the stand and there was just a bank and a wall down that side, so what, the twenties or summat, the same boat, a coracle.' He is losing them, their eyes glaze, fix on their drinks, with this story of his days as a ballboy, on the results of games that have made it through the weather. They toast and drink whenever they hear Irontown mentioned. 'Archie Hill stuck it in the river six times one afternoon, I swear.'

'Archie Hill is a cock,' says Julius.

Archie had dropped him, named the team yesterday, decided to try Kyran up front, and then the rain came.

'I am the curse,' is what Julius had said when he'd had a couple of drinks. 'Archie better believe it.'

Liam can see a man reflected in a mirrored column. He stands near the reception desk, looks uncomfortable, checks a heavy-looking watch, dark blue suit and – this is what has caught Liam's attention – dark glasses. It is pouring with rain in the English Midlands.

'Is that one of the Portuguese?' Liam nods towards the mirror and looks at the other two. When he looks back there is no one there.

'What Portuguese? I'll have another.' Julius rarely drinks, is feeling it.

'Remember,' Liam starts, 'that kid, start of the season, Luis . . .' Then, 'You heard about that club that takes their ground with them, erects a whole stadium? They build the stadium the week of the game out in the desert, out where they don't have football, like Mongolia and places, play their match, then that's it they're away and the ground goes with them, on to the next place.'

'What you on about? Who do they play?'

'You two need to slow down a bit,' Devon says, 'I'll get a round in.'

'They travel round like nomads and that. Wanderers. That's where the team name Wanderers comes from, teams that didn't used to have a home ground.' He says this to no one in particular, sometimes has conversations he thinks he might have with Jari in the future in his head, out loud too now, it seems. If Jari can speak English by then, if Liam can speak Finnish or Swedish or Russian or German or whatever else he might learn.

Liam stands and walks towards the mirror, walks around the column with his drink in his hand, no one there, shakes his head, and walks back to their seats. He'd been sure.

Devon comes back with the drinks on a tray, motions to the TV screen. On the news they show Eusébio's coffin, carried high through weeping streets, into the stadium, out onto the pitch. It is pelting with rain in Lisbon.

. . .

It rained whenever Caesar came.

The shield Nennius used was forged on Manawydan's stone. It swallowed Caesar's sword the first time he came, and Nennius took the sword and cut the invaders down so that the valley filled with blood.

Caesar sailed up the river but the people were ready. They set great iron spikes beneath the still waters. Caesar's ships were drowned and the valley filled with water.

Then Caesar came a third time and the people ran and hid, and the valley filled with ghosts.

There is always a war. Invaders come and go, settle and remain, become the people that live among the valleys and the stones, wait things out, hollow out the hills and burn their black insides. There is always a war, always a fire that burns within, without, and the rivers only ever run with blood.

Arthur died on the muddy, muddy banks.

There was no boat to carry him.

. . .

He needs three or four attempts to get the card in the door lock and then even when he opens it he misses the doorway and walks into the frame. A bump rises on his forehead and he puts his fingers to it to check for blood and this sobers him enough to realise how drunk he is. He giggles and unzips himself and pisses loud and long in the toilet bowl in the dark with the doors open to the corridor, sings 'Oh it's a grand old team to play for,' loudly, and then stops and puts the card in the slot to operate the lights and puts his cock away and zips up carefully and only then closes the door as quietly as he can and then slumps against it and sits down and wonders if he has left a can of beer in the fridge.

He was probably this far gone the night they pulled him up for drink-driving. He had not been playing, had been out with a heel injury and then not back in the side for a couple of months or more, but he kept plugging away in training and got a chance when they played Shrewsbury on a Friday night, live on telly, and he came on with them one-down and getting murdered, only for them to come back and win 3-1 with Liam getting the second himself from a corner.

They'd had a drink in the hotel that night, celebrated, Ally included, with a couple of them with rooms booked because of the late finish. Liam had already been too drunk to drive when he left them and drove back to his house on the hill. He was still trying to live there on his own then and not doing very well at it. So when he got in he turned every light on and got a bottle of wine from cupboard, he'd had intentions at one point of a cellar, and drank that looking out into the dark from the living room, still restless. That was when he went back out for another drive, to see what was happening, Friday night and all that, put some old stuff that he used to listen to with Dee Dee on the stereo as he drove, went back down the hill towards the Anvil Yards with the vague intention of returning to the hotel bar, telling Ally he deserved a start next match.

He drove around, sobering up, he thought, when he saw the young kids queueing to get into a club under the arches in Lowtown that he did not know the name of, did not know existed. And something, in the music and thoughts of the night's match and hating the transition between being surrounded by the crowd and laughter and noise and being on his own in his own silent house and bed, made him keep driving. He thought he might go and bang on Mark's door, go and visit him, had these grand visions of a reconciliation, arms round each other crying, he was crying as he was driving now, of course, but when he got down near the flats he couldn't work out how to drive into them, he had never gone there with a car and Goldie had always parked out here on the main road and he was not stupid or drunk enough to be leaving an almost new BMW parked half-way across the pavement in the Anvil Yards, so he did a couple of circuits, couldn't see any lights on in Stevedore House anyway, and drove off, leaving the big reconciliation for another night. It had been twenty years since they last spoke, after all.

Still, that wasn't enough though, and after driving down to see if the Salamander was still serving, which of course it wasn't as it was after two o'clock by this point, and looking forlornly at the lights on in the upstairs of the pub, even thinking he saw a shape, Dee Dee, pass behind the net curtains, he headed out towards the Heath, past the big cut-out of himself advertising the entrance to Lionel Ahmed's car yard and the reason he was driving a BMW in the first place, just over the hump-backed bridge where he began to list towards the left-hand verge and drove along half in the hedge for thirty yards or so before fully leaving the road. He stayed in the car for a while, might even have slept for a few moments, so peaceful it was here at the Heath's edge in the dead of night. The driver's door was jammed against a branch in the hedgerow and so he was halfway out of the sun-roof, and struggling with this, stiffening up with driving after a match, when a police car came round the corner on its way back to the Lowtown station for a shift-change.

He could have killed someone. The following day his head was full of this. Or he could've killed himself, which at the time felt much the lesser of the evils, he was only a few turns in the road from where Goldie had crashed with Sonia and Alina. In fact, where he was headed in the car at that hour was the clearing in the Goat Wood, to sleep in his car under the trees and think of better days. And he could've gone to prison, something that only really dawned on him on the day of his trial and he couldn't stop his legs shaking when he stood up in court and had to listen to himself described in ways that he did not want to listen to at all. It was a stupid thing to have done, OK but these fuckers in their wigs and with their accents which came from nowhere near the Iron Towns had no right to pass any judgement. Well, there was a judgement, of course, banned for three years, an alcohol aware- ness course, a speed awareness course, a few hundred hours of community service.

'You'll have to stop your drinking now Liam. You could've killed somebody.' His mum's voice that night as he sat in their front room still in his court suit, still in the dock from what he could tell, with his sisters looking at him through the breakfast hatch and his old man not looking at him at all but his lips disap- pearing in that grim smile he used to get just before he'd blow, drop the nut on someone if he had to. As if the drinking was the problem, really. In court, his barrister had talked about the stress of Liam's estrangement from his wife and young child. It wasn't a word he would have used, but it made sense. His own wife and son becoming strangers to him, the same with everyone he had ever known.

'You'll have to smarten up your act, love,' his mum repeated phrases she used to say to him when he was a kid. He smiled at this, a man in his thirties crumpled in the soft armchair in his parents' front room.

'All their furniture is too big for the house,' is something Greta had said to him, and it was true, he'd never noticed before, but it was.

Strangers all of them, to each other, to themselves.

Liam has only ever seen the girl, what, half a dozen times. No more than a few minutes each time. Less than that usually, like when she stood behind the bar the other day and then was gone, like the Portuguese, who are not even Portuguese, in the bar downstairs.

It unnerves him every time, though. He lies on the bed, half-clothed, too pissed to undress. This is what hotels are for, he thinks, is not unhappy right now this moment, but knows he must be pissed to be thinking of it like this.

He thinks of last things, does this sometimes to try to get to sleep, a variation on running through League Cup winners, or trying to remember every player he has ever played with. He thinks of the things that when he dies will go as well, locked inside his head, things that he knows or remembers and, if he lives long enough, will be the last to know.

Such as coal scuttles, the one at his nan and grandad's, the one that still sits in a bucket by his grandad's back door, and dial telephones and houses with no phone at all, like Goldie's all the time they knew him, and Mark's for a good while too, no washing machine; spin dryers; no telly in the daytime or after midnight, black and white, turned on early to warm it up for your programme; copying machines that you got asked to wind the handle of if you were a good boy in class, the print a fading purple; the half-time scores being put up on an old wooden scoreboard under the East Stand, letters of the alphabet that correspond to the day's fixtures; the man in the coracle to fish out any balls that went in the river, and what was his name?

The smell of piss and the sheen of the tiles in the outside toilets; clean, evenly hung net curtains as a sign of something, what?, important to your mum, your position in the world; changes of shift and the men coming up or down the valley like a tide, lines of cars in the rain, a procession huddled along the pavements; seeing Concorde at the air show, a flickering white splinter through the clouds.

They are locked in his head, these last things.

There's the shape of Mark Fala as he sends a volley off the factory wall, then another, then another, always the same poised follow-through, dead still for an instant, like Zidane when he hit that volley at Hampden, like a kid exaggerating a footballer's movements, someone taking the piss, but then you see his face and you know he's for real, the real thing, and the ball hits the same spot time and again. Dee Dee pushing her hair from her face, kneeling over him in that single-bed with the tight white sheets on the top floor of the pub. Sonia, not looking at him, looking at the road, sunshine, then shadow from the trees, then sun again, goading him he tells himself, they shouldn't even be in the car together, have already gone too far.

'I don't believe you want to Liam, I think you're all talk, full of it.'

Last, last things.

. . .

Hengist said he'd bring peace but Hengist brought war. But first he brought his daughter, the most beautiful woman on the island since Elstridis was drowned. Vortigern, the new king, saw her and wanted her, believing in the power of kings.

'What will you offer for my daughter?' Hengist asked.

And Vortigern thought, and he bargained, but what he said and what he thought were different things.

'I will give you the island and everything in it,' is what Hengist heard.

And they burned Vortigern in his tower in the end.

. . .

Liam takes the page from one of the broadsheets that has been left open on the table he sits at for breakfast. Before looking at the paper, he watches the geese that waddle across the car park leaving a trail of green shit. Amir sends cleaners out to scrub the tarmac. The geese used to stay the other side of the water, but Liam reckons they've got scared by the foxes and whatever else is there in the ruins. They aren't stupid, he thinks to himself, as he concentrates on his egg and ignores the newspaper. He likes to watch them fly in formation from out of his window. If only his own back four could maintain some of their awareness of each other.

He doesn't like these newspapers, the accent they are written in, so that they make football sound like something that is theirs and not his own. Ours, theirs, he knew he sounded like his grandad, this reduction to us and them. He looks across to the Anvil Yards. The workers have disappeared. Us and them was how football worked, as well. But the workers have not disappeared, of course, just become invisible most of the time, because here come the cleaners with buckets of soapy water to scrub away the shit so the mobile phone salespeople and the like, workers themselves of course, but god knows how that was work, although more work than chasing a ball across a field maybe, have a nice clean car park to drive on to. One of the cleaners, a woman, older than the two young men with her, wearing a turban above her green uniform shoos the geese with a broom, doesn't speak. One of the geese spreads its wings, hisses, but its heart isn't in the fight and the geese file away towards the canal towpath. Liam knows this woman, nods to her in the foyer and the corridor, where she trails a small vehicle stacked with all sorts of cleaning materials behind her, more a headdress than a turban, and she nods back, doesn't speak. She is African, he supposes, realises that he could not guess one thing about her, what country she is from, who she has at home, how she ended up here. Silence, even in his own head.

He looks at a column on the right-hand side of the page, sees the same picture he'd seen at Tony's, cropped so you could see Luis's face as he runs in the heat in front of some half-built stadium.

A tug of war between Europe's top clubs is underway for football's next big thing. Luis Fonseca Andrade, who hails from Cape Verde but is yet to represent the Blue Sharks at senior level, and who was apparently plucked from the relative obscurity of the Sporting Lisbon B team at the start of the season to sparkle for the nomadic central Asian club Petrosat Tajik Star, plaything of the mysterious gas tycoon Yusuf Khan. Petrosat are not recognised by FIFA or any Asian football federation and any move clubs make for the player will be complicated by this, and by the thorny issue of third party ownership. The player's contracts are managed by Luisito Holdings, registered in the Cayman Islands with investors from three different continents, according to the company website.

None of this seems to be deterring scouts from the Premier League and La Liga heading for the central Asian states (Petrosat are trans-national, with no home ground, one of the many sticking points with FIFA) to watch the slight, tricky, left-footed number 10 (at least that is what he looks like in grainy internet footage) dubbed inevitably 'the new Messi'. If, indeed, the player is actually real. In the virtual world of football gaming, he is already priced in the hundred million euros bracket and yet, 'This player is a sprite, a ghost,' a Sporting Lisbon source suggested yesterday, intimating that a player called Luis Fonseca Andrade had never appeared for any of the club's teams.

As if the player's background and the stories swirling around him were not exotic enough, he began the season, playing in a hastily arranged friendly for League 2 Irontown at their historic Anvil Yards ground, or at least someone with that name did. If even some of the rumours are true, he might be starting next season at Old Trafford or Camp Nou, unless, of course, the player's existence is some sort of elaborate hoax.

The boy is real, that is all he can think. Imagine your whole existence being doubted. Liam thinks of the way he turned and hit the ball in the friendly, the way the boy moved across the defenders, not that any of the Irontown team were going to pick him out with a pass. The real thing, maybe. He pictures men leaving modest flats on the edge of iron towns the world over, and flying on planes to places they would never have believed existed, seekers of something, searching out boys to run through other men's dreams, men looking for lost sons. Maybe that is what he will do when he has finished playing. Wander the earth in search of the one, he thinks. He'll buy a ticket to Finland first.

His only training this morning is to be some stretching and a massage. Archie wants him fit for the weekend, wants him to stay fit, no question of whether he is in or out of the team now.

The woman sloshes soap suds across the tarmac, finishes the mopping. The two boys wait alongside her, and their lives he can well imagine, waiting for the early morning bus from Cowton or the Peng, their mums and grandads telling them they're lucky to have any job at all, and them hating it, hating it, scraping the shit left by other people's shoes, by fucking birds for god's sake, and thinking there must be something else than this, knowing other lads who don't work, fuck that, who get by. They drift back towards the building. They disappear into their headphones and computer games, dream of gold training shoes and Luis Fonseca Andrade. He is suddenly pleased that Jari is two thousand miles away, not here, far from here.

. . .

Because he was the eagle for a long time.

That run angled behind the fullback, the piece of a puzzle falling into place, and Eusébio knows what's going to happen before it does, but then so does everyone by that point, the crowd hoarse now, hushed from cheering the North Koreans into a three-nil lead, these men who've come from nowhere.

And now the English crowds cheer him.

He whips his whole body around the ball, through it, so he hits it across the keeper, right footed, into the far corner, but he knows twenty yards or so before he gets there what will happen.

He moves flat footed almost, this way and that, but those feet barely touch the ground, they kiss it and keep moving, that's the secret, part of it. Don't stay in the same place for too long.

. . .

Liam watches the hooded figure out of the window for a while. He or she – he thinks that the slight frame inside the baggy sweatshirt suggests a thin girl. Something also in her movements, graceful in spite of her clothing, careful, that a man or boy would surely do more clumsily or with more self-conscious bravado – reaches high up the fence panel balancing against a wet trunk and branch, turns the screwdriver methodically. She reaches up and grips the mesh and lifts the panel to drop it against the fence's lower half. She – he has convinced himself now and is already building the picture of a lonely girl living out her days somewhere in these last Anvil Yards streets, maybe a neighbour of Mark Fala himself – has a red scarf wrapped high up her face so just a strip of her eyes shows. He cannot see these from this distance. He remembers the phrase indeterminate ethnicity. There are some binoculars up at his mum and dad's. He should get them, get a chair here at the window, stay in his room.

She jumps inside the fence, a spray can bounces at her hip, attached to her with coiled plastic. She lets it swing as she walks alongside the railway track into the Anvil Yards, looks up and down the track. There will be no train now, for sure, only that long, rumbling goods train that comes through some time after midnight, carrying god knows what to where.

He sees now where she is headed. The bridge that spans the canal and train track at the Greenfield End is not one of Victorian iron. It is poured concrete, and a blank wall reflects in the still water. You might get a glimpse from the road. From the top deck of the buses that rattle past Dee Dee's front room you could get a good look. He feels the sensation of buses and lorries making the rooms above the pub rattle, wonders if he will ever see those rooms again.

She moves quickly, he does not know who she thinks will want to catch her, doesn't know that anyone will care, takes the paint from her hip. He wants a fresco. Diego Rivera in the Anvil Yards. He wants to see some picture emerge that makes him think, yes, of course, this is what it all means, for his life to be changed by this moment. Instead, he gets a quickly scrawled hieroglyph. The girl loses all grace and care in the act, reaches too high up the concrete.

Bobo.

Bobo, of course, perhaps that is what it all means. Tag names mean nothing very much, he knows that, refer only to themselves. I am here, he thinks again. The girl is finished already, has put the cap on the can's nozzle, returned it to her sweatshirt pocket, regained some sense of control. She hurries back along the track. He looks again at the way she moves, on tiptoe and alive, thinks she could've easily climbed the fence quicker than removing the panel. Maybe there is some ritual to it. It only

counts with a set of rusting screws to hold like worry beads as
you spray your imagined name. He wonders if the name has
come to her from Bobby Ahmed. He used to hate it if you ever
reminded him, even when he was still a young boy, missing teeth
that would still grow back, a shadow across his face that used to
seem comical, touching, then, 'Bobby, he would say. Me name's
Bobby.'

Before he went to Finland, Liam had a spell of watching midweek Celtic games, if there was no Irontown match, at the supporters club in Cowton. He wasn't a member but he'd been taken
up there in years gone past with Mark by Mark's dad, and they
recognised him on the door anyway. The big man who looked
after the place would nod to him and he'd follow the same ritual
each time he went, sit on his own with his pint of Guinness, off
to the side of the screen opposite the bar, on a plastic garden
chair, under the green curtains. Not so close to the electric fire
which they turned on full force on winter nights.

'Well up, Bobo.' The voices of the older men would come,
those still with Glaswegian accents, fifty years in the south most
of them, in their suit jackets with pullovers and ties underneath
in muted browns and greys and greens that their wives picked for
them from the stalls at the Lowtown Bull Ring.

Bobo Baldé was the Celtic centre back. Liam watched him,
admired him, knew there was something shared in their movements. He had a faint hope in those days – receding by the game
– that Celtic might come in for him. Not that he'd have said
no to anyone by that point, was desperate to get out, the club
in a shambles, could not really stomach making the break to go

down the road to Hereford or somewhere like it. You'd think it might feel strange in the old men's mouths, this name come from Guinea by way of Marseille, but it didn't at all. And when he skewed a pass that year, stuck it high into the crowd when the ball was on, Larsson somewhere up ahead and spinning into a channel, and this was a weakness in Baldé's game perhaps, and one Liam knew all too well, the old men would admonish him. 'Oh, Bobo,' and fill the syllables with daft affection, like for an errant grandson who knew no better and never would but would be loved always the same.

Liam loved that purred familiarity. He thought back then that it was what he heard himself on a Saturday. Maybe he did, back then.

'That's it, Liam, well up, Liam, go on, Liam, our kid, well in, son.'

When he lost concentration he could hear individual voices, 'Oh Liam, what yer done that for?' When he stuck it onto the roof of the East Stand, the Greenfield End gave an ironic cheer. Even in exasperation, there was a warmth that came through. Then that faded, or he listened in a different way, something, 'That is fucking shite, Corwen', 'How did this bloke get an England cap? Jesus!', the club on the slide again, 'You ain't fit to wear the shirt.' But he wanted to say that even when he played badly he was better than them. That was why they were paying money to watch him. He tried his best, he told himself, even when he didn't. They pay their money, they can say what they like, was what Ally Barr said, but Ally had already gone when Liam left for Finland, coaching in Dubai until they asked him back for a third spell when the club hit rock bottom. There was the year they had four managers, finished bottom of the league, relegated by Easter. Those last few matches, Liam tried to avoid the Main Stand touchline, would sprint as far away as he could to warm up, at least still get a few cheers from the Greenfield End, wouldn't cover his fullback on that side, funny that none of them noticed, these experts who thought they knew it all because they'd paid for a seat. It got bad. He gave them the V-sign late that season when he scored a consolation after they'd booed him, getting a real mauling against Rotherham. His mum stopped going some time that season, couldn't bear to hear it. 'I should think about coaching, Liam, think about what you'll do when you stop playing,' she'd said, dishing out some carrots one Sunday afternoon. Everyone was an expert.

'Finland?' she said. 'What's in Finland? Do they even play football?'

So he did it, he left. That was the hard part, made easier by the angry chorus at the end, the boos in his ears, like he could've done anything about it, saved the club, saved the towns on his own. They still sung Mark Fala's name. Still, today. They'd all had too much faith. It was the year Liam started to believe in the curse. And then he was out of there, free, told himself he was never coming back, and then what had he done?

Greta told him she wanted him out, no reason at all as far as he could see, a break she said, the same week as Ally Barr phoned him, asked him if he'd consider it. A whim, nothing more, she wanted him out, she wanted space, here was some space. 'I need you here, son,' Ally said and that was that. They all stood and clapped when he led them out that first day of the season, all sang his name. He felt vindicated, missed Greta and Jari, kidded himself they'd be with him soon, paced the rooms of his empty house.

. . .

Dee Dee lets the water rise so that the bubbles come up over the bath. Steam fills the room. She slips off her dressing gown and thinks of a lovely silk one that she will buy one day, that she could look for, mention to Alina for her birthday. The water is almost too hot to bear, just as she likes it, and she stretches out so the bubbles come up to her mouth almost, lets the back of her neck rest against the porcelain rim.

She closes her eyes and tries to think of good things, thinks of herself on a beach far from here, no one she knows within hundreds of miles, but her mind drifts towards it like it often does when she stops and tries to relax. She should have told Goldie when he was sat there stinking in the bar. Mali, they were thinking of calling the baby Mali for a while. Rearrange the letters, Goldie, she should've said. You work that out, although you were never the quickest on the uptake. You think about your knives and your anger and who that might be aimed at and you leave Alina alone because she's nothing to do with you, you think about that, you think about what that might mean.

What else might she have said to him? It could have killed him to hear it. All those years she'd been scared he'd come back and then when she saw him, she pitied him, she really did. She knows she'll see him again, come like Mark to the off sales hatch or like that morning to sit in the half-light with his knife in front of him, dressed in rags.

She thinks of Sonia's face, when she said it, when Dee Dee asked her about names.

'We're thinking of Mali,' she said, a kind of innocent look on her face, looking Dee Dee in the eye and smiling.

If she hadn't died, Dee Dee thinks, one of them might have killed her anyway. She shuts her eyes, pushes it all away from her. Too late to stir all this up now. Alina walks past the bathroom door humming something out of tune. She seems happy. Tyrone seems a nice lad. Dee Dee sits and feels the water slowly cool, senses her daughter as she moves through the upstairs rooms.

. . .

When Liam tries to buy the ticket his bank card is refused. There was a message at reception that he phone Amir urgently. He knows it's about the room bill, so he avoids him as best he can. If he asks him to leave he'll have to sleep back at his mum and dad's or ask if he can use Devon's spare room, something. He is not sleeping in his own house ever again. He pictures it full of cobwebs and rats, the thing crumbling into the hillside, which he knows cannot be true as his mum still goes to clean every week, and his dad had been round to look at the damp-proofing. Maybe he could give it to them, to one of his sisters, another grand gesture before he goes. If he goes.

There's a credit card in his wallet that he doesn't have the pin number for, a flight from Heathrow the day after the end of the season. It might take another day to get to the lake house without his own car, doesn't matter. He thinks of unshuttering the lake house, spiders' webs in there to be cleaned out, and the golden light off the lake, the sun through the trees.

This week Greta sent him a video of Jari singing, performing something he has learned at nursery. He looks older, taller, strange words tumbling from his mouth and Liam feels him against him, the boy in his arms from this distance. He tells himself he will get this all over with and be a better man.

He gets a taxi to the car yard, cannot think of a bus that goes anywhere near, feels like he is running out of people to give him lifts. Lionel's office is on the first floor above the showroom, there are cars parked in rows so that you can see them as you drive past. The giant cut-out, Liam twenty foot tall and arms folded, has disappeared since his driving ban. Liam wonders what Lionel has done with it, knows he won't try to find out, scared Lionel has burned him in a back field.

'That ban nearly finished, son? You in for another car.' Lionel sits behind his desk, half-looking at his computer screen. Someone is talking about interest payments in the adjacent office, Liam can hear tools clanking downstairs.

'Morning, Lionel,' he says. 'No, I'm off the road for a while yet.'

'I was gonna say you could have your gaffer's. He'd done a few miles in it, mind you.'

'Ex-gaffer.'

'Ex,' Lionel says, motions for Liam to sit down, then stands up himself, 'I'm surprised he brought that motor back. Gone to Portugal, has he?' and doesn't wait for a reply. 'I don't know, they go to these places, Portugal, Spain, wherever, in the sun, think it'll make them happy, solve their problems. Gracie keeps pestering me about a cruise, Barbados, Miami, Jesus. I say, it's fine, a bit of sun, but you've still got yourself with you, you don't leave yourself behind. All them problems am still the same in the sun. I told our Stan that. He had to leave, I know he did, but still, you can't escape your own self, kid.'

Liam thinks he might be pissed, has second thoughts about talking to him for a moment. He turns in the chair to where Lionel now stands at the window, looking out over the rows of cars, the green hills beyond, small white clouds at the rusted edge of the Iron Towns and a field of four-by-fours and glittering cars worth more than houses in the space below them. These cars were like the sun, he thought, it was still you sitting inside them, they carried you and all your problems with you.

'No, I haven't come about a car,' he says, straight in, he supposes, 'it's about Dee Dee, really. Goldie's come back, went to the pub.'

Lionel turns from the window, goes and shuts the door and then sits back down at his desk. He doesn't say anything for a while.

'You know, I thought it was strange when she asked for them cameras to be fitted,' he says, shakes his head and smiles, 'you know what Dee Dee's like, how stubborn she can be.'

Liam nods.

'When?'

'A good few weeks ago now. Christmas. I wasn't sure what to do. He phoned her a while back, last summer, told her he was coming, threatening, you know.'

'Ex-wives, ex-gaffers,' Lionel says, 'ex-brothers, ex-sons, daughters. I don't know. Any idea what he's up to, where he's staying?'

'He looked in a bad way,' Liam says, remembers he thought it best not to say he'd actually seen him. 'That's what Dee Dee told me, said he had a knife. Homeless, maybe, you know. I don't know if his mum still lives on the Peng or what.'

'She went years ago, son. Got together with a bloke I used to know. Things turned out all right for her. They went to live somewhere near Malaga, I think.' Lionel smiles at this.

'He wants to see Alina.'

'Of course he does, it's only natural, son. Man wants to see his children.' Lionel looks at Liam now, for the first time that morning it seems, Liam looks away, 'Wonder he never come back earlier, really. He knows where they are.'

'You told him you'd kill him.'

Lionel nods. 'We warned him, that's all. We thought that was for the best, give Dee Dee a bit of time and space. We thought of telling you we'd kill you if you didn't stay with her, look after the girl. Then we thought she might be better off without you.'

He says these words very quietly and Liam finds it hard to follow and there's a delay before the shock of what Lionel is saying to him registers, so he sits there and nods his head and feels the colour drain from his face. It strikes him later that Lionel might have been joking.

'Don't worry. I'll sort it,' Lionel says. Liam goes to speak and

Lionel puts his hand up to quieten him, rises from the desk at the same time, 'Don't worry any more about it. We'll smoke him out. The problem will go away.'

'Come on,' Lionel motions down the interior stairs, 'have a look at what you might get when your ban's finished.'

Outside, under the awning, a rainbow forms where they spray the cars clean. Liam sees a figure move quickly around a black jeep, all limbs like a spider, a cloth in each hand, with which he works on the metal. Something in the movement, the way the boy, the man, turns on the balls of his feet makes Liam pause. It's Bobby.

'How's he doing?' Liam says, tries to disguise the shock of seeing him here.

'He's OK. I've got him working down here now, as you can see. I can keep my eye on him. He's doing OK.'

Liam raises his hand to the figure through the window. Bobby moves gracefully with long strides between the cars, stops to peer through the water-splashed glass, grins when he sees Liam, looks like the kid he once was, puts his thumb up to him.

'He's doing OK,' Lionel says again and motions with his head towards the showroom floor. It is quiet. Liam looks at his own reflection in the shiny machines, cars to drive away from everyone he has ever known, to drive past ruins, through hedgerows, to park up in quiet clearings, to drive into the waters of shallow rivers.

.   .   .

Hampden Park, again, April 1956, one hundred and thirty-three thousand people there, Scotland winning until the very last minute. Big Duncan Edwards never gives in. See him now, driving up the pitch out of his own half with the ball at his feet and his head up, looking at Johnny Haynes, as if he is operating in a different time and space to everyone else, as if he has all afternoon, and then he strikes the ball and Haynes is in, and he strokes the ball into the corner and England have equalised. The goal means all four countries share the Home Nations trophy – an unusual enough event – but that is not really the point. When the ball goes in, Duncan gives a little skip, might look strange on a big man, but is the kind of foot movement you see with great boxers, like a kind of Ali shuffle, so balanced and alive, he is a great dancer in fact, and now comes a clenched fist. Sometimes we get the faintest glimmer of who we might truly be.

. . .

'But what is it, all this stuff?'

It's a map, is what Alina wants to say to him, a map of the Anvil Yards and of her own life. She has not thought about it in this way before, but Tyrone is the first person who has asked her what she is doing here. No one has ever known what she is doing before other than a few scraps of film she has put on the internet, a few photos of the huge Greenfield mills with tree branches coming through the roofs and the sun on the gravestones on the far hill in the distance, comments from a lonely girl in Gary, Indiana, from a Japanese man who sent details of the Nowa Huta steelworks in Kraków and posted photos of the workers' broad, sad faces at shift-change, an industrial glow in the sky beyond endless chimneys and blocks of flats, and she was flattered to get any kind of reaction at all but she knew that it was not the places themselves that she wanted to capture. It wasn't about sunsets, it wasn't even about steelworks, not for her, not really.

It was a map, of that she is now convinced. That was why the rope had been important to her. The thread had been something with which to find your way through the labyrinth, to wind yourself up towards the light, to escape the monster. The rope had gone nowhere very fast, another failed piece of work, but it had led her to Tyrone. It was good to feel these separate pieces – the photos of graves and empty buildings, the names she'd tagged on crumbling walls to be glimpsed from passing cars, Bobo and Goldie and Sonia, the artefacts of rusted chain, the apple blossom that blew through giant empty buildings and that no one saw – as part of a whole piece of work, a body, her body. Maybe the work was her own life. The rope had led her to Tyrone, had not had to go anywhere else.

Her own life and everyone else's, and the map spiralled out of the Anvil Yards and out across the Heath and up the hillsides because there was the turn in the road where the car skidded off and there is the river, not even a river, not really, a culvert with steep concrete sides and there is the car within it, there is the dockside where her great-grandad, not really her great-grandad at all, hauled boxes from barges and dreamed of the Bay of Bengal, here are the lanes that pattern the valleys like spiders' webs and maybe give rise to those stories, and here the rows of empty terraces where the people have gone, and tunnels that wind through the hills, and here is the tent of a homeless man, she guesses, empty pill bottles and drink cans scattered around on the banks of the canal, on the land where the navvies pitched their tents in the mud to cut channels between the rivers. And there are the graves and the ash, marked like her mum's, and unmarked like the cholera pits and the body-shaped hollows where the men drank themselves stupid at the Quakers for want of anything else to do and no one seemed to care. And there are the lives, she thought, there are the lives. It is a map of her own life and of innumerable others, to show her the way, to show her who she is.

'It's a kind of map,' she says, takes a deep breath.

. . .

A couple of postponements and the cup matches, which feel a long time in the past now, mean they have three games in hand. Trouble with this kind of thing is that you have to win them. They are bottom of the league now, games running out, games coming twice a week, with a back four with a combined age of one hundred and thirty-four and when did you ever hear anything given as a combined age, when and where in life would that ever be useful? But that is what the *Chronicle* write about the Irontown defence, like they've even got anybody else to stick in there really, and Liam clips the line out of the paper and puts it in his boot bag to use as a kind of charm, a curse. He is going to play for ever.

But what Liam knows is that he has not played two games a week like this for years, he can barely move now, on the pitch or off, but here he is tonight, under the floodlights, heading everything that comes near him. They defend deep, deep, deep, hanging on for a point, the clock ticking down, ticking down, a point takes them off the bottom and that's a start. Archie has not won a match in charge yet and spring is here. You can feel it in the blood-warm earth beneath the pitch. No one has been paid. Supporters' club members collect change in buckets outside the turnstiles in order to pay for the electricity for the floodlights.

Last minute, a nothing ball towards the box and they get a shout of 'Keeper's ball,' that echoes up the empty East Stand. This is their seventh goalkeeper of the season, must be some kind of record. They can't get any more, have been banned from loan deals by the league because they can't pay anybody anything, administration beckons, a points deduction and then it will be all over. Tommy Starr this lad's name is.

'Fuckin' Freddie Starr, more like,' a voice comes to Joey, who sits biting his nails in the stand.

But he's kept a clean sheet tonight and they're heading off the bottom except now, as Tommy shouts, he realises he's misjudged it, is underneath it, and the ball goes over his outstretched hands, and all in one go, Liam has realised this too, and this man who can barely move, who has headed every ball that has come into the box that night is getting back, getting back, stretching, and he gets his toe to the ball just as it hits the sandy goalmouth, as it is about to bounce inside the post, and is able to flick it wide and continues his run full into the post itself and the whole goal frame shakes and he lies crumpled on the floor.

Liam stays down even though he is not hurt, thinks he can

probably eke this out to run down the clock, realises they will still have to defend the corner, so may as well have a breather. He could go to sleep right here curled around the post. Devon has his hand on his shoulder.

'You all right, skipper? Stay down, stay down if you're hurt,' all in one breath. 'Give him some space, eh?' Devon says above him. They are clapping, proper applause, people on their feet, even in the stand.

If Irontown do go down, it will not be through lack of effort on the part of Liam Corwen. He has been a colossus tonight . . . goes Dave Willis's radio voice across the warm night.

'I bet Archie enjoyed that,' Les Martin taps Joey on the shoulder, and Joey nods, but doesn't take his eyes of Liam, not able to tell if he is really hurt, the goal frame is still wobbling, something in Joey's chest and stomach tightens as he claps his hands louder, they should carry him off on a shield, his son, the way he's playing for them, what he's doing, keeping them up with the strength of his will. Another hand thumps Joey on the back from behind. Devon puts his thumbs up to the Greenfield End to signal Liam is OK. They sing *One Liam Corwen, there's only one Liam Corwen* and then *Irontowns, Irontowns, Irontowns.*

But Archie Hill has not enjoyed tonight one bit. In fact Archie did not even see this clearance, there are men wearing luminous jackets running with a stretcher down the touchline, Tyrone running from the other direction with the defibrillator that he prays to God they don't ask him to use, because Archie is lying on his back with the soles of his shoes facing towards the pitch and his heart has stopped.

On the way to the camp Steve Bloomer remembers another train ride years before, how they had changed stations in Birmingham with all their things in a hand cart. Had he really ridden on board like a visiting maharajah?

They had been nailers, his family. Across the river in Cradley Heath they made chain. They'd moved up to Dudley, his mum and dad, come back for his dad to work in the foundry, a puddler. It was a steep hill in the mud and the houses ran in, were falling down.

In Derby the houses were new and the factories lined the railway lines and gleamed in the sun. There was always the sound of metal and the beautiful arc of a ball, these two certainties.

The men work hard to improve the conditions in which they are kept. The winter mud, the threat of dysentery is kept at bay, they sleep in the dry, rooms more sound, perhaps, drier certainly, than the houses they'd flitted from all those years ago, houses that sagged with the water. They organise themselves. They play football, cricket all through the summer to the bemusement of the Germans, write the scores in heavy ledgers.

All his life he's been around hard men, tough men, in Cradley and Derby and Middlesbrough, and now here in Ruhleben, in Spandau. He moves between them. Run into the spaces between them and someone will pass the ball there. There are things that are more simple than they appear.

The war goes on and on, sun and rain and snow. They play

whole league seasons, test matches. He scores a double hundred one afternoon. His eye is good, has never left him. Often it's best to sit and watch and wait, he thinks, move through the gaps when you can.

.   .   .

They got him going on the side of the pitch. They said his heart was stopped and they brought him back to life. He lies with his head on the pillow now with his pyjama top open and pads with wires coming from them stuck onto his chest, a big man with grey skin. Liam watches his body rise and fall gently as they talk, like it will stop if Liam loses concentration.

Just a few minutes, is what the nurses said. It's family visiting only in this hot private room off the ward. Archie's wife, Anne, had gripped Liam's hand at the door when they came in. He heard her say to his dad that she told Archie not to take the job on, let someone else do it, he'd done enough for them over the years, a few weeks in charge and it had almost killed him.

Liam is wearing his club blazer in case there are any photographers about. The crest catches his eye as he moves his arm. He tells Archie that Steve Stringer called him in this morning, after he and Devon had taken training. That he is in charge for these last few games. Tells Archie not to worry, that his job is to get better, to rest. Archie tries to nod his head from the pillow. He's in a bad way.

Liam waited for Archie's autograph once, as a kid, by the Players' Entrance in the rain. Archie was wearing his club blazer, his hair was slicked in a side parting. Liam had never stood next to such a big man, a strong man. Where they sat, the crowd would groan when Archie put a clearance over the stand, the Greenfield End cheered, Liam loved it. He told Archie he played at the back, just like him,

'Remember,' Archie said, as he signed his looping autograph, 'just keep things simple back there. That's the most important thing, the first thing you need to do.'

He still said it sometimes. It was the last thing he'd said before he sent them out the other night.

Keeping things simple is easier said than done, that's for sure, Liam thinks, sighs.

He holds Archie's hand, is surprised by how soft it is. His dad stands behind him, puts his hand on his shoulder, which is his signal that's it's time.

'All right, Archie,' Joey says, 'you take it easy.'

Liam keeps hold of his hand as he gets up from the plastic chair. He can feel his hip, his thigh, there's a bruise that's spread up his leg from where he crashed into the post, from Socrates all the way up to Yashin. He doesn't think he'll be able to play on Saturday. He tries not to limp in the hospital, thinks it looks like he's taking the piss.

'He's in a bad way, Dad, eh?'

'He didn't look very well, son, no.'

They are barely speaking, him and his dad, they sit in the car with the radio on while his dad drives him around. He asks Devon to drive him when he can, gets on the bus, the tram, the drivers and conductors nod to him, ask him when results will improve. He wants to avoid talking to them about Archie, about the side he is going to pick now he's in charge. His mum has barely said a word to him since Christmas.

They parked on the far car park, the one near the old Bethel, which was the workhouse and is now the psychiatric hospital. He sees that lad Tyrone coming down the path, an old woman bent over a walking frame with him. Tyrone the hero, Liam thinks, probably does hospital visiting in his spare time, he got that thing on Archie's chest with the St John's ambulance people, saved his life, everyone said.

Tyrone has the woman's arm and she has both hands on the frame, stares at the path. A blackbird flits past. They can hear the traffic on the flyover.

'Come on, Mum,' he hears Tyrone say, 'you're doing really well.'

He is aware that they have slowed their pace to look at the woman attempt an incline, not get anywhere very far, 'You're doing great,' they hear him say.

At the car his dad asks him if he fancies a pint and he nearly says no, I've got a team to pick, but says, 'Yeah, that would be nice,' and they talk about that time they played Liverpool in the League Cup and Ian Rush kept fouling big Archie, clipping his heels, when the midfield slipped the ball through. Archie got more and more angry but couldn't get anywhere near Rush or Dalglish.

Liam goes back to their house for his tea, asks his dad to pull in so he can pick up some flowers from the Lowtown Bull Ring on the way, tries not to look at the back of the *Chronicle* while they eat. They have printed a kind of doomsday clock above the Anvil Yards, set at five to midnight.

. . .

He moves like a breaking wave, a sense of deep power locked within. Eusébio is broader now, at twenty-six, stronger. Bang the ball in at his chest, his back to goal, and watch him hold the defenders at bay.

He receives the ball in space, side-on to goal, and the couple of strides he takes give him the start he needs. Nobby Stiles hurtles at him, as he does all night, as he had done two years before in the World Cup, a fierce little dog yapping at the tide, but this time Eusébio is gone. He strides past him, over him, lengthening his stride with the ball, until he slows for an instant. Sadler backpedals and keeps going, skittering, as Eusébio pauses. Space opens out around him, even as the United players converge. He looks up, strikes it. The bones of his foot which whip through the ball are called the cuboid, the lateral cuneiform, the metatarsals. They will one day become relics. The ball veers and rises and crashes down and back off the crossbar. Béla Guttmann's curse and the ghosts of Munich fall like dew on the Wembley night.

His free-kicks come back off the United wall, Stiles clatters his ankles again and again. When he glides through the United defence he can't quite get purchase on a left-foot shot on the run. And then the ball falls into his path and he thumps it, the soles of both feet off the ground, and Stepney, the United keeper, clutches it to his chest in mid-air. Eusébio stands and looks and applauds. Then George Best cuts through the Benfica lines, like an elf skipping between summer foxgloves. Eusébio feels heavier. Tides come in and they go out. Time moves one way.

. . .

He sees the news on the ticker on Sports 24, the channel he now leaves on permanently in the room with the sound down low even when he is sleeping. It helps him sleep in fact, the shadows the images make on the wall and the low murmur of voices. He sometimes turns over in the middle of the night to see pictures of luge tobogganing and cliff diving and ultra-distance marathons through a desert somewhere. His body aches and his eyes close.

Real Madrid confirm the signing of Luis Fonseca Andrade from Petrosat Tajik Star for an undisclosed fee. Move to be completed at the end of the season.

He jumps to his feet and laughs, paces up and down the room. He phones Devon but it goes straight to voicemail, starts to blabber on about it, feels embarrassed, not even sure he should be phoning him and talking like this now he's the gaffer, although Devon is his mate, his number two now. 'Real Madrid,' he says, 'just you think about that.'

And with the news they play a clip that someone must have sent in from the dust bowl in the summer, filmed on a phone from the back of the stand, he thinks he can even make out the shape of his dad's head, Liam's hacked clearance wobbles through the air and Luis takes it on his thigh and spins and hits it off the outside of the post and into the hoardings and you see a few people's heads cock like when you try to decide if a car is backfiring or the shooting has begun.

He sits on the edge of the bed. He's got players' names written on a cut-up cereal packet, a tea tray that represents the pitch.

It will be very, very simple. Move Kyran inside and play him off Julius. Hit balls in to Julius and hope it sticks, hit passes into Kyran's feet and let him run at people. If it doesn't work, he can push him out wide again. If it doesn't work he can yank Julius off, stick Shaunie McLaughlin up front to clatter people. Keep it simple, like Archie said. These people have all played with Real Madrid's latest signing. He laughs to himself, the world is beyond all reasoning.

. . .

The Arms Park, 16 March 1896. Billy Meredith looks on from the wing, cannot get the ball, has not touched it, there's an hour gone and not a mark on his kit. To think they fancied their chances in this one, had given Ireland a lesson at the Racecourse Ground. It just shows you how long you get to stay on your perch. He watches the pale arrow on the other side, this young lad Bloomer score one goal after the other. He can't understand why Charlie Parry doesn't kick him, maybe because he just can't get near him, he's like smoke, like a ghost. Nine now, is it? The kid has scored five, half a dozen maybe. Billy thinks the ref blows early, puts them out of their misery.

. . .

Ally looks at the sea below as the taxi climbs the mountainside, up, up out of the city. He's been to the Ronaldo museum to kill some time, enjoyed the photos, enjoyed the chutzpah of a man who opens a museum of himself, wonders idly what he'd put in his own. Ally thinks of what George Best said about Ronaldo, about the passing on of a flame, cannot think for a moment how much he would have seen of him before he died. Ally had been at the funeral, never such a well of emotion had he seen, such love. They said Ronaldo's daddy had been a drinker too. A drinker and a dreamer no doubt, Ally thinks, can afford to let his thoughts drift, to be sentimental. He can afford most things now, of course. He touches the paper of the contracts in the briefcase, his percentage from Luis, money from the Tajiks, from Madrid, all those years of watching and waiting for some kind of break like this. He is a man behind the men now, looks down at the breaking waves through his dark glasses, enjoys the feel of wearing a suit in the hot sun, business to attend to. He thinks of running across cinders in the Finnieston gloom.

Dorothea spends her afternoons on the nursing home terrace, a mirador that overlooks the cliffs. There are ships out on the water that she can't see. Her head lolls over to one side, ninety-nine years old and counting. Her mother's second husband owned a wine exporters, a last crumbling vestige of empire, that's how she ended up here. She was the last baby born at the Greenfield Estate by the Heath. The big house burned down after an air raid late in the war, but everyone always said it had been done for the insurance. They had run out of money even then. Her lawyer and a nurse sit with her in the shade. They all drink lemonade and then a glass of the wine.

She doesn't speak, just nods as they complete the formalities, she signs with a faint spider's leg crawl. Ally has bought plenty of players before but never a whole club. Not that he's really buying this one. She's pretty much giving it him to pass on the debt. But the debt will disappear with the money promised in the briefcase and Iron Towns – he's putting back the s, that's first on the agenda – will rise again, from wherever they find themselves.

'To the Iron Towns,' he says as he raises his glass, sips the warming liquid in the hot afternoon. 'There is one question I have for Dorothea,' he says to the lawyer, a young man with his hair slicked back, he's been warned not to fluster her, to just get the deed done. The lawyer looks not unlike Ronaldo himself, the boy from down the mountain.

'What is it?'

'Why she never sold before. Could maybe have got big money. Was it her love of the club?'

Her voice comes strong out of her tiny frame. Up until now, he has not thought she was entirely with it, assumed the lawyer was offloading the club now for tax reasons.

'No one ever asked, all these years,' she says, and she laughs a hacking laugh, and they all join in. Ally shakes his head, all the stories of the Greenfields' legendary stubbornness, theories of why they wouldn't sell. Money talks, people said. No one even offered. He wonders if she is joking. She raises her hand. The nurse leans forward, sensing something wrong, but the voice goes on.

'No, I lie,' she says, 'Lionel Ahmed asked once, after he forced his brother out. I told him I wouldn't sell to a crook.' And she laughs again and they all join in and Ally turns his face to the sun.

·   ·   ·

At full-time they turn to each other to check the scores from Torquay and Northampton and Bristol Rovers and Wycombe. They have been terrible again, another three-nothing, the crowd too tired to even boo them off. There are hurried conversations and confirmations about the results elsewhere. Still third from bottom, win on Saturday and they still stay up.

'There must be some bad teams in this league if we're still in with a shout,' Les Martin says as the players trudge off. Liam stands at the side of the pitch and applauds the Greenfield End even though there are fingers that jab out of the crowd towards him, some others clapping, fans arguing among themselves.

'We can do it,' Joey mutters, although as he says it, he knows he doesn't believe it.

'Fucked anyway, because of the money. It's been nice knowing you, Joey, eh? Cowton Sports for us next year.'

Les taps his arm.

He thinks the bloke is honestly trying to be nice.

. . .

Dave 'Iron' Willis: Liam, you still believe?

Liam Corwen: A thousand per cent. I opened that dressing-room door and said anyone who doesn't think we can do it should walk through it, go home now. No one did. I'll say the same to the supporters, don't bother next week if you can't get behind us.

He had done nothing of the sort, of course, he'd got back through the door from the ref's office to help Devon pull Tommy Starr off Shaunie McLaughlin. Afterwards, Devon told him he was worried that Tommy would break his hands on Shaunie's head. They haven't got another keeper. He says otherwise he'd have left him to it.

. . .

People are queueing all the way down Chain Street. They did the same for the United match that never came, and here they are again. Steve Stringer himself is at the booth, as they've got no one else in the office to sell tickets any more. Liam gets out of Devon's car and the others follow. This is his idea, the first, the only one he's had in the couple of weeks he's been in charge. Well, that and playing Kyran inside and further forward, and the kid has barely had a kick.

'Thanks for coming down here,' he says to an old bloke five or six places back in the line.

'I want me head examined,' is all the man says but Liam smiles and holds out his hand to shake and he nods to Devon and the others all do the same. A kid in school uniform wants his picture taken with Kyran, there are all manner of things being brought out for them to autograph. He should've phoned Dave Willis, told him what they were doing, dismissed that as too cynical, realises right now that there is no such thing.

'Will you sign this Liam,' he looks up to see Fraser Parks from the fanzine, the young lad who looks fifty if he's a day, hold out a photo of the '93 side, sees his own younger self looking out from the picture, sees Mark standing there next to him, looking nervous just for a team photograph. 'It's not for me,' he says, 'it's to raffle for the children's ward at the Bethel.' That's right, Liam thinks, he does the hospital radio, as well, this lad. Saints, all of them.

'Could do with some of them players on Saturday,' is what Liam says.

'Think we'll do it, Liam?' he asks.

'Course we will,' he says, and he can see in the lad's eyes that he really wants to know, that he really wants it to be true, standing here, selling his home-made magazines with it threatening rain on a Tuesday morning when he should be at work, if he had any work to get to.

'That's great,' he says, 'that's great.'

And maybe it's the tiredness, or the way he says this, like Liam has got any more idea than him of how things will turn out, or the way the line straggles along the broken pavement, mobility scooters and walking sticks and kids bunking school and blokes who look like his dad, his granddad, among them, that makes something shift inside him. Some reversal he thinks. All his life he's had it the other way round, but it's they who are the saints, this ragged line, and those like it, past, present, future.

It is the players who are the pilgrims.

.   .   .

'What do you mean, a different direction? What does that even mean?'

They sit in Tony's studio and look at the brick walls of the yard outside. They sit side by side at the desk for lack of space but also to look at Tony's sketchbook. Liam looks at Tony's reflection in the glass, Tony's face turned towards his.

'How do you want me to talk about it?' Liam says. 'I want to think about what we're heading towards, about how this will finish.'

'What do you mean, finish? There's loads to do yet, you've said yourself. Groups, we talked about. Are we still going more for groups? That's what I want to know.'

There are sketches of the Lisbon Lions, Billy McNeill on a white wall holding the cup aloft, of Brazilians, Pelé stroking the ball into Carlos Alberto's path, of Romáro and Bebeto rocking the baby. There are team photos clipped from old magazines. For months Tony has been looking at groupings, of teammates. This is the work's new phase. They have gone down different routes before, a whole season with Tony sketching famous stadiums only for them to decide it was figures, people they wanted all along.

'Football is a team game. We need to show people together, with their mates,' is what Liam says to him, a change of direction from the big portraits they'd started with, but now he'd thought one step further, about where this was headed. They had never talked about an ending before.

'This is a group,' Liam gestures to the scrap of paper in front of him, pen in hand. 'It's one big group. This is the whole point of it, Tone. Do you get it? It's what we've been working towards.'

'This is a mess.'

'The crowd, the people.'

'I ain't fucking Lowry. What do we want with all these stick men?'

Liam wishes he hadn't tried to draw it. Jari could do better with those giant crayons Greta let him scribble on the floor with. He wanted crowds, the people. He wanted the great crowd to cover the rest of his body, so the players were subsumed into the mass, so they disappeared, so he disappeared too.

'The crowd are what makes them who they are. Don't you see it?'

'I see it, but this is too clever for its own good. It looks shit.'

'Without the crowd they ain't nobody. With no one looking. Football is the people's game.'

'What happened to Pirlo? I've been drawing his fucking miserable face all winter.'

Liam is glad of a bit of levity. Tony doesn't really think he is serious, that's why he's smiling now.

'Pirlo's still playing. He's gonna go on and on like Stanley Matthews. He's missed the boat. There's a cut-off date. They can't still be playing after I finish.'

Tony takes a sip of his green tea and Liam continues talking to the reflection in the window, 'It's an idea, Tone, I want you to think about it. I want it to end when I stop playing, I want it to be complete.'

'It would be like rubbing it out. Years of work, years to come.'

'Just think about it. OK?' Liam pushes his chair back, exhausted suddenly. He honestly thought Tony would think it a good idea. He doesn't even like football, for god's sake. He stands up and looks to go. Tony is still sitting, looking at the sketchbooks laid out on the desk, shaking his head.

'I think this is your problem, Liam, you never see things through.'

'What's that meant to mean? I'm talking about seeing it through, this is seeing it through, this is an idea for an ending.'

He wants to get out of this small room now, does not know why he has even brought this up, thought this visit would be a nice distraction from trying to pick a team for Saturday.

'I just don't think you've got the bottle to stick with things,' Tony says, his back to Liam now, and the way his face appears in the glass, the way he says this, Liam thinks of Dee Dee, some family resemblance, the kind of thing she said to him when she decided to take on Alina.

'You never see anything through, just leave people to pick up after you.'

This was not true. He'd given the biggest part of twenty years to Irontown, he'd come back here for god's sake, stuck by Ally, the club. It wasn't him who left Dee Dee, not really, she chose the girl, he hadn't left Greta and Jari.

'You get too far into things and then get scared and want to pack them in and leave other people to deal with it.'

'Fucking hell, Tone, I'm going, mate. It's only a few pictures. And they'm my tattoos. Jesus.' He clenches and unclenches his fist. There were times when he'd have gone for him. Picked him up by the throat and had him up against the wall. He wishes he'd never mentioned the crowd. It was a great idea, though, how the players would disappear back into the crowd from which they came, it was beautiful, it was what he was going to do at the end of the season, become invisible, start afresh, again. He knows deep down that Tony has a point. It isn't even Tony speaking, Liam thinks, not really. It's Dee Dee.

He turns and moves into the front of the shop. He expects Tony to follow him or say something else but there's nothing. The bell rattles as he opens the door, surprisingly bright outside after the gloom of the studio and the yard. It occurs to him that this might be the end. They can stay on his body as they are, men running through the world, through other men's heads.

. . .

The body of a man found near the Quaker Burial Grounds Burnt Village, has been identified as that of Stephen Williams, 37, of no fixed address. Mr Williams came from a well-known Oxton family and his death has shocked the community.

His sister, Anne Fraser, 33, also of Oxton, told the Chronicle *'This has been the hardest week of my family's lives. We are all devastated. Stevie was a great brother and son. He battled with drink and depression for many years so maybe he is at some sort of peace now but I can't believe we won't see his face again.'*

Iron Town council have received numerous complaints about street drinking and antisocial behaviour in the Quaker Burial Ground area.

'They come up here, sitting around all day and making a nuisance for decent people,' said a local resident who did not wish to be named. 'I've seen a man using a neighbour's front garden as a toilet in the middle of the day. If you say anything you just get abuse. Nothing gets done.'

West Mercia police issued a statement yesterday to the effect that Mr Williams's death was not suspicious, although an inquest will be heard at a date yet to be fixed. It is assumed he died of an alcohol related illness.

Tributes to the dead man have been left along the north wall of the Burial Ground, these include flowers, cards and bottles.

Liz has one last glance at the paper and steps out into the sunshine, Joey is in the car, already looking at his watch again, sighing. He'll have to wait. She knew the Williams family when she was growing up, the Prentices too, the boy's mother, Maggie Prentice as she was, grew up on Red Lion Street, near where the pie shop was on the way to the Bull Ring. Liz had been born on Silver Street. It was named for the brook that ran behind the houses, under some of them, and out into the Chain, right near the bottom end of Lowtown. They'd knocked most of the houses down in the sixties, moved the families out to Cowton and Oxton. The water would rise into the houses in bad weather, in the summer everything smelled of mud and they were rotten with damp. She remembers being sent to peg the washing out as a girl and the mud squeezing up between her toes, being scared of the frogs that lived along the bank and that her brothers used to torture. The smells that came from the factories settled there in the valley, sank into your clothes. People look into the past one-eyed, she thinks, only remember the good parts. She is glad they've torn the place down. At the Heritage Museum they rebuilt one of the terraces, *industrial age slum dwelling, typical of those through Lowtown and the Anvil Yards and still inhabited into the late 1960s*, she'd read on the information card, was shocked to see the word slum at first, her mother kept their curtains nice, the place as spotless as she could, but later thought, why not call it what it was?

She used to look at the hills, at the estates laid out halfway up and the leaded bay windows of Salop and Calon and think that was where she was headed, Maggie Prentice as well, she knew. They kept their ankle socks as white as they could, out of the mud, dreamed of net curtains and broad avenues. And that was what she got, after a fashion. Her dreams had come true. They'd done OK and she'd been lucky with Joey and the girls. And Liam, well, Liam was Liam, was all she'd begun to think now. Tell a boy, a man, how good he is at something, all stand round and clap him on, and watch what happens. He always thought he could do anything, he didn't need grown men egging him on.

Still, she wasn't Maggie Prentice, sitting there in Oxton still, in a house every bit as dilapidated as the kind they grew up in, just in a different way, grieving her lost boy. She remembers seeing her once in the street with a boy who must have been Stephen alongside her, gap-toothed and laughing and helping her with her shopping bags up the hill. She remembered thinking even then that she'd have her work cut out to get Liam to do that, the girls maybe, said as much to Maggie, gave Stephen some change for an ice-cream. There are many ways of being poor, she thinks, has never quite shaken it off, has never got quite far enough up the hill.

She will do a card for Maggie, she thinks, look for when the funeral is, although doubts she'll go, has always wanted to keep her distance, not get dragged back, which is how she's come to think about the football. She hopes they lose and get put out of their misery and she is only going because Eli passed up his ticket, he has not seen them win in the flesh this season and thinks himself a Jonah and so will listen to it on the radio instead as some kind of sacrifice. These boys with their rituals and magic spells. She wishes they would all grow up.

The weather today would suit a wedding better than a funeral, and she guesses that someone will be getting married somewhere today, blossom in the air like confetti, that not everything is concentrated on the Anvil Yards, and she silently wishes them well, while Joey glares at his watch and sighs again and, she can see, wants to sound the horn at her but considers that might make her go even more slowly. There is all the time in the world.

. . .

Cadwallader looks back across the wave-tops, sees the white cliffs fade in the sea spray, sighs. The island is undone, emptied with war and plague and famine. The hills are full of skulls, the rivers run with blood.

Voices come on the wind, faint across the sound of the sea and between the boat's creaking. They say that none of them are dead, not one, that they will come again, from their caves and wooded valleys, that they will take new forms.

. . .

Ally sits in the car for a few seconds before he turns off the engine, the paint that says 'Owner' on the wall above the space has faded so it's almost just a memory. He considers the gateman's wide eyes when he wound the window down, takes a deep breath, reaches into the back for his suit jacket and opens the door.

'Who's parked there?' Steve Stringer asks from his perch high up the stand. 'You know to keep that clear. You can never tell, today might be the day someone turns up.'

In the room along the corridor, the directors and dignitaries, even the mayor is here in a great gold chain, munch on sandwiches and sip their drinks, like the Heath golf club has relocated for the afternoon for the funeral of an old acquaintance they'd all thought had gone years ago.

There's the crackle of a walkie-talkie, words he can't hear. There's a voice behind him that says, 'You're not going to like this, but listen . . .'

. . .

Watching from where they sit is not made any easier by looking at the Morecambe fans dressed as red-and-white shrimps or wearing great sun hats and generally laughing and enjoying themselves no end, beach balls bobbing away above the Chain terracing, nothing to play for, an end of season fancy-dress party with the added bonus of being a part of football history, the last club to play at the Anvil Yards. There were fans swapping scarves outside the Chain End when they came past. They start to sing *We'll meet again*, which Joey thinks is unlikely. The only thing he can hope is that the Morecambe players are already on holiday as well, but he knows things never work like that. They'll probably play like world-beaters.

He keeps his eyes fixed on Liam, who he swears is hiding a limp, and groans inside as he calls the players into a huddle in front of the Greenfield End. These things just look daft. It's noisy, a breeze comes over the East Stand. Liz puts her hand on his.

When the ref whistles Liam sends Devon up for the toss while he speaks to Tommy Starr, holding the keeper's head in his hands, looking him in the eye. He's probably scaring the kid half to death, Joey thinks, just leave him be.

The noise builds, and he needs the toilet but tries not to move, doesn't want Liz have to get up, nods to Les Martin who leans across after he's made a show of giving Liz a kiss and grins and says, 'Thought you'd decided to give it a miss,' and Joey can't even raise a smile.

'Hey,' Les says now, 'have you seen who's here?' and he nods his head over the directors' box barrier.

Joey glances, aware they are about to kick-off and feeling that if he keeps his eyes on Liam then nothing will go wrong, and sees the glint of the chain and assumes Les means the mayor. The box is full for the first time this season, in years, Joey reckons, all come to put the last nail in the coffin.

That's when he sees Ally, sitting there in his blue suit and dark glasses, relaxed as can be. He swears he's got a toothpick in the corner of his mouth.

'He's got some nerve,' is what he says, drowned by the anxious high-pitched keening that greets the kick-off, too nervous, if you ask Joey, that will transmit to the players and whatever happened to the Irontown roar? That was deeper, came from the depths, and they said sounded like a furnace when a door is opened onto it. This was fear. It was what they'd sounded like for years, all of them, Joey thinks, but they all had reasons to be afraid and the fires were all out long ago.

Morecambe play a ball over the top almost straight away and Liam has the back line pressing up the pitch already, too far up, and the ball lands in space behind them and a red-shirted player simply glides in and onto the pass and Joey looks across at the linesman whose flag is down by his knees as he runs parallel with the forward. The keeper is out too, this lad Starr, who extends his yellow arms to make himself look big, and their player thumps it, hits it true. And Tommy Starr tumbles to his left and he saves it, and Joey is on his feet, shouting, 'What a save!' and they are all up with their necks craned to see the ball crash back off Tommy's leaping frame and into Liam's face as he chases the forward and then, everything slows down, as Devon and Liam both stretch their legs and both run after after the ball, and Joey remembers a man on holiday once when he was a kid, chasing a white handkerchief that had blown off his head across the broad green bank of the Great Orme, Joey was scared the man would chase it over the cliff into the sea, and there are Liam and Devon across the goalmouth sand and into the back of the net in a bundle with the ball.

Silence.

Some fucker with a radio on.

Calamity at the Anvil Yards. An own goal after what can only have been, what, twenty seconds of the match . . .

Goldie sees him across the empty factory spaces, his shoulders rolling, his hair wild. He has to think for a moment where he has seen him before, then remembers it's the kid he sold those diazepam tablets to all those months ago, the bottle he'd found in the coat, who he asked about the Ahmeds and the boy had said, 'Know em? I am one, sunshine.'

He comes towards him now, from a hundred yards away he sees him, from out of the shadow of the building opposite, looking all around him, puts his hand to his eyes to shield the sun and looks now at Goldie's building, he kicks at the clumps of grass that grow from the cracked, bleached concrete, not intentionally, but a man in a hurry. Goldie doesn't move, watches the kid approach, stays in the shadows.

The crowd noise stops, all of a sudden, just like someone flicked a switch. Then comes louder again, with *Iron Towns, Iron Towns, Iron Towns* coming across the water against the breeze and echoing off the brick. Goldie has taken to walking down to the edge of the market when they pack up, picking up scraps of all kinds, has seen Liam's face on the back of the paper every night for a week. That fucker doesn't age, in his club blazer, with his gelled hair, and all the rest of them, look at them, look at him. Goldie stares down at his body, pink scars across it, his ribs showing and the jut of his hip-bone above his trousers. He's hoisted them up with a length of wire casing he found out by the docks wall where they've started taking buildings down. He still does not know what he is going to do, story of his life, he supposes.

When he looks up the boy is much nearer, bigger. He wonders if he can see him, he walks with such purpose, sees that he
is holding something up the sleeve of his hooded top, holds a
jerrycan in his other hand, liquid sloshing from the top, which
he guesses must be petrol, perhaps he has run out of petrol, and
he watches from the broken-down wall where he sits, has plans
to watch the light change on the abandoned buildings, until he
realises the boy is very near, his shadow walking with him, and
so Goldie ducks back in through the open factory doorway and
up the concrete steps.

．　．　．

The pub is empty. Paul queued all Tuesday morning, came back
telling her what a genuine bloke he thought Liam was, that he
could understand what she must have seen in him. 'Is that right,
Paul?' is all she said, in as even a tone as she could manage. No
sign even of Mark today and she has bolted the off sales hatch
shut. Alina is working on the stall. Tyrone is bringing a Chinese
with him when he finishes his shift at the ground. They might
wait to eat with her after closing time, sit upstairs at the kitchen
table near to midnight, she told Tony to head round when he's
locked up the shop. They'll sit like a family with the windows
open and the telly on, talking and only half-listening to each
other, and she will want the moment to last for ever.

She lets the radio commentary bleed quietly from the kitchen
into the bar. They are losing. She thinks of Liam, sees him
moving, running across the roof at the flats, Mark, Goldie too,

a long time ago, like they could never fall, like they could fly. She stands under the chandelier, looks at the ticking clock, sings quietly to herself, breaks off every now and then, hopes for an answering call.

. . .

Bobby pulls the knife from his sleeve. It's wrapped in newspaper. He has watched the buildings, knows he's been sleeping in this one, that there's an office on an upstairs floor where there's even a bed. He's been coming over here for years, first on training runs, then when he was off his head, as if he's the full ticket now, he thinks to himself, almost laughs. He tears the newspaper into strips to use as firelighters. Try and smoke him out, is what his old man said, see what you can do. He'll show him, he thinks, he'll show him.

If he sets the fire on this stair he can chase him up and out, down the iron staircase that runs down the back wall, trap him on this side of the canal, although it's wide enough to try to jump it there, he supposes, will take that risk. There's that new rope that someone has brought down here. He plans to tie him up, secure him to one of the iron rings that are worked into the brick, text his dad who is over at the football. He can do what he likes with him then. Bobby doesn't want to know. He never has. When he's done this he reckons his dad will give him a car, some cash, something. Half a chance and he's out of here, he tells himself, they'll never hear from him again. He's tried all sorts of ways of escaping apart from the most obvious, just to leave, to disappear.

He hears something on the stairs above, puts the strips down in among the rubbish that has already swirled with the breeze in the bottom of the stairwell, sloshes some petrol on the pile, there are pipes running out of the wall here and down through the floor, and he pauses for a moment, and then there's another noise above him and he hurries and fumbles with the lighter in his pocket.

. . .

There are fires that have burned all their lives. It's what Mark thinks as he drags the little boat down the bank. He can smell burning from somewhere, he is sure. He can see there's a hole in the bottom of the boat and wonders if he risks drowning and thinks of all the ways to go maybe that would be best. They could all wonder whether he'd meant it or not. But you can stand up in this water and it's only a few yards across. God knows how old the coracle is. It was tied up with fraying rope under the bridge, the one with the graffiti. Frank Hughes must have left it there on his last afternoon, thinking he'd be back for it. Frank's dad had been the boatman before, possibly his dad before that, to fish the balls from the river when they kicked them in there, right back before there even was a stand, just an earth bank where the crowd would assemble after the factory whistle.

When they were ballboys here, Mark and Liam loved to get the East Stand duty, run up and down the empty, splintered wood and have the match played out to themselves. When someone stuck it over the low stand and they heard the ball bouncing across the iron roof they would race each other to the little door at the back which opened out over the water. Frank would be there, paddling slowly after it, wherever it had landed. In his last years he shared the river and the banks with swans, geese; before that the water had been dead, bubbles would rise to its brown surface and pop.

It's the door Mark paddles towards, water sloshing in the bottom of the boat as it knocks against the back of the stand, no more than a hatch really. He thought he would have to force it but the splintered wood pushes open into the gloom and he remembers the smell of the place, pulls himself up and forward and through the hatch like a cat. He does not tie the boat up, let it sink, let it sail down the river to the sea, he thinks, knows it will drift to the bank, stay half submerged, a perch for herons. To get home he might walk across the pitch. Why not? He never really said goodbye. There it is, a strip of green in the sun, the players flicker across it in their red shirts, their Eton Blue shirts, a song starts up again at the Greenfield End. He hears his own name, they want to conjure him up like a spirit, cannot see him, perhaps never did, not who he was, saw who they wanted to see. One–nil down already. Well, he is here again. He thinks of how he used to run across that pitch like his feet didn't touch the ground and sits at the back of the stand where the light makes a pattern through the missing slats. He is not quite alone. The fox sits, alert, upright, down near the Chain End. He has not seen her all winter, since she had her cubs, if it's the same one, there's so many now, her nose in the air. She turns her head towards Mark and then bolts away into the dark. There's a gasp from the crowd as a pass goes awry and the players in red steam forward and there's Liam, who clatters it up onto the roof of the stand and Mark hears the familiar bounce and roll of the ball above him, how he would groan when they did that when he was playing, and gesture to the defenders to knock it into his feet. The crowd cheer Liam who claps his hands, shakes his fist, until a new ball is found and they go again in endless to and fro.

. . .

Bobby waits, crouched on the stained concrete, a coil of smoke comes slowly up the stairwell. He waits for movement, for any sound from the man, knows it must come with the smoke, hears the cries and songs come from the Anvil Yards. He thinks for a moment about how wrong your life must have gone, to be living here in the ruins, in the shadows, getting so thin, becoming invisible. But not so hard to imagine. He hears the crowd cry again, a surge, and he thinks of those fights in the Assembly Rooms and up at the Casino. 'Kill him, Bobby, kill him.' He can sense the man's movements above him, it's like he hunts himself.

. . .

Liam has never known a half go so quick. At least they have kept it at one-nil. They are still in it, that's what he wants to say to them, when they've got their breath, had a drink, resists the urge to say anything too soon. He looks round for Archie at some point, who always checks he's OK at half-time, remembers, thinks of his grey face in the hospital bed. He cannot recall what he said to them before kick-off, or on the pitch in the huddle when he let Devon talk and it was too loud anyway. He is aware of the requirement for some grand speech, although he has never seen them work, the words have never mattered, just goes round the room and looks in their faces, tells them if they are patient it will come, moves Kyran back out wide where he might get some space. He asks Ted Groves to tell Shaunie to get warmed up after the hour, if it's still one-nil. There's nothing doing from the other matches, no favours anywhere, they need to win. He'll throw Shaunie on up front and just sling balls in at him and Julius. He has never claimed to be a tactical genius.

At the mouth of the tunnel is a man talking into a microphone. Liam does not recognise him. He has the newspaper from a couple of weeks ago in his hand, waves it towards the camera.

'Rumours swirling around the ground about a new owner and a dramatic late buyout but the fact remains that as it stands Irontown Football Club – founder members of the Football League – are on their way out of the league and most likely out of business. It's about to strike midnight at the Anvil Yards!!'

It hits him now that this is probably it, his last game, and he bounces on his toes to get the blood running. Kyran sprints past him, late out of the tunnel after getting his ankle taped up. He turns in the middle of the pitch and flicks the ball up, drills it hard towards the reporter. The balls strikes the newspaper and it flies out of his hand. The crowd nearby cheers. The reporter just grins. They've got no shame, these people, Liam thinks, claps his hands. The crowd sing *Iron Towns, Iron Towns, Iron Towns . . .*

'Was trying to get him in the balls,' he hears Kyran shout, who runs on the spot now and pumps his knees high.

. . .

Goldie moves as quietly as he can along the old walkway that looks down on what was the factory floor. A couple of apple trees grow where he guesses they must have ripped out some machine or other, ripped up the concrete too. Blossom foams on their branches and he can smell it when the breeze comes through the open windows. He will pick the apples when the autumn comes, thinks he could stay here for ever, eke out less and less, waste away slowly and disappear.

He thinks of calling out, saying hello. It might be a trick of his imagination that the boy came in here at all, probably on a short cut to fill his car with petrol, or more likely off to set light to something somewhere, it doesn't have to be here. He smells smoke and not blossom, is sure of it, crouches at the top of the stairs, should've tried the door at the end of the walkway, just gone down the rusty fire escape, he thinks, too late, instead waits here with a knife in his hand, looking at the turn in the stairs.

. . .

'You've heard then,' Ally stands at the door to Steve Stringer's office and Steve nods, looks at the desk and the closed computer on it, the folders and old copies of football yearbooks on the shelves, at Chain Street down below, empty. There's an old framed photo of the team with the FA Cup at Hightown Station, the last time they won it, when they brought it back from Crystal Palace on the train, a hundred years gone by and more. He thinks he could take that with him, imagines the bare patch of wall it will leave behind. They hear the shouts when the players emerge back onto the pitch.

Steve waits for the words to come, thinks he might not even stay for the second half, will drive home, and his wife's head will jerk up when he comes through the door at this odd hour, she hates football but will have the commentary on all the same, and he'll tell her that there is no job for him any more, that he is fin-ished, washed up, a familiar old Iron Towns tradition.

'You better get ready to get on the phone, son. When that ban gets lifted we're gonna need to get some new players in for next season, I don't care what league we're in, a lot of that shower have got to go.'

Steve looks at himself in Ally's sunglasses. Ally pats him on the arm.

'Come on,' Ally says to him, as they hear the whistle blow, 'let's get settled for the second half. You look like you've seen a ghost.'

· · ·

And the boy comes up and round the last step with a knife too in his hand, with Goldie crouched there before him, and there's a twitch and a flicker in both of their faces that they might just both turn and run, but where would they even go now? And Goldie springs at him with a sound coming from within him that he cannot fathom. The boy drops the knife, it clatters onto the steps, but his hands are quick and he hits Goldie once, twice, three times and Goldie can see that these are his fists but can't quite believe it, thinks they are lumps of iron, and it's as if the boy is above him now like some great, breaking wave, but he still has the knife in his hand held tight, tight, and the boy goes to kick him and some instinct means he throws his arm at him, feels the knife go in hard, hit something which must be a bone. There was a plan he and Liam made once that they'd go to Spain, to the bull running when the football season ended, but they never did because Liam was always so full of shit.

Goldie knows it's bad straight away, the boy falls backwards, cracks his head on the step, but it's the blood that's the thing, such a spurt of it already, and Goldie saw this once in the dinner queue, inside, when a bloke got stabbed in the neck with one of those plastic shanks people used to make in the workshops, an old Irish fellow it was, who was in for fiddling his pension and got involved in some other kind of scam, only just survived, pints and pint of blood, and Goldie lands on top of him with his momentum and he can see from the boy's eyes straight away that it's no good. It's true that he's an Ahmed, he looks just like Dee Dee, just here, with the colour draining from him, blood everywhere, the smell of smoke and apple blossom all around.

.   .   .

Joey stands and stares at the empty urinal. They've kicked off. He'll tell Liz she's right, been right all along. His old man won't live for ever, although he'll try his best to. They should start looking at what they could get, maybe see about Spain, Portugal, wherever. She's always wanted to leave and she's right, she's right. The girls can come and visit with the children, a bit of sun will do them good. He'll tell her when they get back tonight, whatever the result. Liam can't play for ever, either. He has to look to see if he's actually had a piss or not.

When he gets to the top of the walkway he sees Kyran move, a bit of space at last, and for a second, just a second, it's Mark Fala skipping in from that wing, inside the fullback, running at the centre-half now and inviting a challenge. He hits a shot, a cross more like, but Julius does not move, and it clips the defender with the keeper already moving to his left, and the ball takes a lazy, lovely arc from the deflection and drops into the net, and they've had a bit of luck at last, the first for a hundred years or more from what Joey can tell, and he goes running down the steps past the directors' box with his arms aloft, his flies undone, his tie flailing.

. . .

Bobby lies on the factory steps, huddled, with his hands in his lap and a pool of blood forming fast, too fast, underneath him, spreading and running onto the step below and then the one below that, too fast. Goldie sees a plume of blood that must have sprayed against the wall as the knife hit, a whole wall freckled with blood and he sees it now on his own hands, feels the punches still on his stinging face and head, and he wants to run, and he wants to hold the boy's head and tell him everything will be OK and there is blood pumping away down the step and it cannot go that fast, you cannot lose it at that speed and think anything is going to be all right and Goldie wonders how he got here, cradling the head of a boy he has just stabbed on these dirty steps and he just wants to start over, if he could just start again, he would never leave his room, he would lie on his bed and wait to hear the sound of horses' hooves.

.   .   .

They used to call what is now the East Stand 'The Bank' and what is now the Greenfield End 'The Hill'. The miners would come down the valley and stand on The Hill, those from the port would stand on The Bank, the workers from Greenfields would fill the space in between, so many more of them, and they would all stand as one, but always these differences between them, delineations. They fought among themselves when the miners went out on strike and the factories back to work, although people pretended differently now, if they talked of those days at all. Divide and rule has always been the way to control these islands. Today people bicker over houses and cars and phones. They killed that boy for his trainers. They swam out of drowned Welsh valleys and walked shoeless from Black Country slums. There is the faintest cloud of smoke above the Anvil Yards, as if the fires have started up again.

.   .   .

He can see that the boy is dead, but thinks at the same time, no, and imagines him getting to his feet and prepares himself for another assault but the boy does not move and Goldie can feel his heart beating in his chest and a feeling of dread, a different dread to the one that says to be ready for the boy to get to his feet because he will not, because he is dead, the same one he felt before on that riverbank, looking back at the car with his baby girl in his arms and thinking where's Sonia? Where is Sonia? As if he didn't really know, so that he knew she was in the car and under the water and didn't all at the same time. It is exactly that, because there is the boy lying dead on the concrete steps and Goldie still stands ready with a knife in his hands and looks for the boy to get to his feet.

. . .

The ball bounces towards Tommy Starr and Liam looks at the line, sluggish to move up, the end of the season, the end of time itself he can see, as the ref motions towards the linesman and has the whistle in his mouth. Tommy pumps the ball forward, comes after it, comes to join the party, there was that keeper who scored on the last day to keep Carlisle up, Jimmy Glass, he drives a cab somewhere down south now, the crowd noise has gone up a notch to a kind of slowed-down high-pitch shriek.

Liam jumps and he wins it, he feels it, just the faintest of touches, exactly like when he played for England. They always say he never touched the ball, but he did, just like that, with the lightest of touches as he jumped for a header that took the ball away from his marker. He gets clattered, all arms and legs as he hits the ground and he wants to shout for a foul but can't get the words out as the air is knocked from him.

The ball hits the turf, bounces into the area, and there is Kyran, one last burst, clear of his man and onto the ball. Liam is still on the floor when Kyran pulls back his left foot, Liam sees him there, frozen, both feet off the ground, his head down, thousands of people behind him in a full-throated roar as if he is leaping into the crowd. And he sees the trip, the defender gets back, Kyran lands in a heap, and Liam is back on his feet now, shouting, 'Penalty! Penalty!' along with everyone else in the Anvil Yards, and for a second he thinks the ref is blowing for time but, no, he points with great deliberation towards the spot.

There's a penalty at the Anvil Yards . . . he can hear a radio playing behind the goal, there would always be men when he was a kid with a transistor held to their ear. They would relay scores from other matches, relevant or important or not, a litany of names and numbers, a spell to protect you from the world. *Penalty at the Anvil Yards* . . . he hears, as it plays out into empty bedrooms and rose-filled gardens and across the burning yards themselves, from out of Eli's kitchen window and up over the hill, into Archie Hill's hospital room at the Bethel, from the laptop by Stan Ahmed's bed in his hospital room in Marbella as he slips in and out of the world, their chests rise and fall to its sound, across a patio that overlooks the Atlantic waves, Dorothea's head nodding asleep, into empty rooms in houses up the hill, in the Salamander, where Dee Dee sings.

. . .

They recede into the crowd, not completely, of course, but enough to see them as one of many, a whole people, hundreds of thousands for every one of them, who would walk the factory streets to watch them play. Those who moved to the percussion of clanging metal, of great booms across docks and rivers, of bells and sirens and whistles, along black paths and across green fields, through all the iron towns of the world.

Di Stéfano sits on a cushion in the Bernabeau, George Best sits in the corner of the pub, Eusébio watches the eagle as it soars against the hard blue light and into the shadowed rafters. Billy Meredith stands at the bar of the Stretford Road Hotel, talks with the men that come and go about City, about United, sips orange juice. Steve Bloomer walks on Cromer pier, sees boys fishing for crabs off the sides, looks into the grey northern waters, shoulder to shoulder with men who once cheered his name.

And the crowds recede like an ebbing tide, the iron towns rust, and you might think them all ghosts if you think of them at all, but do not be mistaken, they will not die, they take new forms.

. . .

He can smell petrol that comes off the boy, he is sure now, and there is a curl of smoke that comes up the steps. He should run, needs to run, he understands that. Smoke comes up the steps, a curl of it at first but then a thicker rope of it, as if he could grab hold of it and haul himself to safety and he does put his hand to it, drops the knife which clatters off down the steps and he thinks that this is another mistake because his prints are on the knife.

He does not wear a glove. You see kids now on the back of buses, they wear a golf glove like they're off to play the Sunday medal but everyone knows what it's meant to show and they haven't killed anyone, these boys, they haven't hurt anyone, you can see it in their eyes most of them, but that's what we're left with, he thinks. Everyone wants to be a bad man. He goes to follow the knife but as he turns a corner of the stairs the heat and smoke rise and hit his face like the way Nadine slapped him once, just out of nowhere, while they stood in the kitchen trying to do the dishes.

He turns back and the blood runs through under him, pools on an uneven step and he has to step over the boy who lies at a strange angle, feels something in his stomach and stumbles across the wide floor where they had fought, not even a fight, not really, over in seconds, what the football commentators say is a coming together. There is blood on his hand, a handprint on the concrete, his own blood, must have cut himself as he stabbed him. He is crouched, looks at his own palm print there on the floor and then looks up and tries to rise, sees the smoke above him drifting in the murky light that comes through the skylights. Clumps of moss look like black clouds.

There is something he is aware of now, as he moves away from the heat and starts to run towards the far wall. He remembers the way the stairs just melted in the rain during the storm. He gets to the wall and cannot even see the door that would lead there with the smoke all around him now, filling this great space. It is very hot. He hears a pop from the fire below and a surge in the heat. From beyond the murky skylights he thinks he can hear the shouts of the crowd.

He remembers the way the staircase peeled off the building, nothing but rust, disintegrated in the rain. He can fall or he can burn, he thinks, like some great truth revealed, as if that was always the only choice open to him and he looks up towards the light but there is just thick black smoke now, and the heat, and the sound of the flames getting nearer and he understands there is no way out, probably never was.

.　.　.

We are here.

We come as the creatures from the edges of your dreams, as the griffin and the salamander. We are the ash that will fall on your towns, the pattern of the smoke in the brick, the spores that you will breathe in. We are the iron roar that you thought you'd silenced. We sing of better days. Better days to come.

.　.　.

Liam picks up the ball and puts it on the penalty spot, thinks he sees it move in the breeze which comes stronger now, warm, places it again. He rubs his hands on the turf either side of the ball. The pitch held up well in the end, he thinks, remembers suddenly a story Dee Dee made him read once, a kid winning a prison race who loses on purpose, throws himself down on the floor when he is miles ahead, because he can, because he won't win for the people in power. Liam grins now. He said to Dee Dee, 'Why didn't he just keep running?' and she shook her head and said he didn't understand.

He smells burning. The crowd are still going nuts behind the goal. He cannot ever remember the ground this packed, he sees bodies, arms and legs and heads jumping, writhing, and a great roar coming from them. This is louder now, like something restored, like the days of the old iron roar that he could not even remember if he tried.

There are players still in the box, god knows what anyone is arguing about, as clear a penalty as you might ever see. One of the defenders tries to say something to Liam, he is smiling, it's like he's asking him when the next bus is due, where he's going on his holidays, but Liam cannot hear him and walks close to him to show he is not backing down from anything, his guard will not slip now. Kyran is on his feet he can see, just to the side of the pitch and he tries to beckon him on and looks at the ref but the ref is already pacing out to the side of the ball with the whistle in his mouth, ushers the keeper towards his line and a hush settles. These things are over so quickly, these moments, to be replayed again and again, on television screens and in memories, locked in people's heads.

Liam turns and looks at the ball and looks at the goal, not at the keeper, at the net either side of him. The faces in the Greenfield End merge into one. There is the blur of orange stewards' jackets in front of the hoardings. Everything is still now. The breeze comes again.

Liam takes a breath and then another, moves his hand in front of his face. Is this snow? A shower of white flakes falls through the spring sunshine. Ash. Something is burning. He glances for a moment at the old East Stand, checks the thing isn't in flames. There's a pattern at the back of the stand where there are holes in the concrete and the light shines through like all the stars in the sky, he thinks he can see the shape of a man at the back of the stand, there is a plume of smoke off in the distance somewhere over the Anvil Yards. They had a match in the Pengwern once where there was a burning car in the next field, they played on through the smoke. There are fires that have burned all their lives.

It is silent, all those people and not a murmur, and the referee blows his whistle into the falling ash and the breeze. Liam takes another breath, empties his mind completely of everything other than the only thing he has ever really understood, the shape of a ball struck across a green field.

He knows what to do.

. . .

The fire burned all night. They said there were oil tanks underground that everyone had forgotten about. Old gas cylinders exploded like the sound of gunfire up the valley and there was the deep rumble of walls and ceilings collapsing. Alina thought of the apple trees, of the foxes that would flee from the blaze and streak up the hillsides in the dark, as she dozed in her nana's old chair by the window. Her mum made endless cups of tea. The foxes' tails were alight, spreading fire and mayhem as they ran. She felt strangely calm, shocked maybe, she thought to herself. Her mum looked much the same. Dee Dee stood at the off sales hatch or on the lounge steps with her head craned out to watch the fire-fighters move the cordon nearer and nearer to the pub and then stop not fifty yards or so down the road, a high tide of flame lapping at their doors.

The police used the lounge to co-ordinate things. They had a pub at each corner of the Anvil Yards, kept radioing people in The Magpie three miles distant on a back road into the Heath, which was where the smoke was being blown. Dee Dee hoisted cans of pop from the cellar with Tyrone, bought cups and the kettle down from upstairs. No one slept much and their eyes felt gritty in the morning from the lack of sleep and the smoke that had drifted into everything. The bulk of the smoke hung as a huge black cloud above the Anvil Yards and drifted slowly to the east.

. . .

Sunday morning Alina and Tyrone drove up above the smoke, to the head of the valley where the road dips and runs into the Sheep Folds and the Iron Towns disappear, set a blanket out some way from the roadside with pastries and the flask of coffee that Alina made that morning while listening to the radio, fire crews from as far afield as North Wales and Birmingham is what they said, that the blaze was contained, it would continue to burn but was under control, and a miracle that there had been no injuries.

When they swung the car out of Meeting House Lane they saw the road block and fire-fighters standing on the other side of the temporary fencing, recognised it from when it was erected on the roadside for when the carnival parade came through the

Lowtown Bull Ring. She was shocked at the man standing half in uniform with his arm resting on the top of a police car, his face blackened, like someone made up for a film. The smell was everywhere here. They delivered a last crate of lemonade from the car boot and the fire-fighter grinned through his blackened face as they hoisted the cans over the low fence. She looked at Tyrone for any trace of jealousy and he did look at her and smile but she couldn't work out what the look meant and couldn't decide whether she wanted him jealous or not. Perhaps better not, she thought. She wondered how long the burnt smell would take to leave or if it ever would.

They'd said no casualties but she knew they couldn't be sure. The place was vast, so was the fire, and it would burn for days, maybe weeks they said, but the blaze was under control, the phrase they kept repeating on the radio and TV, so strange to see her own street there on the television screen, all the drama of breaking news. Well, it was broken now. They said no casualties, but there were people living in there, she was certain, she knew it, that tent under the old bridge for one thing, all the drink bottles and rags, and that sense of being watched sometimes, that there were eyes on you in all that space. They meant none of the officials, the fire-fighters and so on. They'd evacuated some flats, some of the houses round and about. They meant those people, but there were others she was sure that no one would account for, and there were people who refused to be evacuated, of course there were, always was. They'd put camp beds in the hall of her old junior school.

Through the Bull Ring there was a sudden shower of ash, soft white flakes fell onto the windscreen and Tyrone put the wipers on with some water and turned it all into a grey, silty wash that meant he had to put his head through the open window in order to see to drive.

There were people out on the hillsides at Cowton, leaning over the walkways and balconies. The sounds of the helicopters now, from the fire brigade, and one that was filming for the TV news. Where they stopped they were above the high-rises, right on the valley-ridge, on the road that ran back down into Black Park. They were above the smoke even, which twisted in the sky as a giant dark plume, the sun coming through it now, and a strange light everywhere.

They spread the picnic blanket out a little way from the car on the sheep-bitten grass. From this distance there were no people and it struck her that this was Greenfield's view, that from the painting, that she had maybe found it at last when she wasn't looking, the lines of the rivers in the valley below, before they entered the smoke, the castle hidden just round the hillside, like the third panel of a triptych, she thought, after the last fire. They'd got the camera with them. Tyrone looked at his phone to see if a picture he'd sent had got on the news.

'We should've taken that fireman,' he said, 'people love that stuff. I reckon he'd blacked his face up on purpose.'

So just the smallest bit of jealousy then, the best sort, she felt, and she squeezed his arm.

It was warm, not just from the fire, but from the sun cutting through the billowing smoke, strange colours at its edge, mauve and purple, chemical smoke.

'But how do they know it's safe? No one remembers what was left in there,' said a voice on the radio this morning after various reassurances about safety and the size of the exclusion cordon.

She phoned her mum to check she was OK. They ate their pastries. There were birds floating on the air that came from the valley. She waited for one to swoop on some unsuspecting prey but they stayed high up and almost out of sight. Tyrone leaned back, one arm around her waist, his other hand holding the newspaper folded open at a picture of Liam with his shirt off on the pitch at full-time just as he disappeared into the crowd. There were a crowd of bodies on his body, a crowd of bodies all around him. They looked like smoke, all of them, the grey swirls on his flesh and the way the people moved towards him, to swallow him, like the way the smoke moved now and swallowed the hillside graves and half of Burnt Village and then drifted over the hill into the rest of England. When they opened the roads she would have to go and clean her mum's plaque. She wondered if the roses would bloom with the colours of the smoke this year, or whether that took ages to happen, genera-tions, evolution, thought of creatures with blackened bodies that lived among soot and ash, and the people in the bottom of the valley in the second painting.

The road was narrow here, a farmer's track really. It ran over the hill and the shape of it, a sudden incline like a breaking wave, made her wonder what was on the other side, even though she knew full well. More roads, more hills. Tyrone saw her looking that way, had finished leafing through the paper.

'We could carry on,' he said, nodding at the brow of the hill.

'Just keep going,'

It was tempting, to choose this moment to leave. Then she looked back at the black smoke in the valley, the charred buildings beneath, a snow of ash falling again on the Iron Towns, charred lives, she thought, my own and everyone that has ever lived here.

'No,' she said. 'No. Let's go home.'